Devilish Doings

Devilish Doings

20 Fiendish Tales by

STEPHEN VINCENT BENÉT,

WASHINGTON IRVING,

EDGAR ALLAN POE,

CHARLES DICKENS,

J. SHERIDAN LE FANU,

MAX BEERBOHM,

AND OTHERS

EDITED BY

Frank J. Finamore

GRAMERCY BOOKS / NEW YORK

Introduction and compilation
Copyright © 1997 by Random House Value Publishing, Inc.
All rights reserved under International and Pan-American
Copyright Conventions.

"The Devil and Daniel Webster" by Stephen Vincent Benét. From *The
Selected Works of Stephen Vincent Benét,* copyright 1936 by The Curtis
Publishing Company. Copyright renewed © 1964 by Thomas C. Benét,
Stephanie B. Mahin, and Rachel Lewis Benét. All rights reserved. Reprinted
by permission of Brandt & Brandt Literary Agents, Inc.

This edition is published by Gramercy Books,
a divison of Random House Value Publishing, Inc.,
201 East 50th Street,
New York, New York 10022.

Gramercy Books and colophon are registered trademarks of
Random House Value Publishing, Inc.

Random House
New York • Toronto • London • Sydney • Auckland
http://www.randomhouse.com

Printed and bound in the United States

A full CIP catalog record of this title can be obtained from the Library of Congress.
Devilish Doings/edited by Frank J. Finamore
ISBN 0-517-18504-0

8 7 6 5 4 3 2 1

Contents

Introduction

As the twentieth century and this millennium come to a close, many people await an apocalypse that they believe will pit the forces of good and evil against each other, and will cause each individual to choose his or her eternal destiny. One sign of this, some point out, is our culture's ever-growing fascination with the Devil.

The great English poet William Blake said of John Milton's epic poem *Paradise Lost* that its author was on the side of Satan—a much more interesting character than God, who is boring in his perfection. We perhaps identify with Satan's imperfections, his pride and his rebelliousness, since they mirror our flawed humanity. We are seduced by the very qualities that he embodies and that our culture admires. The Devil is an underdog who has the tenacity to fight the impossible fight: he must know that it is impossible to defeat God, who created all. He is the ultimate romantic. Satan also has the unconquerable desire to win; he is ever-industrious, as he is always thinking of new ways to ensnare humans for eternal damnation. He believes that the end justifies the means; he stops at nothing to achieve his goal and thus, say some, may be considered the patron saint of the modern politician and businessperson.

Is the Devil some mythical creation from our civilization's collective imagination, or a reality? Only God knows for sure. But whatever the truth, the Devil has been a subject of fascination for countless writers for thousands of years, from the Bible and religious tracts to folktales and fiction. As *Devilish Doings* proves, our enchantment with him is not diminishing. This collection gathers twenty of the world's most famous tales of infernal mischief from a diverse group of writers, many famous, some unknown.

The book begins with a tale by Niccolò Machiavelli (1459–1527), "Belphagor, or the Marriage of the Devil," first published in 1549. Machiavelli is known today as the author of *The Prince,* the most diabolical treatise of political theory ever written. "Belphagor," his only work of fiction, is a droll story that depicts marriage as the irrefutable cause of man's continuous fall from grace.

The next two tales are famous legends from folklore by anonymous hands. "Doctor Faustus" is of German origin and tells of a scholar who sells his soul to the Devil for untold power and knowledge. This legend would later be the source of Christopher Marlowe's play *Doctor Faustus* and Goethe's *Faust.* "The Countess Kathleen O'Shea" is the story of how one of Ireland's legendary heroines sold her soul to save her people.

"The Devil and Tom Walker" (1824) is by Washington Irving (1783–1859), the famed American author of "The Legend of Sleepy

Hollow" and "The Headless Horseman." It is a retelling of a local American legend involving the lost hidden treasure of the pirate Captain Kidd that is guarded by the Devil himself.

"St. John's Eve" (1830) is a folktale from Russia recounted by one of the world's greatest short story writers, Nikolai Vaselevich Gogol (1809–1852). It is the story of a man who sells his soul for gold to enable him to marry his beloved. The title refers to the Christian belief that the Devil can be seen in his true form only on the eve of St. John's birthday.

"The Painter's Devil" (1834), by the great English novelist William Makepeace Thackeray (1811–1863), the author of *Vanity Fair,* brings back the theme of matrimony as the source of man's fall into damnation and how a wife can strike fear into the Devil himself.

There has never been a writer more associated with the macabre than the America's Edgar Allan Poe (1809–1849). He is considered the first master of the supernatural, a writer who dared to unleash man's darkest fantasies onto the printed page with fabulous tales like "The Masque of the Red Death" and "The Tell-Tale Heart." "Bon-Bon" (1835), however, finds Poe in an uncharacteristically light-hearted vein. It tells of an encounter between the Devil and a philosopher-chef as they discuss the Epicurean pleasures that Satan and his cohorts find in human souls.

"The Printer's Devil" (1836), by an unknown hand, is a humorous tour through the topography of the Hell where all books end up. There is an age-old connection between the Devil and books, for it was rumored that the inventor of the printing press, Fust, had dealings with the Evil One.

"The Devil's Mother-in-Law" (1859) is by Fernán Caballero— which was the pen name of Cecilia Böhl de Fabor (1776–1877)—a famous nineteenth-century Spanish writer. It again visits the connection between matrimony and damnation, with the twist that even the Devil is cowered by a mother-in-law.

As anyone who has read *A Christmas Carol* knows, Charles

Dickens (1812–1870), one of English literature's greatest novelists, was no stranger to the supernatural. He credits his nurse, Mary Wells, who used to tell him frightening stories as a child, for beginning his fascination with the macabre. "The Devil and Mr. Chips" (1860) is Dickens's retelling of one of Mary's favorites, a tale of a shipwright who sells his soul for a half-ton of copper and a talking rat.

Charles Baudelaire (1821–1867) is one of France's greatest poets, renowned for his great collection *The Flowers of Evil.* Baudelaire was enamored with the corruption and decadence of society and truly believed in the Devil; as his friend Théophile Gautier noted, he "had a singular prepossession for the Devil as the tempter, in whom he saw a dragon who harried him into sin, infamy, crime, and perversity." In Baudelaire's "The Generous Gambler" (1864), the Devil is a suave Parisian boulevardier who gambles for men's souls.

The Anglo-Irish writer J. Sheridan Le Fanu (1814–1873) is considered by many to be the Victorian era's best author of the supernatural and the forerunner of the modern school of psychological horror. His most famous work is "Carmilla," the brilliant vampire novella. "Sir Dominick's Bargain" (1872) is based on the popular Irish legend of Dunoran and is told in dialect.

The French writer Guy de Maupassant (1850–1893) is one of the world's finest writers of the short story whose most famous works include "The Necklace" and "A Piece of String." "The Legend of Mont St.-Michel" (1888) is a retelling of an old Norman folktale of how St. Michael beat the Devil.

Richard Garnett (1835–1906) was a scholarly writer and minor poet as well as the keeper of printed books at the British Museum. He published one volume of short stories, *Twilight of the Gods: And Other Tales* (1888), from which "Madame Lucifer" is taken. It is a darkly humorous tale in which the Devil's wife proves to be more frightening than the Devil himself. According to Jewish legend, the

Devil married Adam's first wife, Lilith, a woman God created with great beauty but, regrettably, with a heart of ice.

Anatole France was the pen name of Anatole François Thibault (1844–1924). He was the winner of the Nobel Prize for literature in 1921, and his most famous novel today is *Penguin Island* (1908). "Lucifer" (1895) is an amusing story of how the extremely vain Satan visits a Florentine artist to complain about the inaccuracy of depicting him as an appallingly ugly monster and his attempts to convince the artist otherwise.

The Russian writer Maxim Gorky (1868–1936) was born Aleksey Maksimovich Peshkov. He wrote novels and short stories, as well as plays like the famous *The Lower Depths* (1912). He is considered one of the finest writers of Soviet literature. "The Devil" (1899) is an ironically funny tale of how a bored Satan raises a dead author from the grave so he can visit his widow, who has since remarried to a clerk in a millinery shop and is living very well off the sale of her late husband's books.

John Masefield (1878–1967) was a poet, novelist, and playwright who became England's Poet Laureate in 1930. In his youth he went to sea, and his writings are colored by his experiences. "The Devil and the Old Man" (1905) is a tale of how a crusty old sea captain outwits the Devil for the soul of one of his crewmen.

The English author, critic, and artist Max Beerbohm (1872–1956) was a major figure at the beginning of the twentieth century. He was a friend of Oscar Wilde and George Bernard Shaw, and was knighted in 1939. His writing is characterized by his sharp wit and biting satire. "Enoch Soames" (1912) is a clever and very funny story of a mediocre writer who makes a deal with the Devil to travel a hundred years into the future so he can enjoy his posthumous reputation. The only problem, however, is that the single mention of his name he finds is as the title of a "fiction" story by Max Beerbohm.

"The Devil in a Nunnery" by the English writer Francis Oscar

Mann (1885–1964) is a story from his collection *The Devil in a Nunnery, and Other Medieval Tales* (1914). This story is based on the belief of many religious thinkers who assign the origin of music to the Devil. By the sheer sensual and hypnotic power of his voice and cithern, Satan, disguised as a pilgrim, seduces old and youthful nuns alike into a reverie of intoxicating erotic desire and remembrance.

The American writer Stephen Vincent Benét (1898–1943) was one of the most popular short story writers of his day, as well as a famous poet—he won the Pulitzer Prize for poetry in 1928 for *John Brown's Body*. He is remembered today mainly for his marvelous short story "The Devil and Daniel Webster" (1936). In this tale, Benét fashions a timeless American myth. Daniel Webster, one of America's greatest orators, takes on "Old Scratch" in a rhetorical duel for the soul of one of Webster's New Hampshire neighbors.

As this collection proves, the popularity and fascination with the Devil is as strong as ever. But he seems to have become a figure of comic fun rather than the architect of human destruction and damnation. For many of us, Satan has lost much of his diabolical power to invoke true fear and dread in us. The modern secular world seems to have lost the need for such a personification of evil, since we humans are more than capable of outdoing the Devil himself. The imagined torments of damnation and Hell seem rather quaint and innocuous when compared with the horrors we have unleashed upon ourselves in this century alone and what we are quite capable of doing: completely annihilating the world and the human race, something even the Devil himself has never been able to accomplish.

But perhaps our unbelief is only a naive delusion. As Baudelaire writes in "The Generous Gambler," "The loveliest trick of the Devil is to persuade you that he does not exist!" In this "enlightened" modern world, we as a race are even more capable of the evil we once attributed to Satan's diabolical machinations. The Devil has almost disappeared as the perpetrator, leaving us to blame our own sinful impulses. If the Devil exists, he would probably be joyous in his success as the invisible puppet-master leading us through his enticing dance of damnation, as we willingly sell our souls without even realizing we are doing so.

FRANK J. FINAMORE

New York
1997

Belphagor

NICCOLÒ MACHIAVELLI

We read in the ancient archives of Florence the following account, as it was received from the lips of a very holy man, greatly respected by everyone for the sanctity of his manners at the period in which he lived. Happening once to be deeply absorbed in his prayers, such was their efficacy, that he saw an infinite number of condemned souls, belonging to those miserable mortals who had died in their sins, undergoing the punishment due to their offenses in the regions below. He remarked that the greater part of them lamented nothing so bitterly as their folly in having taken wives, attributing to them the whole of their misfortunes. Much surprised at this, Minos and Rhadamanthus, with the rest of the infernal judges, unwilling to credit all the abuse heaped upon the female sex, and wearied from day to day with its repetition, agreed to bring the matter before Pluto. It was then resolved that the conclave of infernal princes should form a committee of inquiry, and should adopt such measures as might be deemed most advisable by the court in order to discover the truth or falsehood of the calumnies which they heard. All being assembled in council, Pluto addressed them as follows: "Dearly beloved demons! though by celestial dispensation and the irreversible decree of fate this kingdom fell to my share, and I might strictly dispense with any kind of celestial or earthly responsibility, yet, as it is more prudent and respectful to consult the laws and to hear the opinion of others, I have resolved to be guided by your advice, particularly in a case that may chance to cast some imputation upon our government. For the souls of all men daily arriving in our kingdom still continue to lay the whole blame upon their wives, and as this appears to us impossible, we must be careful how we decide in such a business, lest we also should come in for a share of their abuse, on account of our too great severity; and yet judgment must be pronounced, lest we be taxed with negligence and with indifference to the interests of justice. Now, as the latter is the fault of a careless, and the former of an unjust judge, we, wishing to avoid the trouble and the blame that might attach to both, yet hardly seeing how to get clear of it, naturally enough apply to you for assistance, in order that you may look to it, and contrive in some way that, as we have hitherto reigned without the slightest imputation upon our character, we may continue to do so for the future."

The affair appearing to be of the utmost importance to all the princes present, they first resolved that it was necessary to ascertain the truth, though they differed as to the best means of accomplishing this object. Some were of opinion that they ought to choose one or more from among themselves, who should be commissioned to pay a visit to the world, and in a human shape endeavor personally to ascertain how far such reports were grounded in truth. To many others it appeared that this might be done without so much trouble merely by compelling some of the wretched souls to confess the truth by the application of a variety of tortures. But the majority being in favor of a journey to the world, they abided by the former proposal. No one, however, being ambitious of undertaking such a task, it was resolved to leave the affair to chance. The lot fell upon the arch-devil Belphagor, who, previous to the Fall, had enjoyed the rank of archangel in a higher world. Though he received his commission with a very ill grace, he nevertheless felt himself constrained by Pluto's imperial mandate, and prepared to execute whatever had been determined upon in council. At the same time he took an oath to observe the tenor of his instructions, as they had been drawn up with all due solemnity and ceremony for the purpose of his mission. These were to the following effect—*Imprimis,* that the better to promote the object in view, he should be furnished with a hundred thousand gold ducats; secondly, that he should make use of the utmost expedition in getting into the world; thirdly, that after assuming the human form he should enter into the marriage state; and lastly, that he should live with his wife for the space of ten years. At the expiration of this period, he was to feign death and return home, in order to acquaint his employers, by the fruits of experience, what really were the respective conveniences and inconveniences of matrimony. The conditions further ran, that during the said ten years he should be subject to all kinds of miseries and disasters, like the rest of mankind, such as poverty, prisons, and diseases into which men are apt to fall, unless, indeed, he could contrive by his own skill and ingenuity to avoid them. Poor Belphagor having signed these conditions and received the money, forthwith came into the world, and having set up his equipage, with a numerous train of servants, he made a very splendid entrance into Florence. He selected this city in preference to all others, as being most favorable for obtaining an usurious interest of his money; and having assumed the name of Roderigo, a native of Castile, he took a house in the suburbs of Ognissanti. And because he was unable to explain the instructions under which he acted, he gave out that he was a merchant, who having had poor prospects in Spain, had gone to Syria, and succeeded in acquiring his fortune at Aleppo, whence he had lastly set out for Italy, with the intention of marrying and settling there, as one of the most polished and agreeable countries he knew.

Roderigo was certainly a very handsome man, apparently about thirty years of age, and he lived in a style of life that showed he was in pretty easy circumstances, if not possessed of immense wealth. Being, moreover, extremely affable and liberal, he soon attracted the notice of many noble citizens blessed with large families of daughters and small incomes. The former of these were soon offered to him, from among whom Roderigo chose a very beautiful girl of the name of Onesta, a daughter of Amerigo Donati, who had also three sons, all grown up, and three more daughters, also nearly marriageable. Though of a noble family and enjoying a good reputation in Florence, his father-in-law was extremely poor, and maintained as poor an establishment. Roderigo, therefore, made very splendid nuptials, and omitted nothing that might tend to confer honor upon such a festival, being liable, under the law which he received on leaving his infernal abode, to feel all kinds of vain and earthly passions. He therefore soon began to enter into all the pomps and vanities of the world, and to aim at reputation and consideration among mankind, which put him to no little expense. But more than this, he had not long enjoyed the society of his beloved Onesta, before he became tenderly attached to her, and was unable to behold her suffer the slightest inquietude or vexation. Now, along with her other gifts of beauty and nobility, the lady had brought into the house of Roderigo such an insufferable portion of pride, that in this respect Lucifer himself could not equal her; for her husband, who had experienced the effects of both, was at no loss to decide which was the most intolerable of the two. Yet it became infinitely worse when she discovered the extent of Roderigo's attachment to her, of which she availed herself to obtain an ascendancy over him and rule him with a rod of iron. Not content with this, when she found he would bear it, she continued to annoy him with all kinds of insults and taunts, in such a way as to give him the most indescribable pain and uneasiness. For what with the influence of her father, her brothers, her friends, and relatives, the duty of the matrimonial yoke, and the love he bore her, he suffered all for some time with the patience of a saint. It would be useless to recount the follies and extravagancies into which he ran in order to gratify her taste for dress, and every article of the newest fashion, in which our city, ever so variable in its nature, according to its usual habits, so much abounds. Yet, to live upon easy terms with her, he was obliged to do more than this; he had to assist his father-in-law in portioning off his other daughters; and she next asked him to furnish one of her brothers with goods to sail for the Levant, another with silks for the West, while a third was to be set up in a goldbeater's establishment at Florence. In such objects the greatest part of his fortune was soon consumed. At length the Carnival season was at hand; the festival of St. John was to be celebrated, and the whole city, as usual, was in a ferment. Numbers of the noblest families were about to vie with each other in the splendor of their parties, and the Lady Onesta, being resolved not to be outshone by her acquaintance, insisted that Roderigo should exceed them all in the richness of their feasts. For the reasons above stated, he submitted to her will; nor, indeed, would he have scrupled at doing much more, however difficult it might have been, could he have flattered himself with a hope of preserving the peace and comfort of his household, and of awaiting quietly the consummation of his ruin. But this was not the case, inasmuch as the arrogant temper

of his wife had grown to such a height of asperity by long indulgence, that he was at a loss in what way to act. His domestics, male
and female, would no longer remain in the house, being unable to
support for any length of time the intolerable life they led. The
inconvenience which he suffered in consequence of having no one to
whom he could intrust his affairs it is impossible to express. Even his
own familiar devils, whom he had brought along with him, had
already deserted him, choosing to return below rather than longer
submit to the tyranny of his wife. Left, then, to himself, amidst this
turbulent and unhappy life, and having dissipated all the ready
money he possessed, he was compelled to live upon the hopes of the
returns expected from his ventures in the East and the West. Being
still in good credit, in order to support his rank he resorted to bills of
exchange; nor was it long before, accounts running against him, he
found himself in the same situation as many other unhappy specula-
tors in that market. Just as his case became extremely delicate, there
arrived sudden tidings both from East and West that one of his
wife's brothers had dissipated the whole of Roderigo's profits in play,
and that while the other was returning with a rich cargo uninsured,
his ship had the misfortune to be wrecked, and he himself was lost.
No sooner did this affair transpire than his creditors assembled, and
supposing it must be all over with him, though their bills had not yet
become due, they resolved to keep a strict watch over him in fear
that he might abscond. Roderigo, on his part, thinking that there
was no other remedy, and feeling how deeply he was bound by the
Stygian law, determined at all hazards to make his escape. So taking
horse one morning early, as he luckily lived near the Prato gate, in
that direction he went off. His departure was soon known; the
creditors were all in a bustle; the magistrates were applied to, and the
officers of justice, along with a great part of the populace, were
dispatched in pursuit. Roderigo had hardly proceeded a mile before
he heard this hue and cry, and the pursuers were soon so close at his

heels that the only resource he had left was to abandon the highroad
and take to the open country, with the hope of concealing himself in
the fields. But finding himself unable to make way over the hedges
and ditches, he left his horse and took to his heels, traversing fields of
vines and canes, until he reached Peretola, where he entered the
house of Matteo del Bricca, a laborer of Giovanna del Bene. Finding
him at home, for he was busily providing fodder for his cattle, our
hero earnestly entreated him to save him from the hands of his
adversaries close behind, who would infallibly starve him to death in
a dungeon, engaging that if Matteo would give him refuge, he would
make him one of the richest men alive, and afford him such proofs
of it before he took his leave as would convince him of the truth of
what he said; and if he failed to do this, he was quite content that
Matteo himself should deliver him into the hands of his enemies.

Now Matteo, although a rustic, was a man of courage, and
concluding that he could not lose anything by the speculation, he
gave him his hand and agreed to save him. He then thrust our hero
under a heap of rubbish, completely enveloping him in weeds; so
that when his pursuers arrived they found themselves quite at a loss,
nor could they extract from Matteo the least information as to his
appearance. In this dilemma there was nothing left for them but to
proceed in the pursuit, which they continued for two days, and then
returned, jaded and disappointed, to Florence. In the meanwhile,
Matteo drew our hero from his hiding place, and begged him to
fulfill his engagement. To this his friend Roderigo replied: "I confess,
brother, that I am under great obligations to you, and I mean to
return them. To leave no doubt upon your mind, I will inform you
who I am"; and he proceeded to acquaint him with all the particu-
lars of the affair: how he had come into the world, and married, and
run away. He next described to his preserver the way in which he
might become rich, which was briefly as follows: As soon as Matteo
should hear of some lady in the neighborhood being said to be

possessed, he was to conclude that it was Roderigo himself who had taken possession of her; and he gave him his word, at the same time, that he would never leave her until Matteo should come and conjure him to depart. In this way he might obtain what sum he pleased from the lady's friends for the price of exorcizing her; and having mutually agreed upon this plan, Roderigo disappeared.

Not many days elapsed before it was reported in Florence that the daughter of Messer Ambrogio Amedei, a lady married to Buonajuto Tebalducci, was possessed by the devil. Her relations did not fail to apply every means usual on such occasions to expel him, such as making her wear upon her head St. Zanobi's cap, and the cloak of St. John of Gualberto; but these had only the effect of making Roderigo laugh. And to convince them that it was really a spirit that possessed her, and that it was no flight of the imagination, he made the young lady talk Latin, hold a philosophical dispute, and reveal the frailties of many of her acquaintance. He particularly accused a certain friar of having introduced a lady into his monastery in male attire, to the no small scandal of all who heard it, and the astonishment of the brotherhood. Messer Ambrogio found it impossible to silence him, and began to despair of his daughter's cure. But the news reaching Matteo, he lost no time in waiting upon Ambrogio, assuring him of his daughter's recovery on condition of his paying him five hundred florins, with which to purchase a farm at Peretola. To this Messer Ambrogio consented; and Matteo immediately ordered a number of masses to be said, after which he proceeded with some unmeaning ceremonies calculated to give solemnity to his task. Then approaching the young lady, he whispered in her ear: "Roderigo, it is Matteo that is come. So do as we agreed upon, and get out." Roderigo replied: "It is all well; but you have not asked enough to make you a rich man. So when I depart I will take possession of the daughter of Charles, king of Naples, and I will not leave her till you come. You may then demand whatever you

please for your reward; and mind that you never trouble me again."
And when he had said this, he went out of the lady, to the no small
delight and amazement of the whole city of Florence.

It was not long again before the accident that had happened to
the daughter of the king of Naples began to be buzzed about the
country, and all the monkish remedies having been found to fail, the
king, hearing of Matteo, sent for him from Florence. On arriving at
Naples, Matteo, after a few ceremonies, performed the cure. Before
leaving the princess, however, Roderigo said: "You see, Matteo, I
have kept my promise and made a rich man of you, and I owe you
nothing now. So, henceforward you will take care to keep out of my
way, lest as I have hitherto done you some good, just the contrary
should happen to you in future." Upon this Matteo thought it best
to return to Florence, after receiving fifty thousand ducats from his
majesty, in order to enjoy his riches in peace, and never once imagined that Roderigo would come in his way again. But in this he was
deceived; for he soon heard that a daughter of Louis, king of France,
was possessed by an evil spirit, which disturbed our friend Matteo
not a little, thinking of his majesty's great authority and of what
Roderigo had said. Hearing of Matteo's great skill, and finding no
other remedy, the king dispatched a messenger for him, whom
Matteo contrived to send back with a variety of excuses. But this did
not long avail him; the king applied to the Florentine council, and
our hero was compelled to attend. Arriving with no very pleasant
sensations at Paris, he was introduced into the royal presence, when
he assured his majesty that though it was true he had acquired some
fame in the course of his demoniac practice, he could by no means
always boast of success, and that some devils were of such a desperate
character as not to pay the least attention to threats, enchantments,
or even the exorcisms of religion itself. He would, nevertheless, do
his majesty's pleasure, entreating at the same time to be held excused
if it should happen to prove an obstinate case. To this the king made

answer, that be the case what it might, he would certainly hang him if he did not succeed. It is impossible to describe poor Matteo's terror and perplexity on hearing these words; but at length mustering courage, he ordered the possessed princess to be brought into his presence. Approaching as usual close to her ear, he conjured Roderigo in the most humble terms, by all he had ever done for him, not to abandon him in such a dilemma, but to show some sense of gratitude for past services and to leave the princess. "Ah! thou traitorous villain!" cried Roderigo, "hast thou, indeed, ventured to meddle in this business? Dost thou boast thyself a rich man at my expense? I will now convince the world and thee of the extent of my power, both to give and to take away. I shall have the pleasure of seeing thee hanged before thou leavest this place." Poor Matteo finding there was no remedy, said nothing more, but, like a wise man, set his head to work in order to discover some other means of expelling the spirit; for which purpose he said to the king, "Sire, it is as I feared: there are certain spirits of so malignant a character that there is no keeping any terms with them, and this is one of them. However, I will make a last attempt, and I trust that it will succeed according to our wishes. If not, I am in your majesty's power, and I hope you will take compassion on my innocence. In the first place, I have to entreat that your majesty will order a large stage to be erected in the center of the great square, such as will admit the nobility and clergy of the whole city. The stage ought to be adorned with all kinds of silks and with cloth of gold, and with an altar raised in the middle. Tomorrow morning I would have your majesty, with your full train of lords and ecclesiastics in attendance, seated in order and in magnificent array, as spectators of the scene at the said place. There, after having celebrated solemn mass, the possessed princess must appear; but I have in particular to entreat that on one side of the square may be stationed a band of men with drums, trumpets, horns, tambours, bagpipes, cymbals, and kettle-drums, and all other

kinds of instruments that make the most infernal noise. Now, when
I take my hat off, let the whole band strike up, and approach with
the most horrid uproar towards the stage. This, along with a few
other secret remedies which I shall apply, will surely compel the
spirit to depart."

These preparations were accordingly made by the royal command; and when the day, being Sunday morning, arrived, the stage
was seen crowded with people of rank and the square with the
people. Mass was celebrated, and the possessed princess conducted
between two bishops, with a train of nobles, to the spot. Now, when
Roderigo beheld so vast a concourse of people, together with all this
awful preparation, he was almost struck dumb with astonishment,
and said to himself, "I wonder what that cowardly wretch is thinking
of doing now? Does he imagine I have never seen finer things than
these in the regions above—ay! and more horrid things below? However, I will soon make him repent it, at all events." Matteo then
approaching him, besought him to come out; but Roderigo replied,
"Oh, you think you have done a fine thing now! What do you mean
to do with all this trumpery? Can you escape my power, think you,
in this way, or elude the vengeance of the king? Thou poltroon
villain, I will have thee hanged for this!" And as Matteo continued
the more to entreat him, his adversary still vilified him in the same
strain. So Matteo, believing there was no time to be lost, made the
sign with his hat, when all the musicians who had been stationed
there for the purpose suddenly struck up a hideous din, and ringing
a thousand peals, approached the spot. Roderigo pricked up his ears
at the sound, quite at a loss what to think, and rather in a perturbed
tone of voice he asked Matteo what it meant. To this the latter
returned, apparently much alarmed: "Alas! dear Roderigo, it is your
wife; she is coming for you!" It is impossible to give an idea of the
anguish of Roderigo's mind and the strange alteration which his
feelings underwent at that name. The moment the name of "wife"

was pronounced, he had no longer presence of mind to consider whether it were probable, or even possible, that it could be her. Without replying a single word, he leaped out and fled in the utmost terror, leaving the lady to herself, and preferring rather to return to his infernal abode and render an account of his adventures, than run the risk of any further sufferings and vexations under the matrimonial yoke. And thus Belphagor again made his appearance in the infernal domains, bearing ample testimony to the evils introduced into a household by a wife; while Matteo, on his part, who knew more of the matter than the devil, returned triumphantly home, not a little proud of the victory he had achieved.

Doctor Faustus

ANONYMOUS

D r. John Faustus was born in Germany: his father was a poor laboring man, not able to give him any manner of education; but he had a brother in the country, a rich man, who having no child of his own, took a fancy to his nephew and resolved to make him a scholar. Accordingly he put him to a grammar school, where he took learning extraordinary well; and afterward to the university to study divinity. But Faustus, not liking that employment, betook himself to the study of necromancy and conjuration, in which arts he made such a proficiency that in a short time none could equal him. However, he studied divinity so far, that he took his doctor's degree in that faculty; after which he threw the Scripture from him and followed his own inclinations.

Faustus, whose restless mind studied day and night, dressed his imagination with the wings of an eagle and endeavored to fly all over the world, and see and know the secrets of heaven and earth. In short, he obtained power to command the Devil to appear before him whenever he pleased.

One day as Dr. Faustus was walking in a wood near Wirtemberg in Germany, having a friend with him who was desirous to see his art and requested him to let him see if he could then and there bring Mephistopheles before them. The doctor immediately called, and the Devil at the first summons made such a hideous noise in the woods as if heaven and earth were coming together. And after this made a roaring as if the wood had been full of wild beasts. Then the doctor made a circle for the Devil, which he danced round with a noise like that of ten thousand wagons running upon paved stones. After this it thundered and lightninged as if the world had been at an end.

Faustus and his friend, amazed at the noise and frightened at the Devil's long stay, would have departed; but the Devil cheered them with such music as they never heard before. This so encouraged Faustus that he began to command Mephistopheles, in the name of the Prince of Darkness, to appear in his own likeness; on which in an instant hung over his head a mighty dragon. Faustus called him again, as he was used, after which there was a cry in the woods as if Hell had been opened and all the tormented souls had been there. Faustus in the meantime asked the Devil many questions and commanded him to show a great many tricks.

Faustus commanded the Spirit to meet him at his own house by ten o'clock the next day. At the hour appointed he came into his chamber demanding what he would have? Faustus told him it was his will and pleasure to conjure him to be obedient to him in all points of these articles, viz.

First, that the Spirit should serve him in all things he asked, from that time till death.

Secondly, whosoever he would have, the Spirit should bring him.

Thirdly, whatsoever he desired for to know he should tell him.

The Spirit told him he had no such power of himself, until he had acquainted his prince that ruled over him. For, said he, we have rulers over us who send us out and call us home when they will; and we can act no farther than the power we receive from Lucifer, who you know for his pride was thrust out of heaven. But I can tell you no more, unless you bind yourself to us. I will have my request, replied Faustus, and yet not be damned with you. Then said the Spirit, you must not, nor shall not have your desire, and yet thou art mine and all the world cannot save thee from my power. Then get you hence, said Faustus, and I conjure thee that thou come to me at night again.

Then the Spirit vanished, and Doctor Faustus began to consider by what means he could obtain his desires without binding himself to the Devil.

While Faustus was in these cogitations, night drew on, and then the Spirit appeared, acquainting him that now he had orders from his prince to be obedient to him and to do for him what he desired, and bid him show what he would have. Faustus replied, his desire was to become a spirit, and that Mephistopheles should always be at his command; that whenever he pleased he should appear invisible to all men. The Spirit answered, his request should be granted if he would sign the articles pronounced to him, viz. That Faustus should give himself over body and soul to Lucifer, deny his Belief, and become an enemy to all good men; and that the writings should be made with his own blood. Faustus agreeing to all this, the Spirit promised he should have his heart's desire, and the power to turn into any shape, and have a thousand spirits at command.

The Spirit, appearing in the morning to Faustus, told him, that now he was come to see the writing executed and give him power. Whereupon Faustus took out a knife, pricked a vein in his left arm, and drew blood, with which he wrote as follows:

I, John Faustus, Doctor in Divinity, do openly acknowledge that in all my studying of the course of nature and the elements, I could never attain to my desire; I, finding men unable to assist me, have made my addresses to the Prince of Darkness, and his messenger Mephistopheles, giving them both soul and body, on condition that they fully execute my desires; the which they have promised me. I do also further grant by these presents, that if I be duly served, when and in what place I command, and have everything that I ask for during the space of twenty-four years, then I agree that at the expiration of the said term, you shall do with Me and Mine, Body and Soul, as you please. Hereby protesting, that I deny God and Christ and all the host of heaven. And as for the further consideration of this my writing, I have subscribed it with my own hand, sealed it with my own seal, and writ it with my own blood.

JOHN FAUSTUS

No sooner had Faustus set his name to the writing but his spirit Mephistopheles appeared all wrapt in fire, and out of his mouth issued fire; and in an instant came a pack of hounds in full cry. Afterward came a bull dancing before him, then a lion and a bear fighting. All these and many spectacles more did the spirit present to the doctor's view, concluding with all manner of music, and some hundreds of spirits dancing before him. This being ended, Faustus looking about saw seven sacks of silver, which he went to dispose of, but could not handle himself, it was so hot.

This diversion so pleased Faustus that he gave Mephistopheles the writing he had made, and kept a copy of it in his own hands. The Spirit and Faustus being agreed, they dwelt together, and the Devil was never absent from his councils.

Faustus having sold his soul to the Devil, it was soon reported among the neighbors, and no one would keep him company but his Spirit, who was frequently with him, playing of strange tricks to please him.

Not far from Faustus's house lived the Duke of Bavaria, the Bishop of Salzburg, and the Duke of Saxony, whose houses and cellars Mephistopheles used to visit and bring from thence the best provision their houses afforded.

One day the Duke of Bavaria had invited most of the gentry of that country to dinner. In an instant came Mephistopheles and took all with him, leaving them full of admiration.

If at any time Faustus had a mind for wild or tame fowl, the Spirit would call whole flocks in at the window. He also taught Faustus to do the like so that no locks nor bolts could hinder them. The Devil also taught Faustus to fly in the air, and act many things that are incredible, and too large for this book to contain.

After Faustus had had a long conference with the Spirit concerning the fall of Lucifer, the state and condition of the fallen angels, he in a dream saw Hell and the devils.

Having seen this sight, he marveled much at it, and having Mephistopheles at his side, he asked him what sort of people they were who lay in the first dark pit? Mephistopheles told him they were those who pretended to be physicians and had poisoned many thousands in trying practices; and now, said the Spirit, they have the very same administered unto them which they prescribed to others, though not with the same effect; for here, said he, they are denied the happiness to die. Over their heads were long shelves full of vials and galipots of poison.

Having passed by them, he came to a long entry exceeding dark, where was a great crowd; I asked what they were? and the Spirit told me they were pickpockets, who, because they loved to be in a crowd in the other world, were also crowded here together. Among these were some padders on the highway, and others of that function.

Walking farther I saw many thousand vintners and some millions of tailors; insomuch there was scarce room enough for them in the place destined for their reception.

A little farther the Spirit opened a cellar door from which issued a smoke almost enough to choke me, with a dismal noise; I asked what they were, and the Spirit told me, they were witches, such as had been pretended saints in the other world, but now having lost their veil, they squabble, fight, and tear one another.

A few steps farther I espied a great number almost hid with smoke; and I asked who they were? The Spirit told me they were millers and bakers; but, good lack! what a noise was there among them! the miller cried to the baker and the baker to the miller for help, but all in vain, for there was none that could help them.

Passing on farther I saw thousands of shopkeepers, some of whom I knew, who were tormented for defrauding and cheating their customers.

Having taken this prospect of Hell, my Spirit Mephistopheles took me up in his arms and carried me home to my own house, where I awaked, amazed at what I had seen in my dream.

Being come to myself I asked Mephistopheles in what place Hell was? He answered, know thou that before the Fall, Hell was ordained: as for the substance or extent of Hell, we devils do not know it; but it is the wrath of God that makes it so furious.

Thirteen students meeting seven more near Faustus's house fell to words and at length to blows; the thirteen were took hard for the seven. The doctor, looking out at a window, saw the fray, and seeing how much the seven were overmatched by the thirteen, he conjured them all blind, so that they could not see each other; and in this manner they continued to fight, and so smote each other as made the public laugh heartily. At length he parted them, leading them all to their own homes, where they immediately recovered their sight, to the great astonishment of all.

There was a gallant young gentleman that was in love with a fair lady, who was of a proper personage, living at Wirtemberg near the doctor's house. This gentleman had long sought this lady in marriage, but could not obtain his desire; and having placed his affections so much upon her, he was ready to pine away, and had certainly died with grief had he not made his affairs known to the doctor, to whom he opened the whole matter. No sooner had the gentleman told his case to the doctor, but he bid him not fear, for his desire should be fulfilled, and he should have her he so much admired, and that the gentlewoman should love none but him, which was done accordingly; for Faustus so changed the mind of the damsel by his practices, that she could think of nothing else but him, whom she before hated; and Faustus's device was thus: He gave him an enchanted ring, which he ordered him to slip on her finger, which he did: and no sooner was it on but her affections began to change and her heart burned with love toward him. She instead of frowns could do nothing else but smile on him, and could not be at rest till she had asked him if he thought he could love her, and make her a good husband. He gladly answered "yes," and he should think he was the happiest man alive; so they were married the next day, and proved a very happy couple.

Faustus walking in the market place saw seven jolly women sitting all on a row, selling butter and eggs; of each of them he bought something and departed; but no sooner was he gone but all their butter and eggs were gone out of their baskets, they knew not how. At last they were told that Faustus had conjured all their goods away; whereupon they ran in haste to the doctor's house and demanded satisfaction for their wares. He resolved to make sport for the townspeople; made them put off all their clothes and dance naked to their baskets; whereupon everyone saw her goods safe and found herself in a humor to put her clothes on again.

Faustus, as he was going one day to Wirtemberg, overtook a country fellow driving a herd of swine, which were very headstrong, some running one way and some another way, so that the driver could not tell how to get them along. Faustus, taking notice of it, made every one of them dance upon their hind legs, with a fiddle in one of their fore feet and a bow in the other, and so dance and fiddle all the way to Wirtemberg, the countryman dancing all the way before them, which made the people wonder. After Faustus had satisfied himself with this sport, he conjured the fiddles away; and the countryman, offering his pigs for sale, soon sold them and got the money; but before he was gone out of the house, Faustus conjured the pigs out of the market and sent them to the countryman's house. The man who had bought them, seeing the swine gone, stopped the man that sold them and forced him to give back the money; on which he returned home very sorrowful, not knowing what to do; but to his great surprise found all the pigs in their sties.

Faustus, having spun out his twenty-four years within a month or two, began to consider what he could do to cheat the Devil, to whom he had made over both body and soul, but he could find no ways to frustrate his miserable end; which now was drawing near. Whereupon in a miserable tone he cried out, O lamentable wretch that I am! I have given myself to the Devil for a few years' pleasure to gratify my carnal and devilish appetites, and now I must pay full dear. Now I must have torment without end. Woe is me, for there is none to help me; I dare not, I cannot look for mercy from God, for I have abandoned him; I have denied him to be my God, and given up myself to the Devil to be his forever; and now the time is almost expired, and I must be tormented forever and ever.

Faustus's full time being come, the Spirit appeared to him, and showed him the writings, and told him that the next day the Devil would fetch him away. This made the doctor's heart to ache; but to divert himself he sent for some doctors, masters, and bachelors of arts, and other students to dine with him, for whom he provided a great store of varieties, with music and the like; but all would not keep up his spirits, for his hour drew near. Whereupon his countenance changing, the doctors asked the reason for his confusion? To which Faustus answered, O! my friends, you have known me these many years, and that I practiced all manner of wickedness. I have been a great conjurer, which art I obtained from the Devil; selling myself to him soul and body, for the term of twenty-four years; which time expiring tonight is the cause of my sorrow. I have called you, my friends, to see my miserable end; and I pray let my fate be a warning to you all not to attempt to search farther into the secrets of nature than is permitted to be known to man, lest your searches lead you to the Devil, to whom I must this night go, whether I will or no.

About twelve o'clock at night the house shook so terribly that they all feared it would have tumbled down on their heads, and suddenly the doors and windows were broke to pieces, and a great hissing was heard as though the house had been full of snakes; Faustus in the meantime calling out for help but all in vain. There was a vast roaring in the hall, as if all the devils in Hell had been there; and then they vanished, leaving the hall besprinkled with blood, which was most terrible to behold.

The Countess Kathleen O'Shea

ANONYMOUS

A very long time ago, there suddenly appeared in old Ireland two unknown merchants of whom nobody had ever heard, and who nevertheless spoke the language of the country with the greatest perfection. Their locks were black, and bound round with gold, and their garments were of rare magnificence.

Both seemed of like age; they appeared to be men of fifty, for their foreheads were wrinkled and their beards tinged with gray.

In the hostelry where the pompous traders alighted it was sought to penetrate their designs; but in vain—they led a silent and retired life. And whilst they stopped there, they did nothing but count over and over again out of their money-bags pieces of gold, whose yellow brightness could be seen through the windows of their lodging.

"Gentlemen," said the landlady one day, "how is it that you are so rich, and that, being able to succor the public misery, you do no good works?"

"Fair hostess," replied one of them, "we didn't like to present alms to the honest poor, in dread we might be deceived by make-believe paupers. Let want knock at our door, we shall open it."

The following day, when the rumor spread that two rich strangers had come, ready to lavish their gold, a crowd besieged their dwelling; but the figures of those who came out were widely different. Some carried pride in their mien; others were shame-faced.

The two chapmen traded in souls for the demon. The souls of the aged were worth twenty pieces of gold, not a penny more; for Satan had had time to make his valuation. The soul of a matron was valued at fifty, when she was handsome, and a hundred when she was ugly. The soul of a young maiden fetched an extravagant sum; the freshest and purest flowers are the dearest.

At that time there lived in the city an angel of beauty, the Countess Kathleen O'Shea. She was the idol of the people and the providence of the indigent. As soon as she learned that these miscreants profited to the public misery to steal away hearts from God, she called to her butler.

"Patrick," said she to him, "how many pieces of gold in my coffers?"

"A hundred thousand."

"How many jewels?"

"The money's worth of the gold."

"How much property in castles, forests, and lands?"

"Double the rest."

"Very well, Patrick; sell all that is not gold; and bring me the account. I only wish to keep this mansion and the demesne that surrounds it."

Two days afterwards the orders of the pious Kathleen were executed, and the treasure was distributed to the poor in proportion to their wants. This, says the tradition, did not suit the purposes of the Evil Spirit, who found no more souls to purchase. Aided by an infamous servant, they penetrated into the retreat of the noble dame, and purloined from her the rest of her treasure. In vain she struggled with all her strength to save the contents of her coffers; the diabolical thieves were the stronger. If Kathleen had been able to make the sign of the Cross, adds the legend, she would have put them to flight, but her hands were captive. The larceny was effected.

Then the poor called for aid to the plundered Kathleen, alas, to no good: she was able to succor their misery no longer; she had to abandon them to the temptation.

Meanwhile, but eight days had to pass before the grain and provender would arrive in abundance from the western lands. Eight such days were an age. Eight days required an immense sum to relieve the exigencies of the dearth, and the poor should either perish in the agonies of hunger, or, denying the holy maxims of the Gospel, vend, for base lucre, their souls, the richest gift from the bounteous hand of the Almighty. And Kathleen hadn't anything, for she had given up her mansion to the unhappy. She passed twelve hours in tears and mourning, rending her sun-tinted hair, and bruising her breast, of the whiteness of the lily; afterwards she stood up, resolute, animated by a vivid sentiment of despair.

She went to the traders in souls.

"What do you want?" they said.

"You buy souls?"

"Yes, a few still, in spite of you. Isn't that so, saint, with the eyes of sapphire?"

"Today I am come to offer you a bargain," replied she.

"What?"

"I have a soul to sell, but it is costly."

"What does that signify if it is precious? The soul, like the diamond, is appraised by its transparency."

"It is mine."

The two emissaries of Satan started. Their claws were clutched under their gloves of leather; their gray eyes sparkled; the soul, pure, spotless, virginal of Kathleen—it was a priceless acquisition!

"Beauteous lady, how much do you ask?"

"A hundred and fifty thousand pieces of gold."

"It's at your service," replied the traders, and they tendered Kathleen a parchment sealed with black, which she signed with a shudder.

The sum was counted out to her.

As soon as she got home she said to the butler, "Here, distribute this: with this money that I give you the poor can tide over the eight days that remain, and not one of their souls will be delivered to the demon."

Afterwards she shut herself up in her room, and gave orders that none should disturb her.

Three days passed; she called nobody, she did not come out.

When the door was opened, they found her cold and stiff; she was dead of grief.

But the sale of this soul, so adorable in its charity, was declared null by the Lord; for she had saved her fellow-citizens from eternal death.

After the eight days had passed, numerous vessels brought into famished Ireland immense provisions in grain. Hunger was no longer possible. As to the traders, they disappeared from their hotel without anyone knowing what became of them. But the fishermen of the Blackwater pretend that they are enchained in a subterranean prison by order of Lucifer, until they shall be able to render up the soul of Kathleen, which escaped from them.

The Devil and Tom Walker

WASHINGTON IRVING

A few miles from Boston, in Massachusetts, there is a deep inlet winding several miles into the interior of the country from Charles Bay, and terminating in a thickly wooded swamp, or morass. On one side of this inlet is a beautiful dark grove; on the opposite side the land rises abruptly from the water's edge, into a high ridge on which grow a few scattered oaks of great age and immense size. Under one of these gigantic trees, according to old stories, there was a great amount of treasure buried by Kidd the pirate. The inlet allowed a facility to bring the money in a boat secretly and at night to the very foot of the hill. The elevation of the place permitted a good look out to be kept that no one was at hand, while the remarkable trees formed good landmarks by which the place might easily be found again. The old stories add, moreover, that the devil presided at the hiding of the money, and took it under his guardianship; but this, it is well known, he always does with buried treasure, particularly when it has been ill gotten. Be that as it may, Kidd never returned to recover his wealth; being shortly after seized at Boston, sent out to England, and there hanged for a pirate.

About the year 1727, just at the time when earthquakes were prevalent in New England, and shook many tall sinners down upon their knees, there lived near this place a meagre miserly fellow of the name of Tom Walker. He had a wife as miserly as himself; they were so miserly that they even conspired to cheat each other. Whatever the woman could lay hands on she hid away: a hen could not cackle but she was on the alert to secure the new laid egg. Her husband was continually prying about to detect her secret hoards, and many and fierce were the conflicts that took place about what ought to have been common property. They lived in a forlorn looking house, that stood alone and had an air of starvation. A few straggling savin trees, emblems of sterility, grew near it; no smoke ever curled from its chimney; no traveller stopped at its door. A miserable horse, whose ribs were as articulate as the bars of a gridiron, stalked about a field where a thin carpet of moss, scarcely covering the ragged beds of pudding stone, tantalized and balked his hunger; and sometimes he would lean his head over the fence, look piteously at the passer by, and seem to petition deliverance from this land of famine. The house and its inmates had altogether a bad name. Tom's wife was a tall termagant, fierce of temper, loud of tongue, and strong of arm. Her voice was often heard in wordy warfare with her husband; and his face sometimes showed signs that their conflicts were not confined to words. No one ventured, however, to interfere between them; the lonely wayfarer shrank within himself at the horrid clamor and clapper clawing; eyed the den of discord askance, and hurried on his way, rejoicing, if a bachelor, in his celibacy.

One day that Tom Walker had been to a distant part of the neighborhood, he took what he considered a short cut homewards through the swamp. Like most short cuts, it was an ill chosen route. The swamp was thickly grown with great gloomy pines and hemlocks, some of them ninety feet high; which made it dark at noonday, and a retreat for all the owls of the neighborhood. It was full of pits and quagmires, partly covered with weeds and mosses; where the green surface often betrayed the traveller into a gulf of black smothering mud; there were also dark and stagnant pools, the abodes of the tadpole, the bull frog, and the water snake, where the trunks of pines and hemlocks lay half drowned, half rotting, looking like alligators, sleeping in the mire.

Tom had long been picking his way cautiously through this treacherous forest; stepping from tuft to tuft of rushes and roots which afforded precarious footholds among deep sloughs; or pacing carefully, like a cat, along the prostrate trunks of trees; startled now and then by the sudden screaming of the bittern, or the quacking of a wild duck, rising on the wing from some solitary pool. At length he arrived at a piece of firm ground, which ran out like a peninsula into the deep bosom of the swamp. It had been one of the strong holds of the Indians during their wars with the first colonists. Here they had thrown up a kind of fort which they had looked upon as almost impregnable, and had used as a place of refuge for their squaws and children. Nothing remained of the old Indian fort but a few embankments gradually sinking to the level of the surrounding earth, and already overgrown in part by oaks and other forest trees, the foliage of which formed a contrast to the dark pines and hemlocks of the swamp.

It was late in the dusk of evening when Tom Walker reached the old fort, and he paused there for a while to rest himself. Any one but he would have felt unwilling to linger in this lonely melancholy place, for the common people had a bad opinion of it from the stories handed down from the time of the Indian wars; when it was asserted that the savages held incantations here and made sacrifices to the evil spirit. Tom Walker, however, was not a man to be troubled with any fears of the kind.

He reposed himself for some time on the trunk of a fallen hemlock, listening to the boding cry of the tree toad, and delving with his walking staff into a mound of black mould at his feet. As he turned up the soil unconsciously, his staff struck against something hard. He raked it out of the vegetable mould, and lo! a cloven skull with an Indian tomahawk buried deep in it, lay before him. The rust on the weapon showed the time that had elapsed since this death blow had been given. It was a dreary memento of the fierce struggle that had taken place in this last foothold of the Indian warriors.

"Humph!" said Tom Walker, as he gave the skull a kick to shake the dirt from it.

"Let that skull alone!" said a gruff voice.

Tom lifted up his eyes and beheld a great black man, seated directly opposite him on the stump of a tree. He was exceedingly surprised, having neither seen nor heard any one approach, and he was still more perplexed on observing, as well as the gathering gloom would permit, that the stranger was neither negro nor Indian. It is true, he was dressed in a rude, half Indian garb, and had a red belt or sash swathed round his body, but his face was neither black nor copper color, but swarthy and dingy and begrimed with soot, as if he had been accustomed to toil among fires and forges. He had a shock of coarse black hair, that stood out from his head in all directions; and bore an axe on his shoulder.

He scowled for a moment at Tom with a pair of great red eyes.

"What are you doing on my grounds?" said the black man, with a hoarse growling voice.

"Your grounds?" said Tom, with a sneer; "no more your grounds than mine: they belong to Deacon Peabody."

"Deacon Peabody be d——d," said the stranger, "as I flatter myself he will be, if he does not look more to his own sins and less to those of his neighbors. Look yonder, and see how Deacon Peabody is faring."

Tom looked in the direction that the stranger pointed, and beheld one of the great trees, fair and flourishing without, but rotten at the core, and saw that it had been nearly hewn through, so that the first high wind was likely to blow it down. On the bark of the tree was scored the name of Deacon Peabody, an eminent man, who had waxed wealthy by driving shrewd bargains with the Indians. He now looked round and found most of the tall trees marked with the name of some great man of the colony, and all more or less scored by the axe. The one on which he had been seated, and which had evidently just been hewn down, bore the name of Crowninshield; and he recollected a mighty rich man of that name, who made a vulgar display of wealth, which it was whispered he had acquired by buccaneering.

"He's just ready for burning!" said the black man, with a growl of triumph. "You see I am likely to have a good stock of firewood for winter."

"But what right have you," said Tom, "to cut down Deacon Peabody's timber?"

"The right of prior claim," said the other. "This woodland belonged to me long before one of your white faced race put foot upon the soil."

"And pray, who are you, if I may be so bold?" said Tom.

"Oh, I go by various names. I am the Wild Huntsman in some countries; the Black Miner in others. In this neighborhood I am known by the name of the Black Woodsman. I am he to whom the red men consecrated this spot, and in honor of whom they now and then roasted a white man by way of sweet smelling sacrifice. Since the red men have been exterminated by you white savages, I amuse myself by presiding at the persecutions of quakers and anabaptists; I am the great patron and prompter of slave dealers, and the grand master of the Salem witches."

"The upshot of all which is, that, if I mistake not," said Tom, sturdily, "you are he commonly called Old Scratch."

"The same at your service!" replied the black man, with a half civil nod.

Such was the opening of this interview, according to the old story, though it has almost too familiar an air to be credited. One would think that to meet with such a singular personage in this wild lonely place, would have shaken any man's nerves: but Tom was a hard minded fellow, not easily daunted, and he had lived so long with a termagant wife, that he did not even fear the devil.

It is said that after this commencement, they had a long and earnest conversation together, as Tom returned homewards. The black man told him of great sums of money buried by Kidd the pirate, under the oak trees on the high ridge not far from the morass. All these were under his command and protected by his power, so that none could find them but such as propitiated his favor. These he offered to place within Tom Walker's reach, having conceived an especial kindness for him: but they were to be had only on certain conditions. What these conditions were, may easily be surmised, though Tom never disclosed them publicly. They must have been very hard, for he required time to think of them, and he was not a man to stick at trifles where money was in view. When they had reached the edge of the swamp the stranger paused.

"What proof have I that all you have been telling me is true?" said Tom.

"There is my signature," said the black man, pressing his finger on Tom's forehead. So saying, he turned off among the thickets of the swamp, and seemed, as Tom said, to go down, down, down, into the earth, until nothing but his head and shoulders could be seen, and so on until he totally disappeared.

When Tom reached home he found the black print of a finger burnt, as it were, into his forehead, which nothing could obliterate.

The first news his wife had to tell him was the sudden death of Absalom Crowninshield the rich buccaneer. It was announced in the papers with the usual flourish, that "a great man had fallen in Israel."

Tom recollected the tree which his black friend had just hewn down, and which was ready for burning. "Let the freebooter roast," said Tom, "who cares!" He now felt convinced that all he had heard and seen was no illusion.

He was not prone to let his wife into his confidence; but as this was an uneasy secret, he willingly shared it with her. All her avarice was awakened at the mention of hidden gold, and she urged her husband to comply with the black man's terms and secure what would make them wealthy for life. However Tom might have felt disposed to sell himself to the devil, he was determined not to do so to oblige his wife; so he flatly refused out of the mere spirit of contradiction. Many and bitter were the quarrels they had on the subject, but the more she talked the more resolute was Tom not to be damned to please her. At length she determined to drive the bargain on her own account, and if she succeeded, to keep all the gain to herself.

Being of the same fearless temper as her husband, she set off for the old Indian fort towards the close of a summer's day. She was many hours absent. When she came back she was reserved and sullen in her replies. She spoke something of a black man whom she had met about twilight, hewing at the root of a tall tree. He was sulky, however, and would not come to terms; she was to go again with a propitiatory offering, but what it was she forbore to say.

The next evening she set off again for the swamp, with her apron heavily laden. Tom waited and waited for her, but in vain: midnight came, but she did not make her appearance; morning, noon, night returned, but still she did not come. Tom now grew uneasy for her safety; especially as he found she had carried off in her apron the silver teapot and spoons and every portable article of value. Another night elapsed, another morning came; but no wife. In a word, she was never heard of more.

What was her real fate nobody knows, in consequence of so many pretending to know. It is one of those facts which have become confounded by a variety of historians. Some asserted that she lost her way among the tangled mazes of the swamp and sank into some pit or slough; others, more uncharitable, hinted that she had eloped with the household booty, and made off to some other province; while others assert that the tempter had decoyed her into a dismal quagmire on top of which her hat was found lying. In confirmation of this, it was said a great black man with an axe on his shoulder was seen late that very evening coming out of the swamp, carrying a bundle tied in a check apron, with an air of surly triumph.

The most current and probable story, however, observes that Tom Walker grew so anxious about the fate of his wife and his property that he set out at length to seek them both at the Indian fort. During a long summer's afternoon he searched about the gloomy place, but no wife was to be seen. He called her name repeatedly, but she was no where to be heard. The bittern alone responded to his voice, as he flew screaming by; or the bull frog croaked dolefully from a neighboring pool. At length, it is said, just in the brown hour of twilight, when the owls began to hoot and the bats to flit about, his attention was attracted by the clamor of carrion crows hovering about a cypress tree. He looked up and beheld a bundle tied in a check apron and hanging in the branches of the tree; with a great vulture perched hard by, as if keeping watch upon it. He leaped with joy, for he recognized his wife's apron, and supposed it to contain the household valuables.

"Let us get hold of the property," said he, consolingly to himself, "and we will endeavor to do without the woman."

As he scrambled up the tree the vulture spread its wide wings, and sailed off screaming into the deep shadows of the forest. Tom seized the check apron, but, woful sight! found nothing but a heart and liver tied up in it.

Such, according to the most authentic old story, was all that was to be found of Tom's wife. She had probably attempted to deal with the black man as she had been accustomed to deal with her husband; but though a female scold is generally considered a match for the devil, yet in this instance she appears to have had the worst of it. She must have died game however; for it is said Tom noticed many prints of cloven feet deeply stamped about the tree, and found handsful of hair, that looked as if they had been plucked from the coarse black shock of the woodsman. Tom knew his wife's prowess by experience. He shrugged his shoulders as he looked at the signs of a fierce clapper clawing. "Egad," said he to himself, "Old Scratch must have had a tough time of it!"

Tom consoled himself for the loss of his property with the loss of his wife; for he was a man of fortitude. He even felt something like gratitude towards the black woodsman, who he considered had done him a kindness. He sought, therefore, to cultivate a further acquaintance with him, but for some time without success; the old black legs played shy, for whatever people may think, he is not always to be had for calling for; he knows how to play his cards when pretty sure of his game.

At length, it is said, when delay had whetted Tom's eagerness to the quick, and prepared him to agree to any thing rather than not gain the promised treasure, he met the black man one evening in his usual woodsman dress, with his axe on his shoulder, sauntering along the edge of the swamp, and humming a tune. He affected to receive Tom's advances with great indifference, made brief replies, and went on humming his tune.

By degrees, however, Tom brought him to business, and they began to haggle about the terms on which the former was to have the pirate's treasure. There was one condition which need not be mentioned, being generally understood in all cases where the devil grants favors; but there were others about which, though of less importance, he was inflexibly obstinate. He insisted that the money found through his means should be employed in his service. He proposed, therefore, that Tom should employ it in the black traffick; that is to say, that he should fit out a slave ship. This, however, Tom resolutely refused; he was bad enough in all conscience; but the devil himself could not tempt him to turn slave dealer.

Finding Tom so squeamish on this point, he did not insist upon it, but proposed instead that he should turn usurer; the devil being extremely anxious for the increase of usurers, looking upon them as his peculiar people.

To this no objections were made, for it was just to Tom's taste.

"You shall open a broker's shop in Boston next month," said the black man.

"I'll do it tomorrow, if you wish," said Tom Walker.

"You shall lend money at two per cent. a month."

"Egad, I'll charge four!" replied Tom Walker.

"You shall extort bonds, foreclose mortgages, drive the merchant to bankruptcy—"

"I'll drive him to the d——l," cried Tom Walker, eagerly.

"You are the usurer for my money!" said the black legs, with delight. "When will you want the rhino?"

"This very night."

"Done!" said the devil.

"Done!" said Tom Walker. So they shook hands, and struck a bargain.

A few days' time saw Tom Walker seated behind his desk in a

counting house in Boston. His reputation for a ready moneyed man, who would lend money out for a good consideration, soon spread abroad. Every body remembers the days of Governor Belcher, when money was particularly scarce. It was a time of paper credit. The country had been deluged with government bills; the famous Land Bank had been established; there had been a rage for speculating; the people had run mad with schemes for new settlements; for building cities in the wilderness; land jobbers went about with maps of grants, and townships, and Eldorados, lying nobody knew where, but which every body was ready to purchase. In a word, the great speculating fever which breaks out every now and then in the country, had raged to an alarming degree, and every body was dreaming of making sudden fortunes from nothing. As usual the fever had subsided; the dream had gone off, and the imaginary fortunes with it; the patients were left in doleful plight, and the whole country resounded with the consequent cry of "hard times."

At this propitious time of public distress did Tom Walker set up as a usurer in Boston. His door was soon thronged by customers. The needy and the adventurous; the gambling speculator; the dreaming land jobber; the thriftless tradesman; the merchant with cracked credit; in short, every one driven to raise money by desperate means and desperate sacrifices, hurried to Tom Walker.

Thus Tom was the universal friend of the needy, and he acted like a "friend in need"; that is to say, he always exacted good pay and good security. In proportion to the distress of the applicant was the hardness of his terms. He accumulated bonds and mortgages; gradually squeezed his customers closer and closer; and sent them at length, dry as a sponge from his door.

In this way he made money hand over hand; became a rich and mighty man, and exalted his cocked hat upon change. He built himself, as usual, a vast house, out of ostentation; but left the greater part of it unfinished and unfurnished out of parsimony. He even set up a carriage in the fullness of his vain glory, though he nearly starved the horses which drew it; and as the ungreased wheels groaned and screeched on the axle trees, you would have thought you heard the souls of the poor debtors he was squeezing.

As Tom waxed old, however, he grew thoughtful. Having secured the good things of this world, he began to feel anxious about those of the next. He thought with regret on the bargain he had made with his black friend, and set his wits to work to cheat him out of the conditions. He became, therefore, all of a sudden, a violent church goer. He prayed loudly and strenuously as if heaven were to be taken by force of lungs. Indeed, one might always tell when he had sinned most during the week, by the clamor of his Sunday devotion. The quiet christians who had been modestly and steadfastly travelling Zionward, were struck with self reproach at seeing themselves so suddenly outstripped in their career by this new made convert. Tom was as rigid in religious, as in money matters; he was a stern supervisor and censurer of his neighbours, and seemed to think every sin entered up to their account became a credit on his own side of the page. He even talked of the expediency of reviving the persecution of quakers and anabaptists. In a word, Tom's zeal became as notorious as his riches.

Still, in spite of all this strenuous attention to forms, Tom had a lurking dread that the devil, after all, would have his due. That he might not be taken unawares, therefore, it is said he always carried a small bible in his coat pocket. He had also a great folio bible on his counting house desk, and would frequently be found reading it when people called on business; on such occasions he would lay his green spectacles in the book, to mark the place, while he turned round to drive some usurious bargain.

Some say that Tom grew a little crack brained in his old days, and that fancying his end approaching, he had his horse new shod, saddled and bridled, and buried with his feet uppermost; because he supposed that at the last day the world would be turned upside down; in which case he should find his horse standing ready for mounting, and he was determined at the worst to give his old friend a run for it. This, however, is probably a mere old wives' fable. If he really did take such a precaution it was totally superfluous; at least so says the authentic old legend which closes his story in the following manner.

One hot afternoon in the dog days, just as a terrible black thundergust was coming up, Tom sat in his counting house in his white linen cap and India silk morning gown. He was on the point of foreclosing a mortgage, by which he would complete the ruin of an unlucky land speculator for whom he had professed the greatest friendship. The poor land jobber begged him to grant a few months' indulgence. Tom had grown testy and irritated and refused another day.

"My family will be ruined and brought upon the parish," said the land jobber. "Charity begins at home," replied Tom, "I must take care of myself in these hard times."

"You have made so much money out of me," said the speculator.

Tom lost his patience and his piety— "The devil take me," said he, "if I have made a farthing!"

Just then there were three loud knocks at the street door. He stepped out to see who was there. A black man was holding a black horse which neighed and stamped with impatience.

"Tom, you're come for!" said the black fellow, gruffly. Tom shrunk back, but too late. He had left his little bible at the bottom of his coat pocket, and his big bible on the desk buried under the mortgage he was about to foreclose: never was sinner taken more unawares. The black man whisked him like a child into the saddle, gave the horse a lash, and away he galloped, with Tom on his back, in the midst of a thunder storm. The clerks stuck their pens behind their ears and stared after him from the windows. Away went Tom Walker, dashing down the streets; his white cap bobbing up and down; his morning gown fluttering in the wind, and his steed striking fire out of the pavement at every bound. When the clerks turned to look for the black man he had disappeared.

Tom Walker never returned to foreclose the mortgage. A countryman who lived on the border of the swamp, reported that in the height of the thunder gust he had heard a great clattering of hoofs and a howling along the road, and running to the window caught sight of a figure, such as I have described, on a horse that galloped like mad across the fields, over the hills and down into the black hemlock swamp towards the old Indian fort; and that shortly after a thunderbolt falling in that direction seemed to set the whole forest in a blaze.

The good people of Boston shook their heads and shrugged their shoulders, but had been so much accustomed to witches and goblins and tricks of the devil in all kinds of shapes from the first settlement of the colony, that they were not so much horror struck as might have been expected. Trustees were appointed to take charge of Tom's effects. There was nothing, however, to administer upon. On searching his coffers all his bonds and mortgages were found reduced to cinders. In place of gold and silver his iron chest was filled with chips and shavings; two skeletons lay in his stable instead of his half starved horses, and the very next day his great house took fire and was burnt to the ground.

Such was the end of Tom Walker and his ill gotten wealth. Let all griping money brokers lay this story to heart. The truth of it is not to be doubted. The very hole under the oak trees, whence he dug Kidd's money is to be seen to this day; and the neighboring swamp and old Indian fort are often haunted in stormy nights by a figure on horseback, in a morning gown and white cap, which is doubtless the troubled spirit of the usurer. In fact, the story has resolved itself into a proverb, and is the origin of that popular saying, prevalent throughout New England, of "The Devil and Tom Walker."

St. John's Eve

NIKOLAI GOGOL

Thoma Grigorovitch had a very strange sort of eccentricity: to the day of his death, he never liked to tell the same thing twice. There were times, when, if you asked him to relate a thing afresh, behold, he would interpolate new matter, or alter it so that it was impossible to recognize it. Once on a time, one of those gentlemen (it is hard for us simple people to put a name to them, to say whether they are scribblers, or not scribblers: but it is just the same thing as the usurers at our yearly fairs; they clutch and beg and steal every sort of frippery, and issue mean little volumes, no thicker than an A B C book, every month, or even every week)—one of these gentlemen wormed this same story out of Thoma Grigorovitch, and he completely forgot about it. But that same young gentleman in the pea-green caftan, whom I have mentioned, and one of whose Tales you have already read, I think, came from Poltava, bringing with him a little book, and, opening it in the middle, shows it to us. Thoma Grigorovitch was on the point of setting his spectacles astride of his nose, but recollected that he had forgotten to wind thread about them, and stick them together with wax, so he passed it over to me. As I understand something about reading and writing, and do not wear spectacles, I undertook to read it. I had not turned two leaves, when all at once he caught me by the hand, and stopped me.

"Stop! tell me first what you are reading."

I confess that I was a trifle stunned by such a question.

"What! what am I reading, Thoma Grigorovitch? These were your very words."

"Who told you that they were my words?"

"Why, what more would you have? Here it is printed: *Related by such and such a sacristan.*"

"Spit on the head of the man who printed that! he lies, the dog of a Moscow peddler! Did I say that? *'Twas just the same as though one hadn't his wits about him!* Listen. I'll tell it to you on the spot."

We moved up to the table, and he began.

My grandfather (the kingdom of heaven be his! may he eat only wheaten rolls and *makovniki* [poppy-seeds cooked in honey, and dried in square cakes] with honey in the other world!) could tell a story wonderfully well. When he used to begin on a tale, you wouldn't stir from the spot all day, but keep on listening. He was no match for the storyteller of the present day, when he begins to lie, with a tongue as though he had had nothing to eat for three days, so that you snatch your cap, and flee from the house. As I now recall it—my old mother was alive then—in the long winter evenings when the frost was crackling out of doors, and had so sealed up hermetically the narrow panes of our cottage, she used to sit before the hackling-comb, drawing out a long thread in her hand, rocking the cradle with her foot, and humming a song, which I seem to hear even now.

The fat-lamp quivering and flaring up as though in fear of something, lighted us within our cottage; the spindle hummed; and all of us children, collected in a cluster, listened to grandfather, who had not crawled off the oven for more than five years, owing to his great age. But the wondrous tales of the incursions of the Zaporozhian Cossacks, the Poles, the bold deeds of Podkova, of Poltor-Kozhukh, and Sagaidatchnii, did not interest us so much as the stories about some deed of eld which always sent a shiver through our frames, and made our hair rise upright on our heads. Sometimes such terror took possession of us in consequence of them, that, from that evening on, Heaven knows what a marvel everything seemed to us. If you chance to go out of the cottage after nightfall for anything, you imagine that a visitor from the other world has lain down to sleep in your bed; and I should not be able to tell this a second time were it not that I had often taken my own smock, at a distance, as it lay at the head of the bed, for the Evil One rolled up in a ball! But the chief thing about grandfather's stories was, that he never had lied in all his life; and whatever he said was so, was so.

I will now relate to you one of his marvelous tales. I know that there are a great many wise people who copy in the courts, and can even read civil documents, who, if you were to put into their hand a simple prayer book, could not make out the first letter in it, and would show all their teeth in derision—which is wisdom. These people laugh at everything you tell them. Such incredulity has spread abroad in the world! What then? (Why, may God and the Holy

Virgin cease to love me if it is not possible that even you will not believe me!) Once he said something about witches; . . . What then? Along comes one of these headbreakers—and doesn't believe in witches! Yes, glory to God that I have lived so long in the world! I have seen heretics, to whom it would be easier to lie in confession than it would to our brothers and equals to take snuff, and those people would deny the existence of witches! But let them just dream about something, and they won't even tell what it was! There's no use in talking about them!

No one could have recognized this village of ours a little over a hundred years ago: a hamlet it was, the poorest kind of a hamlet. Half a score of miserable izbás, unplastered, badly thatched, were scattered here and there about the fields. There was not an enclosure or a decent shed to shelter animals or wagons. That was the way the wealthy lived: and if you had looked for our brothers, the poor— why, a hole in the ground—that was a cabin for you! Only by the smoke could you tell that a God-created man lived there. You ask why they lived so? It was not entirely through poverty: almost everyone led a wandering, Cossack life, and gathered not a little plunder in foreign lands; it was rather because there was no reason for setting up a well-ordered *khata* (wooden house). How many people were wandering all over the country—Crimeans, Poles, Lithuanians! It was quite possible that their own countrymen might make a descent, and plunder everything. Anything was possible.

In this hamlet a man, or rather a devil in human form, often made his appearance. Why he came, and whence, no one knew. He prowled about, got drunk, and suddenly disappeared as if into the air, and there was not a hint of his existence. Then, again, behold, and he seemed to have dropped from the sky, and went flying about the street of the village, of which no trace now remains, and which was not more than a hundred paces from Dikanka. He would collect together all the Cossacks he met; then there were songs, laughter, money in abundance, and vodka flowed like water. . . . He would address the pretty girls, and give them ribbons, earrings, strings of beads—more than they knew what to do with. It is true that the pretty girls rather hesitated about accepting his presents: God knows, perhaps they had passed through unclean hands. My grandfather's aunt, who kept a tavern at that time, in which Basavriuk (as they called that devil-man) often had his carouses, said that no consideration on the face of the earth would have induced her to accept a gift from him. And then, again, how avoid accepting? Fear seized on everyone when he knit his bristly brows, and gave a sidelong glance which might send your feet, God knows whither: but if you accept, then the next night some fiend from the swamp, with horns on his head, comes to call, and begins to squeeze your neck, when there is a string of beads upon it; or bite your finger, if there is a ring upon it; or drag you by the hair, if ribbons are braided in it. God have mercy, then, on those who owned such gifts! But here was the difficulty: it was impossible to get rid of them; if you threw them into the water, the diabolical ring or necklace would skim along the surface, and into your hand.

There was a church in the village—St. Pantelei, if I remember rightly. There lived there a priest, Father Athanasii of blessed memory. Observing that Basavriuk did not come to church, even on Easter, he determined to reprove him, and impose penance upon him. Well, he hardly escaped with his life. "Hark ye, pannótche!" he thundered in reply, "learn to mind your own business instead of meddling in other people's, if you don't want that goat's throat of yours stuck together with boiling kutya." What was to be done with this unrepentant man? Father Athanasii contented himself with announcing that anyone who should make the acquaintance of Basavriuk would be counted a Catholic, an enemy of Christ's church, not a member of the human race.

In this village there was a Cossack named Korzh, who had a laborer whom people called Peter the Orphan—perhaps because no one remembered either his father or mother. The church starost, it is true, said that they had died of the pest in his second year; but my grandfather's aunt would not hear to that, and tried with all her might to furnish him with parents, although poor Peter needed them about as much as we need last year's snow. She said that his father had been in Zaporozhe, taken prisoner by the Turks, underwent God only knows what tortures, and having, by some miracle, disguised himself as a eunuch, had made his escape. Little cared the black-browed youths and maidens about his parents. They merely remarked, that if he only had a new coat, a red sash, a black lambskin cap, with dandified blue crown, on his head, a Turkish saber hanging by his side, a whip in one hand and a pipe with handsome mountings in the other, he would surpass all the young men. But the pity was, that the only thing poor Peter had was a gray svitka with more holes in it than there are gold pieces in a Jew's pocket. And that was not the worst of it, but this: that Korzh had a daughter, such a beauty as I think you can hardly have chanced to see. My deceased grandfather's aunt used to say—and you know that it is easier for a woman to kiss the Evil One than to call anybody a beauty, without malice be it said—that this Cossack maiden's cheeks were as plump and fresh as the pinkest poppy when just bathed in God's dew, and, glowing, it unfolds its petals, and coquets with the rising sun; that her brows were like black cords, such as our maidens buy nowadays, for their crosses and ducats, of the Moscow peddlers who visit the villages with their baskets, and evenly arched as though peeping into her clear eyes; that her little mouth, at sight of which the youths smacked their lips, seemed made to emit the songs of nightingales; that her hair, black as the raven's wing, and soft as young flax (our maidens did not then plait their hair in clubs interwoven with pretty, bright-hued ribbons), fell in curls over her kuntush. Eh! may I never intone another alleluia in the choir, if I would not have kissed her, in spite of the gray which is making its way all through the old wool which covers my pate, and my old woman beside me, like a thorn in my side! Well, you know what happens when young men and maids live side by side. In the twilight the heels of red boots were always visible in the place where Pidórka chatted with her Petrus. But Korzh would never have suspected anything out of the way, only one day—it is evident that none but the Evil One could have inspired him—Petrus took it into his head to kiss the Cossack maiden's rosy lips with all his heart in the passage, without first looking well about him; and that same Evil One—may the son of a dog dream of the holy cross!—caused the old graybeard, like a fool, to open the cottage door at that same moment. Korzh was petrified, dropped his jaw, and clutched at the door for support. Those un-lucky kisses had completely stunned him. It surprised him more than the blow of a pestle on the wall, with which, in our days, the muzhik generally drives out his intoxication for lack of fusees and powder.

Recovering himself, he took his grandfather's hunting whip from the wall, and was about to belabor Peter's back with it, when Pidórka's little six-year-old brother Ivas rushed up from somewhere or other, and, grasping his father's legs with his little hands, screamed out, "Daddy, daddy! don't beat Petrus!" What was to be done? A father's heart is not made of stone. Hanging the whip again upon the wall, he led him quietly from the house. "If you ever show yourself in my cottage again, or even under the windows, look out, Petró! by Heaven, your black mustache will disappear; and your black locks, though wound twice about your ears, will take leave of your pate, or my name is not Terentiy Korzh." So saying, he gave him a little taste of his fist in the nape of his neck, so that all grew dark before Petrus, and he flew headlong. So there was an end of their kissing. Sorrow seized upon our doves; and a rumor was rife in the village, that a certain Pole, all embroidered with gold, with mustaches, saber, spurs, and pockets jingling like the bells of the bag with which our sacristan Taras goes through the church everyday, had begun to frequent Korzh's house. Now, it is well known why the father is visited when there is a black-browed daughter about. So, one day, Pidórka burst into tears, and clutched the hand of her Ivas. "Ivas, my dear! Ivas, my love! fly to Petrus, my child of gold, like an arrow from a bow. Tell him all: I would have loved his brown eyes, I would have kissed his white face, but my fate decrees not so. More than one towel have I wet with burning tears. I am sad, I am heavy at heart. And my own father is my enemy. I will not marry that Pole, whom I do not love. Tell him they are preparing a wedding, but there will be no music at our wedding: ecclesiastics will sing instead of pipes and kobzas. I shall not dance with my bridegroom: they will carry me out. Dark, dark will be my dwelling,—of maple wood; and, instead of chimneys, a cross will stand upon the roof."

Petró stood petrified, without moving from the spot, when the innocent child lisped out Pidórka's words to him. "And I, unhappy man, thought to go to the Crimea and Turkey, win gold and return to thee, my beauty! But it may not be. The evil eye has seen us. I will have a wedding, too, dear little fish, I too; but no ecclesiastics will be at that wedding. The black crow will caw, instead of the pope, over me; the smooth field will be my dwelling; the dark blue clouds my roof-tree. The eagle will claw out my brown eyes: the rain will wash the Cossack's bones, and the whirlwinds will dry them. But what am I? Of whom, to whom, am I complaining? 'Tis plain, God willed it so. If I am to be lost, then so be it!" and he went straight to the tavern.

My late grandfather's aunt was somewhat surprised on seeing Petrus in the tavern, and at an hour when good men go to morning mass; and she stared at him as though in a dream, when he demanded a jug of brandy, about half a pailful. But the poor fellow tried in vain to drown his woe. The vodka stung his tongue like nettles, and tasted more bitter than wormwood. He flung the jug from him upon the ground. "You have sorrowed enough, Cossack," growled a bass voice behind him. He looked round—Basavriuk! Ugh, what a face! His hair was like a brush, his eyes like those of a bull. "I know what you lack: here it is." Then he jingled a leather purse which hung from his girdle, and smiled diabolically. Petró shuddered. "He, he, he! yes, how it shines!" he roared, shaking out ducats into his hand: "he, he, he! and how it jingles! And I only ask one thing for a whole pile of such shiners." "It is the Evil One!" exclaimed Petró: "Give them here! I'm ready for anything!" They struck hands upon it. "See here, Petró, you are ripe just in time: tomorrow is St. John the Baptist's day. Only on this one night in the year does the fern blossom. Delay not. I will await thee at midnight in the Bear's ravine."

I do not believe that chickens await the hour when the woman brings their corn, with as much anxiety as Petrus awaited the evening. And, in fact, he looked to see whether the shadows of the trees were not lengthening, if the sun were not turning red towards setting; and, the longer he watched, the more impatient he grew. How long it was! Evidently, God's day had lost its end somewhere. And now the sun is gone. The sky is red only on one side, and it is already growing dark. It grows colder in the fields. It gets dusky, and more dusky, and at last quite dark. At last! With heart almost bursting from his bosom, he set out on his way, and cautiously descended through the dense woods into the deep hollow called the Bear's ravine. Basavriuk was already waiting there. It was so dark, that you could not see a yard before you. Hand in hand they penetrated the thin marsh, clinging to the luxuriant thorn bushes, and stumbling at almost every step. At last they reached an open spot. Petró looked about him: he had never chanced to come there before. Here Basavriuk halted.

"Do you see, before you stand three hillocks? There are a great many sorts of flowers upon them. But may some power keep you from plucking even one of them. But as soon as the fern blossoms, seize it, and look not round, no matter what may seem to be going on behind thee."

Petró wanted to ask—and behold, he was no longer there. He approached the three hillocks—where were the flowers? He saw nothing. The wild steppe-grass darkled around, and stifled everything in its luxuriance. But the lightning flashed; and before him stood a whole bed of flowers, all wonderful, all strange: and there were also the simple fronds of fern. Petró doubted his senses, and stood thoughtfully before them, with both hands upon his sides.

"What prodigy is this? one can see these weeds ten times in a day: what marvel is there about them? was not devil's face laughing at me?"

Behold! the tiny flower-bud crimsons, and moves as though alive. It is a marvel, in truth. It moves, and grows larger and larger, and flushes like a burning coal. The tiny star flashes up, something bursts softly, and the flower opens before his eyes like a flame, lighting the others about it. "Now is the time," thought Petró, and extended his hand. He sees hundreds of shaggy hands reach from behind him, also for the flower; and there is a running about from place to place, in the rear. He half shut his eyes, plucked sharply at the stalk, and the flower remained in his hand. All became still. Upon a stump sat Basavriuk, all blue like a corpse. He moved not so much as a finger. His eyes were immovably fixed on something visible to him alone: his mouth was half open and speechless. All about, nothing stirred. Ugh! it was horrible!—But then a whistle was heard, which made Petró's heart grow cold within him; and it seemed to him that the grass whispered, and the flowers began to talk among themselves in delicate voices, like little silver bells; the trees rustled in waving contention—Basavriuk's face suddenly became full of life, and his eyes sparkled. "The witch has just returned," he muttered between his teeth. "See here, Petró: a beauty will stand before you in a moment; do whatever she commands; if not—you are lost forever." Then he parted the thorn bush with a knotty stick, and before him stood a tiny izbá, on chicken's legs, as they say. Basavriuk smote it with his fist, and the wall trembled. A large black dog ran out to meet them, and with a whine, transforming itself into a cat, flew straight at his eyes. "Don't be angry, don't be angry, you old Satan!" said Basavriuk, employing such words as would have made a good man stop his ears. Behold, instead of a cat, an old woman with a face wrinkled like a baked apple, and all bent into a bow: her nose and chin were like a pair of nut-crackers. "A stunning beauty!" thought Petró; and cold chills ran down his back. The witch tore the flower from his hand, bent over, and muttered over it for a long time, sprinkling it with some kind of water. Sparks flew from her mouth, froth appeared on her lips.

"Throw it away," she said, giving it back to Petró.

Petró threw it, and what wonder was this? the flower did not fall straight to the earth, but for a long while twinkled like a fiery ball through the darkness, and swam through the air like a boat: at last it began to sink lower and lower, and fell so far away, that the little star, hardly larger than a poppy seed, was barely visible. "Here!" croaked the old woman, in a dull voice: and Basavriuk, giving him a spade, said, "Dig here, Petró: here you will see more gold than you or Korzh ever dreamed of."

Petró spat on his hands, seized the spade, applied his foot, and turned up the earth, a second, a third, a fourth time. . . . There was something hard: the spade clinked, and would go no father. Then his eyes began to distinguish a small, iron-bound coffer. He tried to seize it; but the chest began to sink into the earth, deeper, farther, and deeper still: and behind him he heard a laugh, more like a serpent's hiss. "No, you shall not see the gold until you procure human blood," said the witch, and led up to him a child of six, covered with a white sheet, indicating by a sign that he was to cut off his head. Petró was stunned. A trifle, indeed, to cut off a man's, or even an innocent child's, head for no reason whatever! In wrath he tore off the sheet enveloping his head, and behold! before him stood Ivas. And the poor child crossed his little hands, and hung his head. . . . Petró flew upon the witch with the knife like a madman, and was on the point of laying hands on her. . . .

"What did you promise for the girl?" . . . thundered Basavriuk; and like a shot he was on his back. The witch stamped her foot: a blue flame flashed from the earth; it illumined it all inside, and it was as if molded of crystal; and all that was within the earth became visible, as if in the palm of the hand. Ducats, precious stones in chests and kettles, were piled in heaps beneath the very spot they stood on. His eyes burned, . . . his mind grew troubled. . . . He grasped the knife like a madman, and the innocent blood spurted into his eyes. Diabolical laughter resounded on all sides. Misshaped monsters flew past him in herds. The witch, fastening her hands in the headless trunk, like a wolf, drank its blood. . . . All went round in his head. Collecting all his strength, he set out to run. Everything turned red before him. The trees seemed steeped in blood, and burned and groaned. The sky glowed and glowered. . . . Burning points, like lightning, flickered before his eyes. Utterly exhausted, he rushed into his miserable hovel, and fell to the ground like a log. A deathlike sleep overpowered him.

Two days and two nights did Petró sleep, without once awakening. When he came to himself, on the third day, he looked long at all the corners of his hut; but in vain did he endeavor to recollect; his memory was like a miser's pocket, from which you cannot entice a quarter of a kopek. Stretching himself, he heard something clash at his feet. He looked—two bags of gold. Then only, as if in a dream, he recollected that he had been seeking some treasure, that something had frightened him in the woods. . . . But at what price he had obtained it, and how, he could by no means understand.

Korzh saw the sacks—and was mollified. "Such a Petrus, quite unheard of! yes, and did I not love him? Was he not to me as my own son?" And the old fellow carried on his fiction until it reduced him to tears. Pidórka began to tell him how some passing gypsies had stolen Ivas; but Petró could not even recall him—to such a degree had the Devil's influence darkened his mind! There was no reason for delay. The Pole was dismissed, and the wedding feast prepared; rolls were baked, towels and handkerchiefs embroidered; the young people were seated at table; the wedding-loaf was cut; banduras, cymbals, pipes, kobzi, sounded, and pleasure was rife. . . .

A wedding in the olden times was not like one of the present day. My grandfather's aunt used to tell—what doings!—how the maidens—in festive headdresses of yellow, blue, and pink ribbons, above which they bound gold braid; in thin chemisettes embroidered on all the seams with red silk, and strewn with tiny silver flowers; in morocco shoes, with high iron heels—danced the gorlitza as swimmingly as peacocks, and as wildly as the whirlwind; how the youths—with their shipshaped caps upon their heads, the crowns of gold brocade, with a little slit at the nape where the hairnet peeped through, and two horns projecting, one in front and another behind, of the very finest black lambskin; in kuntushas of the finest blue silk with red borders—stepped forward one by one, their arms akimbo in stately form, and executed the gopak; how the lads—in tall Cossack caps, and light cloth svitkas, girt with silver embroidered belts, their short pipes in their teeth—skipped before them, and talked nonsense. Even Korzh could not contain himself, as he gazed at the young people, from getting gay in his old age. Bandura in hand, alternately puffing at his pipe and singing, a brandy glass upon his head, the gray-beard began the national dance amid loud shouts from the merry-makers. What will not people devise in merry mood! They even began to disguise their faces. They did not look like human beings. They are not to be compared with the disguises which we have at our weddings nowadays. What do they do now? Why, imitate gypsies and Moscow peddlers. No! then one used to dress himself as a Jew, another as the Devil: they would begin by kissing each other, and end by seizing each other by the hair. . . . God be with them! you laughed till you held your sides. They dressed themselves in Turkish and Tatar garments. All upon them glowed like a conflagration, . . . and then they began to joke and play pranks. . . . Well, then away with the saints!

An amusing thing happened to my grandfather's aunt, who was at this wedding. She was dressed in a voluminous Tatar robe, and, wineglass in hand, was entertaining the company. The Evil One instigated one man to pour vodka over her from behind. Another, at the same moment, evidently not by accident, struck a light, and touched it to her; . . . the flame flashed up; poor aunt, in terror, flung her robe from her, before them all. . . . Screams, laughter, jests, arose, as if at a fair. In a word, the old folks could not recall so merry a wedding.

Pidórka and Petrus began to live like a gentleman and lady. There was plenty of everything, and everything was handsome. . . . But honest people shook their heads when they looked at their way of living. "From the Devil no good can come," they unanimously agreed. "Whence, except from the tempter of orthodox people, came this wealth? Where else could he get such a lot of gold? Why, on the very day that he got rich, did Basavriuk vanish as if into thin air?" Say, if you can, that people imagine things! In fact, a month had not passed, and no one would have recognized Petrus. Why, what had happened to him? God knows. He sits in one spot, and says no word to anyone: he thinks continually, and seems to be trying to recall something. When Pidórka succeeds in getting him to speak, he seems to forget himself, carries on a conversation, and even grows cheerful; but if he inadvertently glances at the sacks, "Stop, stop! I have forgotten," he cries, and again plunges into revery, and again strives to recall something. Sometimes when he has sat long in a place, it seems to him as though it were coming, just coming back to mind, . . . and again all fades away. It seems as if he is sitting in the tavern: they bring him vodka; vodka stings him; vodka is repulsive to him. Someone comes along, and strikes him on the shoulder; . . . but beyond that everything is veiled in darkness before him. The perspiration streams down his face, and he sits exhausted in the same place.

What did not Pidórka do? She consulted the sorceress; and they poured out fear, and brewed stomach ache—but all to no avail. And so the summer passed. Many a Cossack had mowed and reaped: many a Cossack, more enterprising than the rest, had set off upon an expedition. Flocks of ducks were already crowding our marshes, but there was not even a hint of improvement.

It was red upon the steppes. Ricks of grain, like Cossacks' caps, dotted the fields here and there. On the highway were to be encountered wagons loaded with brushwood and logs. The ground had become more solid, and in places was touched with frost. Already had the snow begun to besprinkle the sky, and the branches of the trees were covered with rime like rabbit skin. Already on frosty days the redbreasted finch hopped about on the snow-heaps like a foppish Polish nobleman, and picked out grains of corn; and children, with huge sticks, chased wooden tops upon the ice; while their fathers lay quietly on the stove, issuing forth at intervals with lighted pipes in their lips, to growl, in regular fashion, at the orthodox frost, or to take the air, and thresh the grain spread out in the barn. At last the snow began to melt, and the ice rind slipped away: but Petró remained the same; and, the longer it went on, the more morose he grew. He sat in the middle of the cottage as though nailed to the spot, with the sacks of gold at his feet. He grew shy, his hair grew long, he became terrible; and still he thought of but one thing, still he tried to recall something, and got angry and ill-tempered because he could not recall it. Often, rising wildly from his seat, he gesticulates violently, fixes his eyes on something as though desirous of catching it: his lips move as though desirous of uttering some long-forgotten word—and remain speechless. Fury takes possession of him: he gnaws and bites his hands like a man half crazy, and in his vexation tears out his hair by the handful, until, calming down, he falls into forgetfulness, as it were, and again begins to recall, and is again seized with fury and fresh tortures. . . . What visitation of God is this?

Pidórka was neither dead nor alive. At first it was horrible to her to remain alone in the cottage; but, in course of time, the poor woman grew accustomed to her sorrow. But it was impossible to recognize the Pidórka of former days. No blush, no smile: she was thin and worn with grief, and had wept her bright eyes away. Once, someone who evidently took pity on her, advised her to go to the witch who dwelt in the Bear's ravine, and enjoyed the reputation of being able to cure every disease in the world. She determined to try this last remedy: word by word she persuaded the old woman to come to her. This was St. John's Eve, as it chanced. Petró lay insensible on the bench, and did not observe the newcomer. Little by little he rose, and looked about him. Suddenly he trembled in every limb, as though he were on the scaffold: his hair rose upon his head, . . . and he laughed such a laugh as pierced Pidórka's heart with fear. "I have remembered, remembered!" he cried in terrible joy; and, swinging a hatchet round his head, he flung it at the old woman with all his might. The hatchet penetrated the oaken door two *vershok* (three inches and a half). The old woman disappeared; and a child of seven in a white blouse, with covered head, stood in the middle of the cottage. . . . The sheet flew off. "Ivas!" cried Pidórka, and ran to him; but the apparition became covered from head to foot with blood, and illumined the whole room with red light. . . . She ran into the passage in her terror, but, on recovering herself a little, wished to help him; in vain! the door had slammed to behind her so securely that she could not open it. People ran up, and began to knock: they broke in the door, as though there were but one mind among them. The whole cottage was full of smoke; and just in the middle, where Petrus had stood, was a heap of ashes, from which smoke was still rising. They flung themselves upon the sacks: only broken potsherds lay there instead of ducats. The Cossacks stood with staring eyes and open mouths, not daring to move a hair, as if rooted to the earth, such terror did this wonder inspire in them.

I do not remember what happened next. Pidórka took a vow to go upon a pilgrimage, collected the property left her by her father, and in a few days it was as if she had never been in the village. Whither she had gone, no one could tell. Officious old women would have despatched her to the same place whither Petró had gone; but a Cossack from Kief reported that he had seen, in a cloister, a nun withered to a mere skeleton, who prayed unceasingly; and her fellow villagers recognized her as Pidórka, by all the signs— that no one had ever heard her utter a word; that she had come on foot, and had brought a frame for the ikon of God's mother, set with such brilliant stones that all were dazzled at the sight.

But this was not the end, if you please. On the same day that the Evil One made way with Petrus, Basavriuk appeared again; but all fled from him. They knew what sort of a bird he was—none else than Satan, who had assumed human form in order to unearth treasures; and, since treasures do not yield to unclean hands, he seduced the young. That same year, all deserted their earth huts, and collected in a village; but, even there, there was no peace, on account of that accursed Basavriuk. My late grandfather's aunt said that he was particularly angry with her, because she had abandoned her former tavern, and tried with all his might to revenge himself upon her. Once the village elders were assembled in the tavern, and, as the saying goes, were arranging the precedence at the table, in the middle of which was placed a small roasted lamb, shame to say. They chattered about this, that, and the other—among the rest about various marvels and strange things. Well, they saw something; it would have been nothing if only one had seen it, but all saw it; and it was this: the sheep raised his head; his goggling eyes became alive and sparkled; and the black, bristling mustache, which appeared for one instant, made a significant gesture at those present. All, at once, recognized Basavriuk's countenance in the sheep's head: my grandfather's aunt thought it was on the point of asking for vodka. . . . The worthy elders seized their hats, and hastened home.

Another time, the church starost [elder] himself, who was fond of an occasional private interview with my grandfather's brandy glass, had not succeeded in getting to the bottom twice, when he beheld the glass bowing very low to him. "Satan take you, let us make the sign of the cross over you!" . . . And the same marvel happened to his better half. She had just begun to mix the dough in a huge kneading trough, when suddenly the trough sprang up. "Stop, stop! where are you going?" Putting its arms akimbo, with dignity, it went skipping all about the cottage. . . . You may laugh, but it was no laughing matter to our grandfathers. And in vain did Father Athanasii go through all the village with holy water, and chase the Devil through all the streets with his brush; and my late grandfather's aunt long complained, that, as soon as it was dark, someone came knocking at her door, and scratching at the wall.

Well! All appears to be quiet now, in the place where our village stands; but it was not so very long ago—my father was still alive—that I remember how a good man could not pass the ruined tavern, which a dishonest race had long managed for their own interest. From the smoke-blackened chimneys, smoke poured out in a pillar, and rising high in the air, as if to take an observation, rolled off like a cap, scattering burning coals over the steppe; and Satan (the son of a dog should not be mentioned) sobbed so pitifully in his lair, that the startled ravens rose in flocks from the neighboring oak-wood, and flew through the air with wild cries.

The Painter's Bargain

WILLIAM MAKEPEACE THACKERAY

Simon Gambouge was the son of Solomon Gambouge; and, as all the world knows, both father and son were astonishingly clever fellows at their profession. Solomon painted landscapes, which nobody bought; and Simon took a higher line, and painted portraits to admiration, only nobody came to sit to him.

As he was not gaining five pounds a year by his profession, and had arrived at the age of twenty, at least, Simon determined to better himself by taking a wife—a plan which a number of other wise men adopt, in similar years and circumstances. So Simon prevailed upon a butcher's daughter (to whom he owed considerably for cutlets) to quit the meat-shop and follow him. Griskinissa—such was the fair creature's name—"was as lovely a bit of mutton," her father said, "as ever a man would wish to stick a knife into." She had sat to the painter for all sorts of characters; and the curious who possess any of Gambouge's pictures will see her as Venus, Minerva, Madonna, and in numberless other characters: Portrait of a Lady—Griskinissa; Sleeping Nymph—Griskinissa, without a rag of clothes, lying in a forest; Maternal Solicitude—Griskinissa again, with young Master Gambouge, who was by this time the offspring of their affections.

The lady brought the painter a handsome little fortune of a couple of hundred pounds; and as long as this sum lasted no woman could be more lovely or loving. But want began speedily to attack their little household; bakers' bills were unpaid; rent was due, and the relentless landlord gave no quarter; and, to crown the whole, her father, unnatural butcher! suddenly stopped the supplies of mutton-chops; and swore that his daughter, and the dauber her husband, should have no more of his wares. At first they embraced tenderly, and, kissing and crying over their little infant, vowed to Heaven that they would do without: but in the course of the evening Griskinissa grew peckish, and poor Simon pawned his best coat.

When this habit of pawning is discovered, it appears to the poor a kind of Eldorado. Gambouge and his wife were so delighted, that they, in the course of a month, made away with her gold chain, her great warming-pan, his best crimson plush inexpressibles, two wigs, a washhand basin and ewer, fire-irons, window curtains, crockery, and armchairs. Griskinissa said, smiling, that she had found a second father in *her uncle*—a base pun, which showed that her mind was corrupted, and that she was no longer the tender simple Griskinissa of other days.

I am sorry to say that she had taken to drinking: she swallowed the warming-pan in the course of three days, and fuddled herself one whole evening with the crimson plush breeches.

Drinking is the devil—the father, that is to say, of all vices. Griskinissa's face and her mind grew ugly together; her good-humor changed to bilious bitter discontent; her pretty fond epithets, to foul abuse and swearing; her tender blue eyes grew watery and blear, and the peach color on her cheeks fled from its old habitation, and crowded up into her nose, where, with a number of pimples, it stuck fast. Add to this a dirty draggle-tailed chintz; long matted hair, wandering into her eyes, and over her lean shoulders, which were once so snowy, and you have the picture of drunkenness and Mrs. Simon Gambouge.

Poor Simon, who had been a gay lively fellow enough in the days of his better fortune, was completely cast down by his present ill luck, and cowed by the ferocity of his wife. From morning till night the neighbors could hear this woman's tongue, and understand her doings; bellows went skimming across the room, chairs were flumped down on the floor, and poor Gambouge's oil and varnish pots went clattering through the windows, or down the stairs. The baby roared all day; and Simon sat pale and idle in a corner, taking a small sup at the brandy bottle, when Mrs. Gambouge was out of the way.

One day, as he sat disconsolately at his easel, furbishing up a picture of his wife, in the character of Peace, which he had commenced a year before, he was more than ordinarily desperate, and cursed and swore in the most pathetic manner. "O miserable fate of genius!" cried he, "was I, a man of such commanding talents, born for this—to be bullied by a fiend of a wife; to have my masterpieces neglected by the world, or sold only for a few pieces? Cursed be the love which has misled me; cursed be the art which is unworthy of me! Let me dig or steal, let me sell myself as a soldier, or sell myself to the Devil, I should not be more wretched than I am now!"

"Quite the contrary," cried a small cheery voice.

"What!" exclaimed Gambouge, trembling and surprised. "Who's there?—where are you?—who are you?"

"You were just speaking of me," said the voice.

Gambouge held, in his left hand, his palette; in his right, a bladder of crimson lake, which he was about to squeeze out upon the mahogany. "Where are you?" cried he again.

"S-q-u-e-e-z-e!" exclaimed the little voice.

Gambouge picked out the nail from the bladder, and gave a squeeze; when, as sure as I am living, a little imp spurted out from the hole upon the palette, and began laughing in the most singular and oily manner.

When first born he was little bigger than a tadpole; then he grew to be as big as a mouse; then he arrived at the size of a cat; and then he jumped off the palette, and, turning head over heels, asked the poor painter what he wanted with him.

The strange little animal twisted head over heels, and fixed himself at last upon the top of Gambouge's easel—smearing out, with his heels, all the white and vermilion which had just been laid on the allegoric portrait of Mrs. Gambouge.

"What!" exclaimed Simon, "is it the ——"

"Exactly so; talk of me, you know, and I am always at hand: besides, I am not half so black as I am painted, as you will see when you know me a little better."

"Upon my word," said the painter, "it is a very singular surprise which you have given me. To tell truth, I did not even believe in your existence."

The little imp put on a theatrical air, and, with one of Mr. Macready's best looks, said—

"There are more things in heaven and earth, Gambogio,
    Than are dreamed of in your philosophy."

Gambouge, being a Frenchman, did not understand the quotation, but felt somehow strangely and singularly interested in the conversation of his new friend.

Diabolus continued: "You are a man of merit, and want money: you will starve on your merit; you can only get money from me. Come, my friend, how much is it? I ask the easiest interest in the world: old Mordecai, the usurer, has made you pay twice as heavily before now: nothing but the signature of a bond, which is a mere ceremony, and the transfer of an article which, in itself, is a supposition—a valueless, windy, uncertain property of yours, called, by some poet of your own, I think, an *animula vagula, blandula*—bah! there is no use beating about the bush—I mean *a soul*. Come, let me have it: you know you will sell it some other way, and not get such good pay for your bargain!"—and, having made this speech, the Devil pulled out from his fob a sheet as big as a double *Times,* only there was a different *stamp* in the corner.

It is useless and tedious to describe law documents: lawyers only love to read them; and they have as good in Chitty as any that are to be found in the Devil's own; so nobly have the apprentices emulated the skill of the master. Suffice it to say, that poor Gambouge read over the paper, and signed it. He was to have all he wished for seven years, and at the end of that time was to become the property of the ——; *Provided* that, during the course of the seven years, every single wish which he might form should be gratified by the other of the contracting parties; otherwise the deed became null and non-avenue, and Gambouge should be left "to go to the —— his own way."

"You will never see me again," said Diabolus, in shaking hands with poor Simon, on whose fingers he left such a mark as is to be seen at this day—"never, at least, unless you want me; for everything you ask will be performed in the most quiet and everyday manner: believe me, it is best and most gentlemanlike, and avoids anything like scandal. But if you set me about anything which is extraordinary, and out of the course of nature, as it were, come I must, you know; and of this you are the best judge." So saying, Diabolus disappeared; but whether up the chimney, through the keyhole, or by any other aperture or contrivance, nobody knows. Simon Gambouge was left in a fever of delight, as, Heaven forgive me! I believe many a worthy man would be, if he were allowed an opportunity to make a similar bargain.

"Heigho!" said Simon. "I wonder whether this be a reality or a dream. I am sober, I know; for who will give me credit for the means to be drunk? and as for sleeping, I'm too hungry for that. I wish I could see a capon and a bottle of white wine."

"Monsieur Simon!" cried a voice on the landing place.

"C'est ici," quoth Gambouge, hastening to open the door. He did so; and lo! there was a *restaurateur's* boy at the door, supporting a tray, a tin-covered dish, and plates on the same; and, by its side, a tall amber-colored flask of Sauterne.

"I am the new boy, sir," exclaimed this youth, on entering; "but I believe this is the right door, and you asked for these things."

Simon grinned, and said, "Certainly, I did *ask for* these things." But such was the effect which his interview with the demon had had on his innocent mind, that he took them, although he knew that they were for old Simon, the Jew dandy, who was mad after an opera girl, and lived on the floor beneath.

"Go, my boy," he said; "it is good: call in a couple of hours, and remove the plates and glasses."

The little waiter trotted downstairs, and Simon sat greedily down to discuss the capon and the white wine. He bolted the legs, he devoured the wings, he cut every morsel of flesh from the breast—seasoning his repast with pleasant drafts of wine, and caring nothing for the inevitable bill, which was to follow all.

"Ye gods!" said he, as he scraped away at the backbone, "what a dinner! what wine!—and how gaily served up too!" There were silver forks and spoons, and the remnants of the fowl were upon a silver dish. "Why, the money for this dish and these spoons," cried Simon, "would keep me and Mrs. G. for a month! I WISH"—and here Simon whistled, and turned round to see that nobody was peeping—"I wish the plate were mine."

Oh, the horrid progress of the Devil! "Here they are," thought Simon to himself; "why should not I *take them?*" And take them he did. "Detection," said he, "is not so bad as starvation; and I would as soon live at the galleys as live with Madame Gambouge."

So Gambouge shoveled dish and spoons into the flap of his surtout, and ran downstairs as if the Devil were behind him—as, indeed, he was.

He immediately made for the house of his old friend the pawn-broker—that establishment which is called in France the Mont de Piété. "I am obliged to come to you again, my old friend," said Simon, "with some family plate, of which I beseech you to take care."

The pawnbroker smiled as he examined the goods. "I can give you nothing upon them," said he.

"What!" cried Simon; "not even the worth of the silver?"

"No; I could buy them at that price at the 'Café Morisot,' Rue de la Verrerie, where, I suppose, you got them a little cheaper." And, so saying, he showed to the guilt-stricken Gambouge how the name of that coffeehouse was inscribed upon every one of the articles which he had wished to pawn.

The effects of conscience are dreadful indeed. Oh! how fearful is retribution, how deep is despair, how bitter is remorse for crime— *when crime is found out!*—otherwise, conscience takes matters much more easily. Gambouge cursed his fate, and swore henceforth to be virtuous.

"But, hark ye, my friend," continued the honest broker, "there is no reason why, because I cannot lend upon these things, I should not buy them: they will do to melt, if for no other purpose. Will you have half the money?—speak, or I peach."

Simon's resolves about virtue were dissipated instantaneously.

"Give me half," he said, "and let me go.—What scoundrels are these pawnbrokers!" ejaculated he, as he passed out of the accursed shop, "seeking every wicked pretext to rob the poor man of his hard-won gain."

When he had marched forwards for a street or two, Gambouge counted the money which he had received, and found that he was in possession of no less than a hundred francs. It was night as he reckoned out his equivocal gains, and he counted them at the light of a lamp. He looked up at the lamp, in doubt as to the course he should next pursue: upon it was inscribed the simple number, 152. "A gambling house," thought Gambouge. "I WISH I had half the money that is now on the table, upstairs."

He mounted, as many a rogue has done before him, and found half a hundred persons busy at a table of *rouge et noir*. Gambouge's five napoleons looked insignificant by the side of the heaps which were around him; but the effects of the wine, of the theft, and of the detection by the pawnbroker, were upon him, and he threw down his capital stoutly upon the 0 0.

It is a dangerous spot that 0 0, or double zero; but to Simon it was more lucky than to the rest of the world. The ball went spinning round—in "its predestined circle rolled," as Shelley has it, after Goethe—and plumped down at last in the double zero. One hundred and thirty-five gold napoleons (louis they were then) were counted out to the delighted painter. "Oh, Diabolus!" cried he, "now it is that I begin to believe in thee! Don't talk about merit," he cried; "talk about fortune. Tell me not about heroes for the future—tell me of *zeroes*." And down went twenty napoleons more upon the 0.

The Devil was certainly in the ball: round it twirled, and dropped into zero as naturally as a duck pops its head into a pond. Our friend received five hundred pounds for his stake; and the croupiers and lookers-on began to stare at him.

There were twelve thousand pounds on the table. Suffice it to say, that Simon won half, and retired from the Palais Royal with a thick bundle of bank notes crammed into his dirty three-cornered hat. He had been but half-an-hour in the place, and he had won the revenues of a prince for half a year!

Gambouge, as soon as he felt that he was a capitalist, and that he had a stake in the country, discovered that he was an altered man. He repented of his foul deed, and his base purloining of the restaurateur's plate. "O honesty!" he cried, "how unworthy is an action like this of a man who has a property like mine!" So he went back to the pawnbroker with the gloomiest face imaginable. "My friend," said he, "I have sinned against all that I hold most sacred: I have forgotten my family and my religion. Here is thy money. In the name of Heaven, restore me the plate which I have wrongfully sold thee!"

But the pawnbroker grinned, and said, "Nay, Mr. Gambouge, I will sell that plate for a thousand francs to you, or I never will sell it at all."

"Well," said Gambouge, "thou art an inexorable ruffian, Trois-boules; but I will give thee all I am worth." And here he produced a billet of five hundred francs. "Look," said he, "this money is all I own; it is the payment of two years' lodging. To raise it, I have toiled for many months; and, failing, I have been a criminal. O Heaven! I *stole* that plate that I might pay my debt, and keep my dear wife from wandering houseless. But I cannot bear this load of ignominy—I cannot suffer the thought of this crime. I will go to the person to whom I did wrong. I will starve, I will confess: but I will, I *will* do right!"

The broker was alarmed. "Give me thy note," he cried; "here is the plate."

"Give me an acquittal first," cried Simon, almost brokenhearted; "sign me a paper, and the money is yours." So Troisboules wrote according to Gambouge's dictation: "Received, for thirteen ounces of plate, twenty pounds."

"Monster of iniquity!" cried the painter, "fiend of wickedness! thou art caught in thine own snares. Hast thou not sold me five pounds' worth of plate for twenty? Have I it not in my pocket? Art thou not a convicted dealer in stolen goods? Yield, scoundrel, yield thy money, or I will bring thee to justice!"

The frightened pawnbroker bullied and battled for a while; but he gave up his money at last, and the dispute ended. Thus it will be seen that Diabolus had rather a hard bargain in the wily Gambouge. He had taken a victim prisoner, but he had assuredly caught a Tartar. Simon now returned home, and, to do him justice, paid the bill for his dinner, and restored the plate.

And now I may add (and the reader should ponder upon this, as a profound picture of human life), that Gambouge, since he had grown rich, grew likewise abundantly moral. He was a most exemplary father. He fed the poor, and was loved by them. He scorned a base action. And I have no doubt that Mr. Thurtell, or the late lamented Mr. Greenacre, in similar circumstances, would have acted like the worthy Simon Gambouge.

There was but one blot upon his character—he hated Mrs. Gam. worse than ever. As he grew more benevolent, she grew more virulent: when he went to plays, she went to Bible societies, and *vice versâ:* in fact, she led him such a life as Xantippe led Socrates, or as a dog leads a cat in the same kitchen. With all his fortune—for, as may be supposed, Simon prospered in all worldly things—he was the most miserable dog in the whole city of Paris. Only on the point of drinking did he and Mrs. Simon agree: and for many years, and during a considerable number of hours in each day, he thus dissipated, partially, his domestic chagrin. O philosophy! we may talk of thee: but, except at the bottom of the wine cup, where thou liest like truth in a well, where shall we find thee?

He lived so long, and in his worldly matters prospered so much, there was so little sign of devilment in the accomplishment of his wishes, and the increase of his prosperity, that Simon, at the end of six years, began to doubt whether he had made any such bargain at all, as that which we have described at the commencement of this history. He had grown, as we said, very pious and moral. He went regularly to mass, and had a confessor into the bargain. He resolved, therefore, to consult that reverend gentleman, and to lay before him the whole matter.

"I am inclined to think, holy sir," said Gambouge, after he had concluded his history, and shown how, in some miraculous way, all his desires were accomplished, "that, after all, this demon was no other than the creation of my own brain, heated by the effects of that bottle of wine, the cause of my crime and my prosperity."

The confessor agreed with him, and they walked out of church comfortably together, and entered afterwards a *café,* where they sat down to refresh themselves after the fatigues of their devotion.

A respectable old gentleman, with a number of orders at his buttonhole, presently entered the room, and sauntered up to the marble table, before which reposed Simon and his clerical friend. "Excuse me, gentlemen," he said, as he took a place opposite them, and began reading the papers of the day.

"Bah!" said he, at last—"sont-ils grands ces journaux Anglais? Look, sir," he said, handing over an immense sheet of the *Times* to Mr. Gambouge, "was ever anything so monstrous?"

Gambouge smiled politely, and examined the proffered page. "It is enormous," he said; "but I do not read English."

"Nay," said the man with the orders, "look closer at it, Signor Gambouge; it is astonishing how easy the language is."

Wondering, Simon took the sheet of paper. He turned pale as he looked at it, and began to curse the ices and the waiter. "Come, M. l'Abbé," he said; "the heat and glare of this place are intolerable."

* * *

The stranger rose with them. "Au plaisir de vous revoir, mon cher monsieur," said he; "I do not mind speaking before the Abbé here, who will be my very good friend one of these days; but I thought it necessary to refresh your memory, concerning our little business transaction six years since; and could not exactly talk of it *at church,* as you may fancy."

Simon Gambouge had seen, in the double-sheeted *Times,* the paper signed by himself, which the little Devil had pulled out of his fob.

There was no doubt on the subject; and Simon, who had but a year to live, grew more pious, and more careful than ever. He had consultations with all the doctors of the Sorbonne and all the lawyers of the Palais. But his magnificence grew as wearisome to him as his poverty had been before; and not one of the doctors whom he consulted could give him a pennyworth of consolation.

Then he grew outrageous in his demands upon the Devil, and put him to all sorts of absurd and ridiculous tasks; but they were all punctually performed, until Simon could invent no new ones, and the Devil sat all day with his hands in his pockets doing nothing.

One day, Simon's confessor came bounding into the room, with the greatest glee. "My friend," said he, "I have it! Eureka!—I have found it. Send the Pope a hundred thousand crowns, build a new Jesuit College at Rome, give a hundred gold candlesticks to St. Peter's; and tell his Holiness you will double all, if he will give you absolution!"

Gambouge caught at the notion, and hurried off a courier to Rome *ventre à terre.* His Holiness agreed to the request of the petition, and sent him an absolution, written out with his own fist, and all in due form.

"Now," said he, "foul fiend, I defy you! arise, Diabolus! your contract is not worth a jot: the Pope has absolved me, and I am safe on the road to salvation." In a fervor of gratitude he clasped the hand of his confessor, and embraced him: tears of joy ran down the cheeks of these good men.

They heard an inordinate roar of laughter, and there was Diabolus sitting opposite to them, holding his sides, and lashing his tail about, as if he would have gone mad with glee.

"Why," said he, "what nonsense is this! do you suppose I care about *that?*" and he tossed the Pope's missive into a corner. "M. l'Abbé knows," he said, bowing and grinning, "that though the Pope's paper may pass current *here,* it is not worth twopence in our country. What do I care about the Pope's absolution? You might just as well be absolved by your under-butler."

"Egad," said the Abbé, "the rogue is right—I quite forgot the fact, which he points out clearly enough."

"No, no, Gambouge," continued Diabolus, with horrid familiarity, "go thy ways, old fellow, that *cock won't fight.*" And he retired up the chimney, chuckling at his wit and his triumph. Gambouge heard his tail scuttling all the way up, as if he had been a sweeper by profession.

Simon was left in that condition of grief in which, according to the newspapers, cities and nations are found when a murder is committed, or a lord ill of the gout—a situation, we say, more easy to imagine than to describe.

To add to his woes, Mrs. Gambouge, who was now first made acquainted with his compact, and its probable consequences, raised such a storm about his ears, as made him wish almost that his seven years were expired. She screamed, she scolded, she swore, she wept, she went into such fits of hysterics, that poor Gambouge, who had completely knocked under to her, was worn out of his life. He was allowed no rest, night or day: he moped about his fine house, solitary and wretched, and cursed his stars that he ever had married the butcher's daughter.

It wanted six months of the time.

A sudden and desperate resolution seemed all at once to have taken possession of Simon Gambouge. He called his family and his friends together—he gave one of the greatest feasts that ever was known in the city of Paris—he gaily presided at one end of his table, while Mrs. Gam., splendidly arrayed, gave herself airs at the other extremity.

After dinner, using the customary formula, he called upon Diabolus to appear. The old ladies screamed, and hoped he would not appear naked; the young ones tittered, and longed to see the monster: everybody was pale with expectation and affright.

A very quiet gentlemanly man, neatly dressed in black, made his appearance, to the surprise of all present, and bowed all round to the company. "I will not show my *credentials*," he said, blushing, and pointing to his hoofs, which were cleverly hidden by his pumps and shoebuckles, "unless the ladies absolutely wish it; but I am the person you want, Mr. Gambouge; pray tell me what is your will."

"You know," said that gentleman, in a stately and determined voice, "that you are bound to me, according to our agreement, for six months to come?"

"I am," replied the newcomer.

"You are to do all that I ask, whatsoever it may be, or you forfeit the bond which I gave you?"

"It is true."

"You declare this before the present company?"

"Upon my honor, as a gentleman," said Diabolus, bowing, and laying his hand upon his waistcoat.

A whisper of applause ran round the room: all were charmed with the bland manners of the fascinating stranger.

"My love," continued Gambouge, mildly addressing his lady, "will you be so polite as to step this way? You know I must go soon, and I am anxious, before this noble company, to make a provision for one who, in sickness as in health, in poverty as in riches, has been my truest and fondest companion."

Gambouge mopped his eyes with his handkerchief—all the company did likewise. Diabolus sobbed audibly, and Mrs. Gambouge sidled up to her husband's side, and took him tenderly by the hand. "Simon!" said she, "is it true? and do you really love your Griskinissa?"

Simon continued solemnly: "Come hither, Diabolus; you are bound to obey me in all things for the six months during which our contract has to run; take, then, Griskinissa Gambouge, live alone with her for half a year, never leave her from morning till night, obey all her caprices, follow all her whims, and listen to all the abuse which falls from her infernal tongue. Do this, and I ask no more of you; I will deliver myself up at the appointed time."

Not Lord G——— when flogged by Lord B——— in the House— not Mr. Cartlitch, of Astley's Amphitheatre, in his most pathetic passages, could look more crestfallen, and howl more hideously, than Diabolus did now. "Take another year, Gambouge," screamed he; "two more—ten more—a century; roast me on Lawrence's grid-iron, boil me in holy water, but don't ask that: don't, don't bid me live with Mrs. Gambouge!"

Simon smiled sternly. "I have said it," he cried; "do this, or our contract is at an end."

The Devil, at this, grinned so horribly that every drop of beer in the house turned sour; he gnashed his teeth so frightfully that every person in the company well-nigh fainted with the colic. He slapped down the great parchment upon the floor, trampled upon it madly, and lashed it with his hoofs and his tail: at last, spreading out a mighty pair of wings as wide as from here to Regent Street, he slapped Gambouge with his tail over one eye, and vanished, abruptly, through the keyhole.

*   *   *

Gambouge screamed with pain and started up. "You drunken lazy scoundrel!" cried a shrill and well-known voice, "you have been asleep these two hours:" and here he received another terrific box on the ear.

It was too true, he had fallen asleep at his work; and the beautiful vision had been dispelled by the thumps of the tipsy Griskinissa. Nothing remained to corroborate his story, except the bladder of lake, and this was spurted all over his waistcoat and breeches.

"I wish," said the poor fellow, rubbing his tingling cheeks, "that dreams were true;" and he went to work again at his portrait.

My last accounts of Gambouge are, that he has left the arts, and is footman in a small family. Mrs. Gam. takes in washing; and it is said that her continual dealings with soapsuds and hot water have been the only things in life which have kept her from spontaneous combustion.

Bon-Bon

EDGAR ALLAN POE

Quand un bon vin meuble mon estomac,
Je suis plus savant que Balzac—
Plus sage que Pibrac;
Mon bras seul faisant l'attaque
De la nation Cossaque,
La mettroit au sac;
De Charon Je passerois le lac
En dormant dans son bac;
J'irois au fier Eac,
Sans que mon cœur fit tic ni tac,
Presenter du tabac.

French Vaudeville

That Pierre Bon-Bon was a *restaurateur* of uncommon qualifications, no man who, during the reign of ———, frequented the little Câfé in the cul-de-sac Le Febvre at Rouen, will, I imagine, feel himself at liberty to dispute. That Pierre Bon-Bon was, in an equal degree, skilled in the philosophy of that period is, I presume, still more especially undeniable. His *patés à la fois* were beyond doubt immaculate; but what pen can do justice to his essays *sur la Nature*—his thoughts *sur l'Ame*—his observations *sur l'Esprit?* If his *omelettes*—if his *fricandeaux* were inestimable, what *littérateur* of that day would not have given twice as much for an *"Idée de Bon-Bon"* as for all the trash of all the *"Idées"* of all the rest of the *savants?* Bon-Bon had ransacked libraries which no other man had ransacked—had read more than any other would have entertained a notion of reading—had understood more than any other would have conceived the possibility of understanding; and although, while he flourished, there were not wanting some authors at Rouen to assert "that his *dicta* evinced neither the purity of the Academy, nor the depth of the Lyceum"—although, mark me, his doctrines were by no means very generally comprehended, still it did not follow that they were difficult of comprehension. It was, I think, on account of their self-evidency that many persons were led to consider them abstruse. It is to Bon-Bon—but let this go no farther—it is to Bon-Bon that Kant himself is mainly indebted for his metaphysics. The former was indeed not a Platonist, nor strictly speaking an Aristotelian—nor did he, like the modern Leibnitz, waste those precious hours which might be employed in the invention of a *fricasée,* or, *facili gradú,* the analysis of a sensation, in frivolous attempts at reconciling the obstinate oils and waters of ethical discussion. Not at all. Bon-Bon was Ionic—Bon-Bon was equally Italic. He reasoned *à priori*—He reasoned also *à posteriori*. His ideas were innate—or otherwise. He believed in George of Trebizond—He believed in Bossarion. Bon-Bon was emphatically a—Bon-Bonist.

I have spoken of the philosopher in his capacity of *restaurateur*. I would not, however, have any friend of mine imagine that, in fulfilling his hereditary duties in that line, our hero wanted a proper estimation of their dignity and importance. Far from it. It was impossible to say in which branch of his profession he took the greater pride. In his opinion the powers of the intellect held intimate connection with the capabilities of the stomach. I am not sure, indeed, that he greatly disagreed with the Chinese, who hold that the soul lies in the abdomen. The Greeks at all events were right, he thought, who employed the same word for the mind and the diaphragm. By this I do not mean to insinuate a charge of gluttony, or indeed any other serious charge to the prejudice of the metaphysician. If Pierre Bon-Bon had his failings—and what great man has not a thousand?—if Pierre Bon-Bon, I say, had his failings, they were failings of very little importance—faults indeed which, in other tempers, have often been looked upon rather in the light of virtues. As regards one of these foibles, I should not even have mentioned it in this history but for the remarkable prominency—the extreme *alto relievo*—in which it jutted out from the plane of his general disposition.—He could never let slip an opportunity of making a bargain.

Not that he was avaricious—no. It was by no means necessary to the satisfaction of the philosopher, that the bargain should be to his own proper advantage. Provided a trade could be effected—a trade of any kind, upon any terms, or under any circumstances—a triumphant smile was seen for many days thereafter to enlighten his countenance, and a knowing wink of the eye to give evidence of his sagacity.

At any epoch it would not be very wonderful if a humor so peculiar as the one I have just mentioned, should elicit attention and remark. At the epoch of our narrative, had this peculiarity *not* attracted observation, there would have been room for wonder indeed. It was soon reported that, upon all occasions of the kind, the smile of

Bon-Bon was wont to differ widely from the downright grin with which he would laugh at his own jokes, or welcome an acquaintance. Hints were thrown out of an exciting nature; stories were told of perilous bargains made in a hurry and repented of at leisure; and instances were adduced of unaccountable capacities, vague longings, and unnatural inclinations implanted by the author of all evil for wise purposes of his own.

The philosopher had other weaknesses—but they are scarcely worthy our serious examination. For example, there are few men of extraordinary profundity who are found wanting in an inclination for the bottle. Whether this inclination be an exciting cause, or rather a valid proof, of such profundity, it is a nice thing to say. Bon-Bon, as far as I can learn, did not think the subject adapted to minute investigation—nor do I. Yet in the indulgence of a propensity so truly classical, it is not to be supposed that the *restaurateur* would lose sight of that intuitive discrimination which was wont to characterize, at one and the same time, his *essais* and his *omelettes*. In his seclusions the Vin de Bourgogne had its allotted hour, and there were appropriate moments for the Côtes du Rhone. With him Sauterne was to Medoc what Catullus was to Homer. He would sport with a syllogism in sipping St. Peray, but unravel an argument over Clos de Vougeot, and upset a theory in a torrent of Chambertin. Well had it been if the same quick sense of propriety had attended him in the peddling propensity to which I have formerly alluded— but this was by no means the case. Indeed, to say the truth, *that* trait of mind in the philosophic Bon-Bon *did* begin at length to assume a character of strange intensity and mysticism, and appeared deeply tinctured with the *diablerie* of his favorite German studies.

To enter the little *Cáfé* in the *Cul-de-Sac* Le Febvre was, at the period of our tale, to enter the *sanctum* of a man of genius. Bon-Bon was a man of genius. There was not a *sous-cuisinier* in Rouen, who could not have told you that Bon-Bon was a man of genius. His very cat knew it, and forbore to whisk her tail in the presence of the man of genius. His large water-dog was acquainted with the fact, and upon the approach of his master, betrayed his sense of inferiority by a sanctity of deportment, a debasement of the ears, and a dropping of the lower jaw not altogether unworthy of a dog. It is, however, true that much of this habitual respect might have been attributed to the personal appearance of the metaphysician. A distinguished exterior will, I am constrained to say, have its weight even with a beast; and I am willing to allow much in the outward man of the *restaurateur* calculated to impress the imagination of the quadruped. There is a peculiar majesty about the atmosphere of the little great—if I may be permitted so equivocal an expression—which mere physical bulk alone will be found at all times inefficient in creating. If, however, Bon-Bon was barely three feet in height, and if his head was diminutively small, still it was impossible to behold the rotundity of his stomach without a sense of magnificence nearly bordering upon the sublime. In its size both dogs and men must have seen a type of his acquirements—in its immensity a fitting habitation for his immortal soul.

I might here—if it so pleased me—dilate upon the matter of habiliment, and other mere circumstances of the external metaphysician. I might hint that the hair of our hero was worn short, combed smoothly over his forehead, and surmounted by a conical-shaped white flannel cap and tassels—that his pea-green jerkin was not after the fashion of those worn by the common class of *restaurateurs* at that day—that the sleeves were something fuller than the reigning costume permitted—that the cuffs were turned up, not as usual in that barbarous period, with cloth of the same quality and color as the garment, but faced in a more fanciful manner with the particolored velvet of Genoa—that his slippers were of a bright purple, curiously filagreed, and might have been manufactured in Japan, but for the exquisite pointing of the toes, and the brilliant tints of the binding and embroidery—that his breeches were of the yellow satin-like material called *aimable*—that his sky-blue cloak, resembling in form a dressing-wrapper, and richly bestudded all over with crimson devices, floated cavalierly upon his shoulders like a mist of the morning—and that his *tout ensemble* gave rise to the remarkable words of Benevenuta, the Improvisatrice of Florence, "that it was difficult to say whether Pierre Bon-Bon was indeed a bird of Paradise, or the rather a very Paradise of perfection."—I might, I say, expatiate upon all these points if I pleased—but I forbear—merely personal details may be left to historical novelists—they are beneath the moral dignity of matter-of-fact.

I have said that "to enter the *Café* in the *Cul-de-Sac* Le Febvre was to enter the *sanctum* of a man of genius"—but then it was only the man of genius who could duly estimate the merits of the *sanctum*. A sign consisting of a vast folio swung before the entrance. On one side of the volume was painted a bottle; on the reverse a *paté*. On the back were visible in large letters the words *Œuvres de Bon-Bon*. Thus was delicately shadowed forth the twofold occupation of the proprietor.

Upon stepping over the threshold the whole interior of the building presented itself to view. A long, low-pitched room of antique construction, was indeed all the accommodation afforded by the *Café*. In a corner of the apartment stood the bed of the metaphysician. An array of curtains, together with a canopy *à la Greque,* gave it an air at once classic and comfortable. In the corner diagonally opposite, appeared, in direct family communion, the properties of the kitchen and the *bibliotheque*. A dish of polemics stood peacefully upon the dresser. Here lay an oven-full of the latest ethics—there a kettle of duodecimo *melanges*. Volumes of German morality were hand and glove with the gridiron—a toasting fork might be discovered by the side of Eusebius—Plato reclined at his ease in the frying pan—and contemporary manuscripts were filed away upon the spit.

In other respects the *Câfé de Bon-Bon* might be said to differ little from the usual *restaurants* of the period. A large fireplace yawned opposite the door. On the right of the fireplace an open cupboard displayed a formidable array of labelled bottles.

It was here, about twelve o'clock one night, during the severe winter of ——, that Pierre Bon-Bon, after having listened for some time to the comments of his neighbors upon his singular propensity—that Pierre Bon-Bon, I say, having turned them all out of his house, locked the door upon them with an oath, and betook himself in no very pacific mood to the comforts of a leather-bottomed armchair, and a fire of blazing faggots.

It was one of those terrific nights which are only met with once or twice during a century. It snowed fiercely, and the house tottered to its center with the floods of wind that, rushing through the crannies in the wall, and pouring impetuously down the chimney, shook awfully the curtains of the philosopher's bed, and disorganized the economy of his paté-pans and papers. The huge folio sign that swung without, exposed to the fury of the tempest, creaked ominously, and gave out a moaning sound from its stanchions of solid oak.

It was in no placid temper, I say, that the metaphysician drew up his chair to its customary station by the hearth. Many circumstances of a perplexing nature had occurred during the day, to disturb the serenity of his meditations. In attempting *des œufs à la Princesse* he had unfortunately perpetrated an *omelette à la Reine;* the discovery of a principle in ethics had been frustrated by the overturning of a stew; and last, not least, he had been thwarted in one of those admirable bargains which he at all times took such especial delight in bringing to a successful termination. But in the chafing of his mind at these unaccountable vicissitudes, there did not fail to be mingled some degree of that nervous anxiety which the fury of a boisterous night is so well calculated to produce. Whistling to his more immediate vicinity the large black water-dog we have spoken of before, and settling himself uneasily in his chair, he could not help casting a wary and unquiet eye towards those distant recesses of the apartment whose inexorable shadows not even the red firelight itself could more than partially succeed in overcoming. Having completed a scrutiny whose exact purpose was perhaps unintelligible to himself, he drew close to his seat a small table covered with books and papers, and soon became absorbed in the task of retouching a voluminous manuscript, intended for publication on the morrow.

He had been thus occupied for some minutes when "I am in no hurry, Monsieur Bon-Bon," suddenly whispered a whining voice in the apartment.

"The devil!" ejaculated our hero, starting to his feet, overturning the table at his side, and staring around him in astonishment.

"Very true," calmly replied the voice.

"Very true!—what is very true?—how came you here?" vociferated the metaphysician, as his eye fell upon something which lay stretched at full length upon the bed.

"I was saying," said the intruder, without attending to the interrogatories, "I was saying that I am not at all pushed for time—that the business upon which I took the liberty of calling is of no pressing importance—in short that I can very well wait until you have finished your Exposition."

"My Exposition!—there now!—how do *you* know—how came *you* to understand that I was writing an exposition?—good God!"

"Hush!" replied the figure in a shrill undertone: and, arising quickly from the bed, he made a single step towards our hero, while an iron lamp that depended overhead swung convulsively back from his approach.

The philosopher's amazement did not prevent a narrow scrutiny of the stranger's dress and appearance. The outlines of a figure, exceedingly lean, but much above the common height, were rendered minutely distinct by means of a faded suit of black cloth which fitted tight to the skin, but was otherwise cut very much in the style

of a century ago. These garments had evidently been intended for a
much shorter person than their present owner. His ankles and wrists
were left naked for several inches. In his shoes, however, a pair of
very brilliant buckles gave the lie to the extreme poverty implied by
the other portions of his dress. His head was bare, and entirely bald,
with the exception of the hinder part, from which depended a *queue*
of considerable length. A pair of green spectacles, with side glasses,
protected his eyes from the influence of the light, and at the same
time prevented our hero from ascertaining either their color or their
conformation. About the entire person there was no evidence of a
shirt; but a white cravat, of filthy appearance, was tied with extreme
precision around the throat, and the ends, hanging down formally
side by side, gave (although I dare say unintentionally) the idea of an
ecclesiastic. Indeed, many other points both in his appearance and
demeanor might have very well sustained a conception of that nature. Over his left ear, he carried, after the fashion of a modern clerk,
an instrument resembling the *stylus* of the ancients. In a breast-
pocket of his coat appeared conspicuously a small black volume
fastened with clasps of steel. This book, whether accidentally or not,
was so turned outwardly from the person as to discover the words
"*Rituel Catholique*" in white letters upon the back. His entire physi-
ognomy was interestingly saturnine—even cadaverously pale. The
forehead was lofty, and deeply furrowed with the ridges of contem-
plation. The corners of the mouth were drawn down into an expression of the most submissive humility. There was also a clasping of
the hands, as he stepped towards our hero—a deep sigh—and altogether a look of such utter sanctity as could not have failed to be
unequivocally prepossessing. Every shadow of anger faded from the
countenance of the metaphysician, as, having completed a satisfactory survey of his visitor's person, he shook him cordially by the
hand, and conducted him to a seat.

There would however be a radical error in attributing this in-
stantaneous transition of feeling in the philosopher, to any one of

those causes which might naturally be supposed to have had an influence. Indeed Pierre Bon-Bon, from what I have been able to understand of his disposition, was of all men the least likely to be imposed upon by any speciousness of exterior deportment. It was impossible that so accurate an observer of men and things should have failed to discover, upon the moment, the real character of the personage who had thus intruded upon his hospitality. To say no more, the conformation of his visitor's feet was sufficiently remark-able—he maintained lightly upon his head an inordinately tall hat—there was a tremulous swelling about the hinder part of his breeches—and the vibration of his coattail was a palpable fact. Judge then with what feelings of satisfaction our hero found himself thrown thus at once into the society of a person for whom he had at all times entertained the most unqualified respect. He was, however, too much of the diplomatist to let escape him any intimation of his suspicions in regard to the true state of affairs. It was not his cue to appear at all conscious of the high honor he thus unexpectedly enjoyed, but by leading his guest into conversation, to elicit some important ethical ideas, which might, in obtaining a place in his contemplated publication, enlighten the human race, and at the same time immortalize himself—ideas which, I should have added, his visitor's great age, and well known proficiency in the science of morals, might very well have enabled him to afford.

Actuated by these enlightened views, our hero bade the gen-tleman sit down, while he himself took occasion to throw some faggots upon the fire, and place upon the now reestablished table some bottles of Mousseux. Having quickly completed these opera-tions, he drew his chair *vis-à-vis* to his companion's and waited until the latter should open the conversation. But plans even the most skillfully matured are often thwarted in the outset of their applica-tion, and the *restaurateur* found himself *nonplussed* by the very first words of his visitor's speech.

"I see you know me, Bon-Bon," said he: "ha! ha! ha!—he! he!

he!—hi! hi! hi!—ho! ho! ho!—hu! hu! hu!"—and the devil, dropping at once the sanctity of his demeanor, opened to its fullest extent a mouth from ear to ear, so as to display a set of jagged and fanglike teeth, and throwing back his head, laughed long, loudly, wickedly, and uproariously, while the black dog, crouching down upon his haunches, joined lustily in the chorus, and the tabby cat, flying off at a tangent, stood up on end and shrieked in the farthest corner of the apartment.

Not so the philosopher; he was too much a man of the world either to laugh like the dog, or by shrieks to betray the indecorous trepidation of the cat. It must be confessed, he felt a little astonishment to see the white letters which formed the words *"Rituel Catholique"* on the book in his guest's pocket, momently changing both their color and their import, and in a few seconds, in place of the original title, the words *Régitre des Condamnés* blaze forth in characters of red. This startling circumstance, when Bon-Bon replied to his visitor's remark, imparted to his manner an air of embarrassment which probably might not otherwise have been observed.

"Why, sir," said the philosopher, "why, sir, to speak sincerely—I believe you are—upon my word—the d——dest—that is to say I think—I imagine—I *have* some faint—some *very* faint idea—of the remarkable honor—"

"Oh!—ah!—yes!—very well!" interrupted his Majesty, "say no more—I see how it is." And hereupon, taking off his green spectacles, he wiped the glasses carefully with the sleeve of his coat, and deposited them in his pocket.

If Bon-Bon had been astonished at the incident of the book, his amazement was now much increased by the spectacle which here presented itself to view. In raising his eyes, with a strong feeling of curiosity to ascertain the color of his guest's, he found them by no means black, as he had anticipated—nor gray, as might have been imagined—nor yet hazel nor blue—nor indeed yellow nor red—nor purple—nor white—nor green—nor any other color in the heavens above, or in the earth beneath, or in the waters under the earth. In short Pierre Bon-Bon not only saw plainly that his Majesty had no eyes whatsoever, but could discover no indications of their having existed at any previous period; for the space where eyes should naturally have been, was, I am constrained to say, simply a dead level of flesh.

It was not in the nature of the metaphysician to forbear making some inquiry into the sources of so strange a phenomenon, and the reply of his Majesty was at once prompt, dignified, and satisfactory.

"Eyes! my dear Bon-Bon, eyes! did you say?—oh! ah! I perceive. The ridiculous prints, eh? which are in circulation, have given you a false idea of my personal appearance. Eyes!!—true. Eyes, Pierre Bon-Bon, are very well in their proper place—*that,* you would say, is the head?—right—the head of a worm. To *you* likewise these optics are indispensable—yet I will convince you that my vision is more pene-trating than your own. There is a cat, I see in the corner—a pretty cat!—look at her!—observe her well! Now, Bon-Bon, do you behold the thoughts—the thoughts, I say—the ideas—the reflections—which are being engendered in her pericranium? There it is now!—you do not. She is thinking we admire the length of her tail and the profundity of her mind. She has just concluded that I am the most distinguished of ecclesiastics, and that you are the most superfluous of metaphysicians. Thus you see I am not altogether blind: but to one of my profession the eyes you speak of would be merely an incumbrance, liable at any time to be put out by a toasting iron or a pitchfork. To you, I allow, these optical affairs are indispensable. Endeavor, Bon-Bon, to use them well; *my* vision is the soul."

Hereupon the guest helped himself to the wine upon the table, and pouring out a bumper for Bon-Bon, requested him to drink it without scruple, and make himself perfectly at home.

"A clever book that of yours, Pierre," resumed his Majesty,

tapping our friend knowingly upon the shoulder, as the latter put down his glass after a thorough compliance with his visitor's injunction. "A clever book that of yours, upon my honor. It's a work after my own heart. Your arrangement of matter, I think, however, might be improved, and many of your notions remind me of Aristotle. That philosopher was one of my most intimate acquaintances. I liked him as much for his terrible ill temper, as for his happy knack at making a blunder. There is only one solid truth in all that he has written, and for that I gave him the hint out of pure compassion for his absurdity. I suppose, Pierre Bon-Bon, you very well know to what divine moral truth I am alluding."

"Cannot say that I—"

"Indeed!—why it was I who told Aristotle that by sneezing men expelled superfluous ideas through the proboscis."

"Which is—hiccup!—undoubtedly the case," said the metaphysician, while he poured out for himself another bumper of Mousseux, and offered his snuffbox to the fingers of his visitor.

"There was Plato, too," continued his Majesty, modestly declining the snuffbox and the compliment it implied, "there was Plato, too, for whom I, at one time, felt all the affection of a friend. You knew, Plato, Bon-Bon?—ah! no, I beg a thousand pardons. He met me at Athens, one day, in the Parthenon, and told me he was distressed for an idea. I bade him write down that ο νους εςτιν αυλος. He said that he would do so, and went home, while I stepped over to the pyramids. But my conscience smote me for having uttered a truth, even to aid a friend, and hastening back to Athens, I arrived behind the philosopher's chair as he was inditing the 'αυλος.' Giving the lambda a fillip with my finger I turned it upside down. So the sentence now reads 'ο νους εςτιν αυγος.' and is, you perceive, the fundamental doctrine in his metaphysics."

"Were you ever at Rome?" asked the *restaurateur* as he finished his second bottle of Mousseux, and drew from the closet a larger supply of Chambertin.

"But once, Monsieur Bon-Bon, but once. There was a time"—
said the devil, as if reciting some passage from a book—"there was a
time when occurred an anarchy of five years, during which the
republic, bereft of all its officers, had no magistracy besides the
tribunes of the people, and these were not legally vested with any
degree of executive power—at that time, Monsieur Bon-Bon—at
that time *only* I was in Rome, and I have no earthly acquaintance,
consequently, with any of its philosophy."

"What do you think of—what do you think of—hiccup!—
Epicurus?"

"What do I think of *whom?*" said the devil in astonishment,
"you cannot surely mean to find any fault with Epicurus! What do I
think of Epicurus! Do you mean me, sir?—*I* am Epicurus. I am the
same philosopher who wrote each of the three hundred treatises
commemorated by Diogenes Laertes."

"That's a lie!" said the metaphysician, for the wine had gotten a
little into his head.

"Very well!—very well, sir!—very well indeed, sir," said his Majesty, apparently much flattered.

"That's a lie!" repeated the *restaurateur* dogmatically, "that's a—
hiccup!—a lie!"

"Well, well! have it your own way," said the devil pacifically: and
Bon-Bon, having beaten his Majesty at an argument, thought it his
duty to conclude a second bottle of Chambertin.

"As I was saying," resumed the visitor, "as I was observing a
little while ago, there are some very *outré* notions in that book of
yours, Monsieur Bon-Bon. What, for instance, do you mean by all
that humbug about the soul? Pray, sir, what *is* the soul?"

"The—hiccup!—soul," replied the metaphysician, referring to
his MS., "is undoubtedly—"

"No, sir!"

"Indubitably—"

"No, sir!"

"Indisputably—"

"No, sir!"

"Evidently—"

"No, sir!"

"Incontrovertibly—"

"No sir!"

"Hiccup!—"

"No, sir!"

"And beyond all question a—"

"No, sir! the soul is no such thing." (Here, the philosopher looking daggers, took occasion to make an end, upon the spot, of his third bottle of Chambertin.)

"Then—hic-cup!—pray, sir—what—what is it?"

"That is neither here nor there, Monsieur Bon-Bon," replied his Majesty, musingly. "I have tasted—that is to say, I have known some very bad souls, and some too—pretty good ones." Here he smacked his lips, and, having unconsciously let fall his hand upon the volume in his pocket, was seized with a violent fit of sneezing.

He continued:

"There was the soul of Cratinus—passable: Aristophanes—racy: Plato—exquisite—not *your* Plato, but Plato the comic poet; your Plato would have turned the stomach of Cerberus—laugh! Then let me see! there were Nœvius, and Andronicus, and Plautus, and Terentius. Then there were Lucilius, and Catullus, and Naso, and Quintius Flaccus—dear Quinty! as I called him when he sung a *seculare* for my amusement, while I toasted him, in pure good humor, on a fork. But they want *flavor* these Romans. One fat Greek is worth a dozen of them, and besides will *keep*, which cannot be said of a Quirite.—Let us taste your Sauterne."

Bon-Bon had by this time made up his mind to the *nil admirari*, and endeavored to hand down the bottles in question. He was, however, conscious of a strange sound in the room like the wagging of a tail. Of this, although extremely indecent in his Majesty, the philosopher took no notice—simply kicking the dog, and requesting him to be quiet. The visitor continued:

"I found that Horace tasted very much like Aristotle—you know I am fond of variety. Terentius I could not have told from Menander. Naso, to my astonishment, was Nicander in disguise. Virgilius had a strong twang of Theocritus. Martial put me much in mind of Archilochus—and Titus Livius was positively Polybius and none other."

"Hic-cup!" here replied Bon-Bon, and his Majesty proceeded:

"But if I *have* a *penchant,* Monsieur Bon-Bon—if I *have* a *penchant,* it is for a philosopher. Yet, let me tell you, sir, it is not every dev—I mean it is not every gentleman who knows how to *choose* a philosopher. Long ones are *not* good; and the best, if not carefully shelled, are apt to be a little rancid on account of the gall."

"Shelled!!"

"I mean taken out of the carcass."

"What do you think of a—hic-cup!—physician?"

"*Don't* mention them!—ugh! ugh!" (Here his Majesty retched violently.) "I never tasted but one—that rascal Hippocrates!—smelt of asafœtida—ugh! ugh! ugh!—caught a wretched cold washing him in the Styx—and after all he gave me the cholera morbus."

"The—hiccup!—wretch!" ejaculated Bon-Bon, "the—hiccup!—abortion of a pillbox!"—and the philosopher dropped a tear.

"After all," continued the visitor, "after all, if a dev—if a gentleman wishes to *live,* he must have more talents than one or two; and with us a fat face is an evidence of diplomacy."

"How so?"

"Why we are sometimes exceedingly pushed for provisions. You must know that, in a climate so sultry as mine, it is frequently impossible to keep a spirit alive for more than two or three hours; and after death, unless pickled immediately, (and a pickled spirit is *not* good,) they will—smell—you understand, eh? Putrefaction is always to be apprehended when the souls are consigned to us in the usual way."

"Hiccup!—hiccup!—good God! how *do* you manage?"

Here the iron lamp commenced swinging with redoubled violence, and the devil half started from his seat—however, with a slight sigh, he recovered his composure, merely saying to our hero in a low tone, "I tell you what, Pierre Bon-Bon, we *must* have no more swearing."

The host swallowed another bumper, by way of denoting thorough comprehension and acquiescence, and the visitor continued:

"Why there are *several* ways of managing. The most of us starve: some put up with the pickle: for my part I purchase my spirits *vivente corpore,* in which case I find they keep very well."

"But the body!—hiccup!—the body!!!"

"The body, the body—well, what of the body?—oh! ah! I perceive. Why, sir, the body is not *at all* affected by the transaction. I have made innumerable purchases of the kind in my day, and the parties never experienced any inconvenience. There were Cain and Nimrod, and Nero, and Caligula, and Dionysius, and Pisistratus, and—and a thousand others, who never knew what it was to have a soul during the latter part of their lives; yet, sir, these men adorned society. Why isn't there A——, now, whom you know as well as I? Is *he* not in possession of all his faculties, mental and corporeal? Who writes a keener epigram? Who reasons more wittily? Who—but, stay! I have his agreement in my pocketbook."

Thus saying, he produced a red leather wallet, and took from it a number of papers. Upon some of these Bon-Bon caught a glimpse of the letters *Machi—Maza—Robesp*—with the words *Caligula, George, Elizabeth.* His Majesty selected a narrow slip of parchment, and from it read aloud the following words:

"In consideration of certain mental endowments which it is

unnecessary to specify, and in farther consideration of one thousand louis d'or, I, being aged one year and one month, do hereby make over to the bearer of this agreement all my right, title, and appurtenance in the shadow called my soul. (Signed) A . . . . . (Here his Majesty repeated a name which I do not feel myself justified in indicating more unequivocally.)

"A clever fellow that," resumed he; "but like you, Monsieur Bon-Bon, he was mistaken about the soul. The soul a shadow truly! The soul a shadow! Ha! ha! ha!—he! he! he!—hu! hu! hu! Only think of a fricasséed shadow!"

"*Only* think—hiccup!—of a fricasséed shadow!" exclaimed our hero, whose faculties were becoming much illuminated by the profundity of his Majesty's discourse.

"Only think of a—hiccup!—fricasséed shadow!! Now, damme!—hiccup!—humph! If *I* would have been such a—hiccup!—nincompoop. *My* soul, Mr.—humph!"

"*Your* soul, Monsieur Bon-Bon?"

"Yes, sir—hiccup!—*my* soul is—"

"What, sir?"

"*No* shadow, damme!"

"Did you mean to say—"

"Yes, sir, *my* soul is—hiccup!—humph!—yes, sir."

"Did not intend to assert—"

"*My* soul is—hiccup!—peculiarly qualified for—hiccup!—a—"

"What, sir?"

"Stew."

"Ha!"

"Soufflée."

"Eh?"

"Fricassée."

"Indeed!"

"Ragout and fricandeau—and see here, my good fellow! I'll let you have it—hiccup!—a bargain." Here the philosopher slapped his Majesty upon the back.

"Couldn't think of such a thing," said the latter calmly, at the same time rising from his seat. The metaphysician stared.

"Am supplied at present," said his Majesty.

"Hiccup!—e-h?" said the philosopher.

"Have no funds on hand."

"What?"

"Besides, very unhandsome in me—"

"Sir!"

"To take advantage of—"

"Hiccup!"

"Your present disgusting and ungentlemanly situation."

Here the visitor bowed and withdrew—in what manner could not precisely be ascertained—but in a well-concerted effort to discharge a bottle at "the villain," the slender chain was severed that depended from the ceiling, and the metaphysician prostrated by the downfall of the lamp.

The Printer's Devil

ANONYMOUS

As I was sitting in my armchair and preparing an essay on the Devil in literature, sleep overpowered me; the pen fell from my hands, and my head reclined upon the desk. I had been thinking so much about the Devil in my waking hours, that the same idea pursued me after I had fallen asleep. I heard a gentle rap at the door, and having bawled out as usual, "Come in," a little gentleman entered, wrapped in a large blue cloth cloak, with a slouched hat, and goggles over his eyes. After bowing and scraping with considerable ceremony, he took off his hat, and threw his cloak over the back of a chair, when I immediately perceived that my visitor was no mortal. His face was hideously ugly; the skin appearing very much like wet paper, and the forehead covered with those cabalistic signs whose wondrous significance is best known to those who correct the press. On the end of his long hooked nose there seemed to me to be growing, like a carbuncle, the first letter of the alphabet, glittering with ink and ready to print. I observed, also, that each of his fingers and toes, or rather claws, was in the same manner terminated by one of the letters of the alphabet; and as he slashed round his tail to brush a fly off his nose, I noticed that the letter Z formed the extremity of that useful member. While I was looking with no small astonishment and some trepidation at my extraordinary visitor, he took occasion to inform me that he had taken liberty to call, as he was afraid I might forget him in the treatise which I was writing—an omission which he assured me would cause him no little mortification. "In me," says he, "you behold the prince and patron of printer's devils. My province is to preside over the hell of books; and if you will only take the trouble to accompany me a little way, I will show you some of the wonders of that world." As my imagination had lately been much excited by perusing Dante's *Inferno,* I was delighted with an adventure which promised to turn out something like his wonderful journey, and I readily consented to visit my new friend's dominions, and we sallied forth together. As we pursued our way, my conductor endeavored to give me some information respecting the world I was about to enter, in order to prepare me for the wonders I should encounter there. "You must know," remarked he, "that books have souls as well as men; and the moment any work is published, whether successful or not, its soul appears in precisely the same form in another world; either in this domain, which is subject to me, or in a better region, over which I have no control. I have power only to exhibit the place of punishment for bad books, periodicals, pamphlets, and, in short, publications of every kind."

We now arrived at the mouth of a cavern, which I did not remember to have ever noticed before, though I had repeatedly passed the spot in my walks. It looked to me more like the entrance to a coalmine than anything else, as the sides were entirely black. Upon examining them more closely, I found that they were covered with a black fluid which greatly resembled printer's ink, and which seemed to corrode and wear away the rocks of the cavern wherever it touched them. "We have lately received a large supply of political publications," said my companion; "and hell is perfectly saturated with their maliciousness. We carry on a profitable trade upon the earth, by retailing this ink to the principal political editors. Unfortunately, it is not found to answer very well for literary publications, though they have tried it with considerable success in printing the London *Quarterly* and several of the other important reviews."

The cavern widened as we advanced, and we came presently into a vast open plain, which was bounded on one side by a wall so high that it seemed to reach the very heavens. As we approached the wall I observed a vast gateway before us, closed up by folding doors. The gates opened at our approach, and we entered. I found myself in a warm sandy valley, bounded on one side by a steep range of mountains. A feeble light shone upon it, much like that of a sick chamber, and the air seemed confined and stifling like that of the abode of illness. My ears were assailed by a confused whining noise, as if all the litters of new-born puppies, kittens with their eyes unopened, and babes just come to light, in the whole world, were brought into one spot, and were whelping, mewing, and squalling at once. I turned in mute wonder to my guide for explanation; and he informed me that I now beheld the destined abode of all still-born and abortive publications; and the infantine noises which I heard were only their feeble wailing for the miseries they had endured in being brought into the world. I now saw what the feebleness of the light had prevented my observing before, that the soil was absolutely covered with books of every size and shape, from the little diamond almanac up to the respectable quarto. I saw folios there. These books were crawling about and tumbling over each other like blind whelps, uttering, at the same time, the most mournful cries. I observed one, however, which remained quite still, occasionally groaning a little, and appeared like an overgrown toad oppressed with its own heaviness. I drew near, and read upon the back, "*Resignation,* a Novel." The cover flew open, and the title-page immediately began to address me. I walked off, however, as fast as possible, only distinguishing a few words about "the injustice and severity of critics;" "bad taste of the public;" "very well considering;" "first effort;" "feminine mind," etc., etc. I presently discovered a very important-looking little book, stalking about among the rest in a great passion, kicking the others out of the way, and swearing like a trooper; till at length, apparently exhausted with its efforts, it sunk down to rise no more. "Ah ha!" exclaimed my little diabolical friend, "here is a new comer; let's see who he is"; and coming up, he turned it over with his foot so that we could see the back of it, upon which was printed "*The Monikins,* by the Author of, etc., etc." I noticed that the book had several marks across it, as if some one had been flogging the unfortunate work. "It is only the marks of the scourge," said my companion, "which the critics have used rather more severely, I think, than was necessary." I expected, after all the passion I had seen, and the great importance of feeling, arrogance, and vanity the little work had manifested, that it would have some pert remarks to make to us; but it was so much exhausted that it could not say a word. At the bottom of the valley was a small pond of a milky hue, from which there issued a perfume very much like the smell of bread and butter. An immense number of thin, prettily bound manuscript books were soaking in this pond of milk, all of which, I was informed, were *Young Ladies' Albums,* which it was necessary to souse in the slough, to prevent them from stealing passages from the various works about them. As soon as I heard what they were, I ran away with all my speed, having a mortal dread of these books.

We had now traversed the valley, and, approaching the barrier of mountains, we found a passage cut through, which greatly resembled the Pausilipo, near Naples; it was closed on the side towards the valley, only with a curtain of white paper, upon which were printed the names of the principal reviews, which my conductor assured me were enough to prevent any of the unhappy works we had seen from coming near the passage.

As we advanced through the mountains, occasional gleams of light appeared before us, and immediately vanished, leaving us in darkness. My guide, however, seemed to be well acquainted with the way, and we went on fearlessly till we emerged into an open field, lighted up by constant flashes of lightning, which glared from every side; the air was hot, and strongly impregnated with sulphur. "Each department of my dominions," said the Devil, "receives its light from the works which are sent there. You are now surrounded by the glittering but evanescent coruscations of the more recent novels. This department of hell was never very well supplied till quite lately, though Fielding, Smollett, Maturin, and Godwin, did what they could for us. Our greatest benefactors have been Disraeli, Bulwer, and Victor Hugo; and this glare of light, so painful to our eyes, proceeds chiefly from their books." There was a tremendous noise like the rioting of an army of drunken men, with horrible cries and imprecations, and fiend-like laughing, which made my blood curdle; and such a scrambling and fighting among the books, as I never saw before. I could not imagine at first what could be the cause of this, till I discovered at last a golden hill rising up like a cone in the midst of the plain, with just room enough for one book on the summit; and I found that the novels were fighting like so many devils for the occupation of this place. One work, however, had gained possession of it, and seemed to maintain its hold with a strength and resolution which bade defiance to the rest. I could not at first make out the name of this book, which seemed to stand upon its golden throne like the Prince of Hell; but presently the whole arch of the heavens glared with new brilliancy, and the magic name of *Vivian Grey* flashed from the book in letters of scorching light. I was much afraid, however, that *Vivian* would not long retain his post; for I saw *Pelham* and *Peregrine Pickle,* and the terrible *Melmoth* with his glaring eyes, coming together to the assault, when a whirlwind seized them all four and carried them away to a vast distance, leaving the elevation vacant for some other competitor. "There is no peace to the wicked, you see," said my Asmodeus. "These books are longing for repose, and they can get none on account of the insatiable vanity of their authors, whose desire for distinction made them careless of the sentiments they expressed and the principles they advocated. The great characteristic of works of this stamp is action, intense, painful action. They have none of that beautiful serenity which shines in Scott and Edgeworth; and they are condemned to illustrate, by an eternity of contest here, the restless spirit with which they are inspired."

While I was looking on with fearful interest in the mad combat before me, the horizon seemed to be darkened, and a vast cloud rose up in the image of a gigantic eagle, whose wings stretched from the east to the west till he covered the firmament. In his talons he carried an open book, at the sight of which the battle around me was calmed; the lightnings ceased to flash, and there was an awful stillness. Then suddenly there glared from the book a sheet of fire, which rose in columns a thousand feet high, and filled the empyrean with intense light; the pillars of flame curling and wreathing themselves into monstrous letters, till they were fixed in one terrific glare, and I read—"BYRON." Even my companion quailed before the awful light, and I covered my face with my hands. When I withdrew them, the cloud and the book had vanished, and the contest was begun again—"You have seen the Prince of this division of hell," said my guide.

We now began rapidly to descend into the bowels of the earth; and, after sinking some thousand feet, I found myself on terra firma again, and walking a little way, we came to a gate of massive ice, over which was written in vast letters—"My heritage is despair." We passed through, and immediately found ourselves in a vast basin of lead, which seemed to meet the horizon on every side. A bright light shone over the whole region; but it was not like the genial light of the sun. It chilled me through; and every ray that fell upon me seemed like the touch of ice. The deepest silence prevailed; and though the valley was covered with books, not one moved or uttered a sound. I drew near to one, and I shivered with intense cold as I read upon it—"Voltaire." "Behold," said the demon, "the hell of infidel books; the light which emanates from them is the light of reason, and they are doomed to everlasting torpor." I found it too cold to pursue my investigations any farther in this region, and I gladly passed on from the leaden gulf of Infidelity.

I had no sooner passed the barrier which separated this department from the next, than I heard a confused sound like the quacking of myriads of ducks and geese, and a great flapping of wings; of which I soon saw the cause. "You are in the hell of newspapers," said my guide. And sure enough, when I looked up I saw thousands of newspapers flying about with their great wooden back-bones, and the padlock dangling like a bobtail at the end, flapping their wings and hawking at each other like mad. After circling about in the air for a little while, and biting and tearing each other as much as they could, they plumped down, head first, into a deep black-looking pool, and were seen no more. "We place these newspapers deeper in hell than the Infidel publications," said the Devil; "because they are so much more extensively read, and thereby do much greater mischief. It is a kind of pest of which there is no end; and we are obliged to allot the largest portion of our dominions to containing them."

We now came to an immense pile of a leaden hue, which I found at last to consist of old worn-out type, which was heaped up to form the wall of the next division. A monstrous u, turned bottom upwards (in this way: ∩) formed the arch of a gateway through which we passed; and then traversed a draw-bridge, which was thrown across a river of ink, upon whose banks millions of horrible little demons were sporting. I presently saw that they were employed in throwing into the black stream a quantity of books which were heaped up on the shore. As I looked down into the stream, I saw that they were immediately devoured by the most hideous and disgusting monsters which were floundering about there. I looked at one book, which had crawled out after being thrown into the river; it was dripping with filth, but I distinguished on the back the words—*Don Juan.* It had hardly climbed up the bank, however, when one of the demons gave it a kick, and sent it back into the stream, where it was immediately swallowed. On the back of some of the books which the little imps were tossing in, I saw the name of—*Rochester,* which showed me the character of those which were sent into this division of the infernal regions.

Beyond this region rose up a vast chain of mountains, which we were obliged to clamber over. After toiling for a long time, we reached the summit, and I looked down upon an immense labyrinth built upon the plain below, in which I saw a great number of large folios, stalking about in solemn pomp, each followed by a number of small volumes and pamphlets, like so many pages or footmen watching the beck of their master. "You behold here," said the demon, "all the false works upon theology which have been written since the beginning of the Christian era. They are condemned to wander about to all eternity in the hopeless maze of this labyrinth, each folio drawing after it all the minor works to which it gave origin." A faint light shone from these ponderous tomes; but it was like the shining of a lamp in a thick mist, shorn of its rays, and illuminating nothing around it. And if my companion had not held a torch before me, I should not have discerned the outlines of this department of the Infernal world. As my eye became somewhat accustomed to the feeble light, I discovered beyond the labyrinth a thick mist, which appeared to rise from some river or lake. "That," said my companion, "is the distinct abode of German Metaphysical works, and other treatises of a similar unintelligible character. They are all obliged to pass through a press; and if there is any sense in them, it is thus separated from the mass of nonsense in which it is imbedded, and is allowed to escape to a better world. Very few of the works, however, are found to be materially diminished by passing through the press." We had now crossed the plain, and stood near the impenetrable fog, which rose up like a wall before us. In front of it was the press managed by several ugly little demons, and surrounded by an immense number of volumes of every size and shape, waiting for the process which all were obliged to undergo. As I was watching their operations, I saw two very respectable German folios, with enormous clasps, extended like arms, carrying between them a little volume, which they were fondling like a pet child with marks of doting affection. These folios proved to be two of the most abstruse, learned, and incomprehensible of the metaphysical productions of Germany; and the bantling which they seemed to embrace with so much affection, was registered on the back—*"Records of a School."* I did not find that a single ray of intelligence had been extracted from either of the two after being subjected to the press. As soon as the volumes had passed through the operation of yielding up all the little sense they contained, they plunged into the intense fog, and disappeared for ever.

We next approached the verge of a gulf, which appeared to be

bottomless; and there was dreadful noise, like the war of the elements, and forked flames shooting up from the abyss, which re-
minded me of the crater of Vesuvius. "You have now reached the
ancient limits of hell," said the demon, "and you behold beneath
your feet the original chaos on which my domains are founded. But
within a few years we have been obliged to build a yet deeper
division beyond the gulf, to contain a class of books that were
unknown in former times." "Pray, what class can be found," I asked,
"worse than those which I have already seen, and for which it
appears hell was not bad enough?" "They are American reprints of
English publications," replied he, "and they are generally works of
such a despicable character, that they would have found their way
here without being republished; but even where the original work
was good, it is so degenerated by the form under which it reappears
in America, that its merit is entirely lost, and it is only fit for the
seventh and lowest division of hell."

I now perceived a bridge spanning over the gulf, with an arch
that seemed as lofty as the firmament..We hastily passed over, and
found that the farthest extremity of the bridge was closed by a gate,
over which was written three words. "They are the names of the
three furies who reign over this division," said my guide. I of course
did not contradict him; but the words looked very much like some I
had seen before; and the more I examined them, the more difficult
was it to convince myself that the inscription was not the same thing
as the sign over a certain publishing house in Philadelphia.

"These," said the Devil, "are called the three furies of the hell of
books; not from the mischief they do there to the works about them,
but for the unspeakable wrong they did to the same works upon the
earth, by re-printing them in their hideous brown paper editions."
As soon as they beheld me, they rushed towards me with such
piteous accents and heart-moving entreaties, that I would intercede
to save them from their torment, that I was moved with the deepest

compassion, and began to ask my conductor if there were no relief for them. But he hurried me away, assuring me that they only wanted to sell me some of their infernal editions, and the idea of owning any such property was so dreadful that it woke me up directly.

The Devil's Mother-in-Law

FERNÁN CABALLERO

In a town named Villagañanes, there was once an old widow uglier than the sergeant of Utrera, who was considered as ugly as ugly could be; drier than hay; older than foot-walking, and more yellow than the jaundice. Moreover, she had so crossgrained a disposition that Job himself could not have tolerated her. She had been nicknamed "Mother Holofernes," and she had only to put her head out of doors to put all the lads to flight. Mother Holofernes was as clean as a new pin, and as industrious as an ant, and in these respects suffered no little vexation on account of her daughter Panfila, who was, on the contrary, so lazy, and such an admirer of the Quietists, that an earthquake would not move her. So it came to pass that Mother Holofernes began quarrelling with her daughter almost from the day that the girl was born.

"You are," she said, "as flaccid as Dutch tobacco, and it would take a couple of oxen to draw you out of your room. You fly work as you would the pest, and nothing pleases you but the window, you shameless girl. You are more amorous than Cupid himself, but, if I have any power, you shall live as close as a nun."

On hearing all this, Panfila got up, yawned, stretched herself, and turning her back on her mother, went to the street door. Mother Holofernes, without paying attention to this, began to sweep with most tremendous energy, accompanying the noise of the broom with a monologue of this tenor:—

"In my time girls had to work like men."

The broom gave the accompaniment of *shis, shis, shis.*

"And lived as secluded as nuns."

And the broom went *shis, shis, shis.*

"Now they are a pack of fools."—*Shis, shis.*

"Of idlers."—*Shis, shis.*

"And think of nothing but husbands.—*Shis, shis.*

"And are a lot of good-for-nothings."

The broom following with its chorus.

By this time she had nearly reached the street door, when she saw her daughter making signs to a youth; and the handle of the broom, as the handiest implement, descended upon the shoulders of Panfila, and effected the miracle of making her run. Next, Mother Holofernes, grasping the broom, made for the door; but scarcely had the shadow of her head appeared, than it produced the customary effect, and the aspirant disappeared so swiftly that it seemed as if he must have had wings on his feet.

"Drat that fellow!" shouted the mother; "I should like to break all the bones in his body."

"What for? Why should I not think of getting married?"

"What are you saying? You get married, you fool! not while I live!"

"Why were you married, madam? and my grandmother? and my great grandmother?"

"Nicely I have been repaid for it, by you, you saucebox! And understand me, that if I chose to get married, and your grandmother also, and your great grandmother also, I do not intend that you shall marry; nor my granddaughter, nor my great granddaughter! Do you hear me?"

In these gentle disputes the mother and daughter passed their lives, without any other result than that the mother grumbled more and more every day, and the daughter became daily more and more desirous of getting a husband.

Upon one occasion, when Mother Holofernes was doing the washing, and as the lye was on the point of boiling, she had to call her daughter to help her lift the caldron, in order to pour its contents on to the tub of clothes. The girl heard her with one ear, but with the other was listening to a well-known voice which sang in the street:

> "I would like to love thee,
>   Did thy mother let me woo!
> May the demon meddle
>   In all she tries to do!"

The sound outside being more attractive for Panfila than the caldron within, she did not hasten to her mother, but went to the window. Mother Holofernes, meanwhile, seeing that her daughter did not come, and that time was passing, attempted to lift the caldron by herself, in order to pour the water upon the linen; and as the good woman was small, and not very strong, it turned over, and burnt her foot. On hearing the horrible groans Mother Holofernes made, her daughter went to her.

"Wretch, wretch!" cried the enraged Mother Holofernes to her daughter, "may you love Barabbas! And as for marrying—may Heaven grant you may marry the Evil One himself!"

Sometime after this accident an aspirant presented himself: he was a little man, young, fair, red-haired, well-mannered, and had well-furnished pockets. He had not a single fault, and Mother Holofernes was not able to find any in all her arsenal of negatives. As for Panfila, it wanted little to send her out of her senses with delight. So the preparations for the wedding were made, with the usual grumbling accompaniment on the part of the bridegroom's future mother-in-law. Everything went on smoothly straightforward, and without a break—like a railroad—when, without knowing why, the popular voice—a voice which is as the personification of conscience,—began to rise in a murmur against the stranger, despite the fact that he was affable, humane, and liberal; that he spoke well and sang better; and freely took the black and horny hands of the laborers between his own white and beringed fingers. They began to feel neither honored nor overpowered by so much courtesy; his reasoning was always so coarse, although forcible and logical.

"By my faith!" said Uncle Blas; "why does this ill-faced gentleman call me Mr. Blas, as if that would make me any better? What does it look like to you?"

"Well, as for me," said Uncle Gil, "did he not come to shake hands with me as if we had some plot between us? Did he not call me citizen? I, who have never been out of the village, and never want to go."

As for Mother Holofernes, the more she saw of her future son-in-law, the less regard she had for him. It seemed to her that between that innocent red hair and the cranium were located certain protuberances of a very curious kind; and she remembered with emotion that malediction she had uttered against her daughter on that ever memorable day on which her foot was injured and her washing spoilt.

At last, the wedding day arrived. Mother Holofernes had made pastry and reflections—the former sweet, the latter bitter; a great *olla podrida* for the food, and a dangerous project for supper; she had prepared a barrel of wine that was generous, and a line of conduct that was not. When the bridal pair were about to retire to the nuptial chamber, Mother Holofernes called her daughter aside, and said: "When you are in your room, be careful to close the door and windows; shut all the shutters, and do not leave a single crevice open but the keyhole of the door. Take with you this branch of consecrated olive, and beat your husband with it as I advise you; this ceremony is customary at all marriages, and signifies that the woman is going to be master, and is followed in order to sanction and establish the rule."

Panfila, for the first time obedient to her mother, did everything that she had prescribed.

No sooner did the bridegroom espy the branch of consecrated olive in the hands of his wife, than he attempted to make a precipitous retreat. But when he found the doors and windows closed, and every crevice stopped up, seeing no other means of escape than by passing through the keyhole, he crept into that; this spruce, red-and-white, and well-spoken bachelor being, as Mother Holofernes had suspected, neither more nor less than the Evil One himself, who, availing himself of the right given him by the anathema launched against Panfila by her mother, thought to amuse himself with the pleasures of a marriage, and encumber himself with a wife of his own, whilst so many husbands were supplicating him to take theirs off their hands.

But this gentleman, despite his reputation for wisdom, had met with a mother-in-law who knew more than he did; and Mother

Holofernes was not the only specimen of that genus. Therefore, scarcely had his lordship entered into the keyhole, congratulating himself upon having, as usual, discovered a method of escape, than he found himself in a phial, which his foreseeing mother-in-law had ready on the other side of the door; and no sooner had he got into it than the provident old dame sealed the vessel hermetically. In a most tender voice, and with most humble supplications, and most pathetic gestures, her son-in-law addressed her, and desired that she would grant him his liberty. But Mother Holofernes was not to be deceived by the demon, nor disconcerted by orations, nor imposed upon by honeyed words; she took charge of the bottle and its contents, and went off to a mountain. The old lady vigorously climbed to the summit of this mountain, and there, on its most elevated crest, in a rocky and secluded spot, deposited the phial, taking leave of her son-in-law with a shake of her closed fist as a farewell greeting.

And there his lordship remained for ten years. What years those ten were! The world was as quiet as a pool of oil. Everybody attended to his own affairs, without meddling in those of other people. Nobody coveted the position, nor the wife, nor the property of other persons; theft became a word without signification; arms rusted; powder was only consumed in fireworks; prisons stood empty; finally, in this decade of the golden age, only one single deplorable event occurred . . . the lawyers died from hunger and quietude.

Alas! that so happy a time should have an end! But everything has an end in this world, even the discourses of the most eloquent fathers of the country. At last the much-to-be-envied decade came to a termination in the following way.

A soldier named Briónes had obtained permission for a few days' leave to enable him to visit his native place, which was Villagañanes. He took the road which led to the lofty mountain upon whose summit the son-in-law of Mother Holofernes was cursing all mothers-in-law, past, present, and future, promising as soon as ever he regained his power to put an end to that class of vipers, and by a very simple method—the abolition of matrimony. Much of his time was spent in composing and reciting satires against the invention of washing linen, the primal cause of his present trouble.

Arrived at the foot of the mountain, Briónes did not care to go round the mountain like the road, but wished to go straight ahead, assuring the carriers who were with him, that if the mountain would not go to the right-about for him he would pass over its summit, although it were so high that he should knock his head against the sky.

When he reached the summit, Briónes was struck with amazement on seeing the phial borne like a pimple on the nose of the mountain. He took it up, looked through it, and on perceiving the demon, who with years of confinement and fasting, the sun's rays, and sadness, had dwindled and become as dried as a prune, exclaimed in surprise:

"Whatever vermin is this? What a phenomenon!"

"I am an honorable and meritorious demon," said the captive, humbly and courteously. "The perversity of a treacherous mother-in-law, into whose clutches I fell, has held me confined here during the last ten years; liberate me, valiant warrior, and I will grant any favor you choose to solicit."

"I should like my demission from the army," said Briónes.

"You shall have it; but uncork, uncork quickly, for it is a most monstrous anomaly to have thrust into a corner, in these revolutionary times, the first revolutionist in the world."

Briónes drew the cork out slightly, and a noxious vapor issued from the bottle and ascended to his brain. He sneezed, and immediately replaced the stopper with such a violent blow from his hand that the cork was suddenly depressed, and the prisoner, squeezed down, gave a shout of rage and pain.

"What are you doing, vile earthworm, more malicious and perfidious than my mother-in-law?" he exclaimed.

"There is another condition," responded Briónes, "that I must add to our treaty; it appears to me that the service I am going to do you is worth it."

"And what is this condition, tardy liberator?" inquired the demon.

"I should like for thy ransom four dollars daily during the rest of my life. Think of it, for upon that depends whether you stay in or come out."

"Miserable avaricious one!" exclaimed the demon, "I have no money."

"Oh!" replied Briónes, "what an answer from a great lord like you! Why, friend, that is the Minister of War's answer! If you can't pay me I cannot help you."

"Then you do not believe me," said the demon, "only let me out, and I will aid you to obtain what you want as I have done for many others. Let me out, I say, let me out."

"Gently," responded the soldier, "there is nothing to hurry about. Understand me that I shall have to hold you by the tail until you have performed your promise to me; and if not, I have nothing more to say to you."

"Insolent, do you not trust me then!" shouted the demon.

"No," responded Briónes.

"What you desire is contrary to my dignity," said the captive, with all the arrogance that a being of his size could express.

"Now I must go," said Briónes.

"Good-bye," said the demon, in order not to say *adieu.*

But seeing that Briónes went off, the captive made desperate jumps in the phial, shouting loudly to the soldier.

"Return, return, dear friend," he said; and muttered to himself, "I should like a four-year-old bull to overtake you, you soulless

fool!" and then he shouted, "Come, come, beneficent fellow, liberate me, and hold me by the tail, or by the nose, valiant warrior"; and
then muttered to himself, "Some one will avenge me, obstinate
soldier; and if the son-in-law of Mother Holofernes is not able to do
it, there are those who will burn you both, face to face, in the same
bonfire, or I have little influence."

On hearing the demon's supplications Briónes returned and
uncorked the bottle. Mother Holofernes's son-in-law came forth like
a chick from its shell, drawing out his head first and then his body,
and lastly his tail, which Briónes seized; and the more the demon
tried to contract it the firmer he held it.

After the ex-captive, who was somewhat cramped, had occasionally stopped to stretch his arms and legs, they took the road to court,
the demon grumbling and following the soldier, who carried the tail
well secured in his hands.

On their arrival they went to court, and the demon said to his
liberator:

"I am going to put myself into the body of the princess, who is
extremely beloved by her father, and I shall give her pains that no
doctor will be able to cure; then you present yourself and offer to
cure her, demanding for your recompense four dollars daily, and
your discharge. I will then leave her to you, and our accounts will be
settled."

Everything happened as arranged and foreseen by the demon,
but Briónes did not wish to let go his hold of the tail, and he said:

"Well devised, sir, but four dollars are a ransom unworthy of
you, of me, and of the service that we have undertaken. Find some
method of showing yourself more generous. To do this will give you
honor in the world, where, pardon my frankness, you do not enjoy
the best of characters."

"Would that I could get rid of you!" said the demon to himself,
"but I am so weak and so numbed that I am not able to go alone. I

must have patience! that which men call a virtue. Oh, now I understand why so many fall into my power for not having practised it.
Forward then for Naples, for it is necessary to submit in order to
liberate my tail. I must go and submit to the arbitration of fate for
the satisfaction of this new demand."

Everything succeeded according to his wish. The princess of
Naples fell a victim to convulsive pains and took to her bed. The
king was greatly afflicted. Briónes presented himself with all the
arrogance his knowledge that he would receive the demon's aid
could give him. The king was willing to make use of his services, but
stipulated that if within three days he had not cured the princess, as
he confidently promised to, he should be hanged. Briónes, certain of
a favorable result, did not raise the slightest objection.

Unfortunately, the demon heard this arrangement made, and
gave a leap of delight at seeing within his hands the means of
avenging himself.

The demon's leap caused the princess such pain that she begged
them to take the doctor away.

The following day this scene was repeated. Briónes then knew
that the demon was at the bottom of it, and intended to let him be
hanged. But Briónes was not a man to lose his head.

On the third day, when the pretended doctor arrived, they were
erecting the gallows in front of the very palace door. As he entered
the princess's apartment, the invalid's pains were redoubled and she
began to cry out that they should put an end to that impostor.

"I have not exhausted all my resources yet," said Briónes gravely,
"deign, your Royal Highness, to wait a little while." He then went
out of the room and gave orders in the princess's name that all the
bells of the city should be rung.

When he returned to the royal apartment, the demon, who has a
mortal hatred of the sound of bells, and is, moreover, inquisitive,
asked Briónes what the bells were ringing for.

"They are ringing," responded the soldier, "because of the ar-rival of your mother-in-law, whom I have ordered to be sum-moned."

Scarcely had the demon heard that his mother-in-law had ar-rived, than he flew away with such rapidity that not even a sun's ray could have caught him. Proud as a peacock, Briónes was left in victorious possession of the field.

The Devil and Mr. Chips

CHARLES DICKENS

There was once a shipwright, and he wrought in a Government Yard, and his name was Chips. And his father's name before him was Chips, and *his* father's name before *him* was Chips, and they were all Chipses. And Chips the father had sold himself to the Devil for an iron pot and a bushel of tenpenny nails and half a ton of copper and a rat that could speak; and Chips the grandfather had sold himself to the Devil for an iron pot and a bushel of tenpenny nails and half a ton of copper and a rat that could speak; and Chips the great-grandfather had disposed of himself in the same direction, on the same terms; and the bargain had run in the family for a long,

long time. So one day, when young Chips was at work in the Dock Slip all alone, down in the dark hold of an old Seventy-four that was haled up for repairs, the Devil presented himself, and remarked:

> "A Lemon has pips,
> And a Yard has ships,
> And I'll have Chips!"

(I don't know why, but this fact of the Devil's expressing himself in rhyme was peculiarly trying to me.) Chips looked up when he heard the words, and there he saw the Devil, with saucer eyes that squinted on a terrible great scale, and that struck out sparks of blue fire continually. And whenever he winked his eyes, showers of blue sparks came out, and his eyelashes made a clattering like flints and steels striking lights. And hanging over one of his arms by the handle was an iron pot, and under that arm was a bushel of tenpenny nails, and under his other arm was a half ton of copper, and sitting on one of his shoulders was a rat that could speak. So the Devil said again:

> "A Lemon has pips,
> And a Yard has ships,
> And I'll have Chips!"

(The invariable effect of this alarming tautology on the part of the Evil Spirit was to deprive me of my senses for some moments.) So Chips answered never a word, but went on with his work. "What are you doing, Chips?" said the rat that could speak. "I am putting in new planks where you and your gang have eaten old away," said Chips. "But we'll eat them too," said the rat that could speak: "and we'll let in the water and drown the crew, and we'll eat them too." Chips, being only a shipwright, and not a Man-of-war's man said, "You are welcome to it." But he couldn't keep his eyes off the half a ton of copper or the bushel of tenpenny nails; for nails and copper are a shipwright's sweethearts, and shipwrights will run away with them whenever they can. So the Devil said, "I see what you are looking at, Chips. You had better strike the bargain. You know the terms. Your father before you was well acquainted with them, and so were your grandfather and great-grandfather before him." Says Chips, "I like the copper, and I like the nails, and I don't mind the pot, but I don't like the rat." Says the Devil, fiercely, "You can't have the metal without him—and he's a curiosity. I'm going." Chips, afraid of losing the half a ton of copper and the bushel of nails, then said, "Give us hold!" So he got the copper and the nails and the pot, and the rat that could speak, and the Devil vanished. Chips sold the copper, and he sold the nails, and he would have sold the pot, but whenever he offered it for sale, the rat was in it, and the dealers dropped it, and would have nothing to say to the bargain. So Chips resolved to kill the rat, and, being at work in the Yard one day, with a great kettle of hot pitch on one side of him and the iron pot with the rat in it on the other, he turned the scalding pitch into the pot, and filled it full. Then he kept his eye upon it till it cooled and hardened, and then he let it stand for twenty days, and then he heated the pitch again, and turned it back into the kettle, and then he sank the pot in water for twenty days more, and then he got the smelters to put it in the furnace for twenty days more, and then they gave it him out, red-hot, and looking like red-hot glass instead of iron,—yet there was the rat in it, just the same as ever! And the moment it caught his eye, it said with a jeer:

"A Lemon has pips,
And a Yard has ships,
And I'll have Chips!"

(For this Refrain I had waited since its last appearance with inexpressible horror, which now culminated.) Chips now felt certain in his own mind that the rat would stick to him; the rat, answering his thought, said, "I will—like pitch!"

Now, as the rat leaped out of the pot when it had spoken, and made off, Chips began to hope that it wouldn't keep its word. But a terrible thing happened next day. For when dinner-time came and the Dock-bell rang to strike work, he put his rule into the long pocket at the side of his trousers, and there he found a rat—not that rat, but another rat. And in his hat he found another; and in his pocket-handkerchief another; and in the sleeves of his coat, when he pulled it on to go to dinner, two more. And from that time he found himself so frightfully intimate with all the rats in the Yard, that they climbed up his legs when he was at work, and sat on his tools while he used them. And they could all speak to one another, and he understood what they said. And they got into his lodging, and into his bed, and into his teapot, and into his beer, and into his boots. And he was going to be married to a corn-chandler's daughter; and when he gave her a work-box he had himself made for her a rat jumped out of it; and when he put his arm round her waist, a rat clung about her; so the marriage was broken off, though the banns were already twice put up—which the parish clerk well remembers, for, as he handed the book to the clergyman for the second time of asking, a large fat rat ran over the leaf. (By this time a special cascade of rats was rolling down my back, and the whole of my small listening person was overrun with them. At intervals ever since I have been morbidly afraid of my own pocket, lest my exploring hand should find a specimen or two of those vermin in it.)

You may believe that all this was very terrible to Chips; but even all this was not the worst. He knew, besides, what the rats were doing, wherever they were. So sometimes he would cry aloud, when he was at his club at night, "O, keep the rats out of the convicts' burying-ground! Don't let them do that!" or, "There's one of them at the cheese down stairs!" or, "There's two of them smelling at the baby in the garret!" or other things of that sort. At last he was voted mad, and lost his work in the Yard, and could get no other work. But King George wanted men, so before very long he got pressed for a sailor. And so he was taken off in a boat one evening to his ship, lying at Spithead, ready to sail. And so the first thing he made out in her, as he got near her, was the figure-head of the old Seventy-four, where he had seen the Devil. She was called the "Argonaut," and they rowed right under the bowsprit where the figure-head of the Argonaut, with a sheep-skin in his hand and a blue gown on, was looking out to sea; and sitting staring on his forehead was the rat who could speak, and his exact words were these: "Chips ahoy! Old boy! We've pretty well eat them too, and we'll drown the crew, and will eat them too!" (Here I always became exceedingly faint, and would have asked for water but that I was speechless.)

The ship was bound for the Indies; and if you don't know where that is, you ought to it, and angels will never love you. (Here I felt myself an outcast from a future state.) The ship set sail that very night, and she sailed, and sailed, and sailed. Chips's feelings were dreadful. Nothing ever equalled his terrors. No wonder. At last, one day, he asked leave to speak to the Admiral. The Admiral giv' leave. Chips went down on his knees in the Great State Cabin. "Your Honor, unless your Honor, without a moment's loss of time, makes sail for the nearest shore, this is a doomed ship, and her name is the Coffin!" "Young man, your words are a madman's words." "Your Honor, no; they are nibbling us away." "They?" "Your Honor, them dreadful rats. Dust and hollowness where solid oak ought to be! Rats nibbling a grave for every man on board! Oh! Does your Honor love your lady and your pretty children?" "Yes, my man, to be sure." "Then, for God's sake, make for the nearest shore; for at this present moment the rats are all stopping in their work, and are all looking straight towards you with bare teeth, and are all saying to one another that you shall never, never, never, never see your lady and your children more." "My poor fellow, you are a case for the doctor. Sentry, take care of this man!"

So he was bled, and he was blistered, and he was this and that, for six whole days and nights. So then he again asked leave to speak to the Admiral. The Admiral giv' leave. He went down on his knees in the Great State Cabin. "Now, Admiral, you must die! You took no warning; you must die! The rats are never wrong in their calculations, and they make out that they'll be through at twelve tonight. So you must die!—with me and all the rest!" And so at twelve o'clock there was a great leak reported in the ship, and a torrent of water rushed in and nothing could stop it; and they all went down, every living soul. And what the rats—being water-rats—left of Chips at last floated to shore, and sitting on him was an immense overgrown rat, laughing, that dived when the corpse touched the beach, and never came up. And there was a deal of sea-weed on the remains. And if you get thirteen bits of sea-weed, and dry them and burn them in the fire, they will go off like in these thirteen words as plain as plain can be:

> "A Lemon has pips,
> And a Yard has ships,
> And *I*'ve got Chips!"

The Generous Gambler

CHARLES PIERRE BAUDELAIRE

Yesterday, across the crowd of the boulevard, I found myself touched by a mysterious Being I had always desired to know, and who I recognized immediately, in spite of the fact that I had never seen him. He had, I imagined, in himself, relatively as to me, a similar desire, for he gave me, in passing, so significant a sign in his eyes that I hastened to obey him. I followed him attentively, and soon I descended behind him into a subterranean dwelling, astonishing to me as a vision, where shone a luxury of which none of the actual houses in Paris could give me an approximate example. It seemed to me singular that I had passed so often that prodigious retreat without having discovered the entrance. There reigned an exquisite, an almost stifling atmosphere, which made one forget almost instantaneously all the fastidious horrors of life; there I breathed a sombre sensuality, like that of opium-smokers when, set on the shore of an enchanted island, over which shone an eternal afternoon, they felt born in them, to the soothing sounds of melodious cascades, the desire of never again seeing their households, their women, their children, and of never again being tossed on the decks of ships by storms.

There were there strange faces of men and women, gifted with so fatal a beauty that I seemed to have seen them years ago and in countries which I failed to remember, and which inspired in me that curious sympathy and that equally curious sense of fear that I usually discover in unknown aspects. If I wanted to define in some fashion or other the singular expression of their eyes, I would say that never had I seen such magic radiance more energetically expressing the horror of *ennui* and of desire—of the immortal desire of feeling themselves alive.

As for mine host and myself, we were already, as we sat down, as perfect friends as if we had always known each other. We drank immeasurably of all sorts of extraordinary wines, and—a thing not less bizarre—it seemed to me, after several hours, that I was no more intoxicated than he was.

However, gambling, this superhuman pleasure, had cut, at various intervals, our copious libations, and I ought to say that I had gained and lost my soul, as we were playing, with an heroical carelessness and light-heartedness. The soul is so invisible a thing, often useless and sometimes so troublesome, that I did not experience, as to this loss, more than that kind of emotion I might have, had I lost my visiting card in the street.

We spent hours in smoking cigars, whose incomparable savor and perfume give to the soul the nostalgia of unknown delights and sights, and, intoxicated by all these spiced sauces, I dared, in an access of familiarity which did not seem to displease him, to cry, as I lifted a glass filled to the brim with wine: "To your immortal health, Old He-Goat!"

We talked of the universe, of its creation and of its future destruction; of the leading ideas of the century—that is to say, of Progress and Perfectibility—and, in general, of all kinds of human infatuations. On this subject his Highness was inexhaustible in his irrefutable jests, and he expressed himself with a splendor of diction and with a magnificence in drollery such as I have never found in any of the most famous conversationalists of our age. He explained to me the absurdity of different philosophies that had so far taken possession of men's brains, and deigned even to take me in confidence in regard to certain fundamental principles, which I am not inclined to share with any one.

He complained in no way of the evil reputation under which he lived, indeed, all over the world, and he assured me that he himself was of all living beings the most interested in the destruction of *Superstition,* and he avowed to me that he had been afraid, relatively as to his proper power, once only, and that was on the day when he had heard a preacher, more subtle than the rest of the human herd, cry in his pulpit: "My dear brethren, do not ever forget, when you hear the progress of lights praised, that the loveliest trick of the Devil is to persuade you that he does not exist!"

The memory of this famous orator brought us naturally on the subject of Academies, and my strange host declared to me that he didn't disdain, in many cases, to inspire the pens, the words, and the consciences of pedagogues, and that he almost always assisted in person, in spite of being invisible, at all the scientific meetings.

Encouraged by so much kindness I asked him if he had any news of God—who has not his hours of impiety?—especially as the old friend of the Devil. He said to me, with a shade of unconcern united with a deeper shade of sadness: "We salute each other when we meet." But, for the rest, he spoke in Hebrew.

It is uncertain if his Highness has ever given so long an audience to a simple mortal, and I feared to abuse it.

Finally, as the dark approached shivering, this famous personage, sung by so many poets, and served by so many philosophers who work for his glory's sake without being aware of it, said to me: "I want you to remember me always, and to prove to you that I—of whom one says so much evil—am often enough *bon diable,* to make use of one of your vulgar locutions. So as to make up for the irremediable loss that you have made of your soul, I shall give you back the stake you ought to have gained, if your fate had been fortunate—that is to say, the possibility of solacing and of conquering, during your whole life, this bizarre affection of *ennui,* which is the source of all your maladies and of all your miseries. Never a desire shall be formed by you that I will not aid you to realize; you will reign over your vulgar equals; money and gold and diamonds, fairy palaces, shall come to seek you and shall ask you to accept them without your having made the least effort to obtain them; you can change your abode as often as you like; you shall have in your power all sensualities without lassitude, in lands where the climate is always hot, and where the women are as scented as the flowers." With this he rose up and said good-bye to me with a charming smile.

If it had not been for the shame of humiliating myself before so immense an assembly, I might have voluntarily fallen at the feet of this generous Gambler, to thank him for his unheard-of munificence. But, little by little, after I had left him, an incurable defiance entered into me; I dared no longer believe in so prodigious a happiness; and as I went to bed, making over again my nightly prayer by means of all that remained in me in the matter of faith, I repeated in my slumber: "My God, my Lord, my God! Do let the Devil keep his word with me!"

Sir Dominick's Bargain

J. SHERIDAN LE FANU

In the early autumn of the year 1838, business called me to the south of Ireland. The weather was delightful, the scenery and people were new to me, and sending my luggage on by the mail-coach route in charge of a servant, I hired a serviceable nag at a posting-house, and, full of the curiosity of an explorer, I commenced a leisurely journey of five-and-twenty miles on horseback, by sequestered cross-roads, to my place of destination. By bog and hill, by plain and ruined castle, and many a winding stream, my picturesque road led me.

I had started late, and having made little more than half my journey, I was thinking of making a short halt at the next convenient place, and letting my horse have a rest and a feed, and making some provision also for the comforts of his rider.

It was about four o'clock when the road, ascending a gradual steep, found a passage through a rocky gorge between the abrupt termination of a range of mountains to my left and a rocky hill, that rose dark and sudden at my right. Below me lay a little thatched village, under a long line of gigantic beech-trees, through the boughs of which the lowly chimneys sent up their thin turf-smoke. To my left, stretched away for miles, ascending the mountain range I have mentioned, a wild park, through whose sward and ferns the rock broke, time-worn and lichen-stained. This park was studded with straggling wood, which thickened to something like a forest, behind and beyond the little village I was approaching, clothing the irregular ascent of the hillsides with beautiful, and in some places discolored, foliage.

As you descend, the road winds slightly, with the gray park-wall, built of loose stone, and mantled here and there with ivy, at its left, and crosses a shallow ford; and as I approached the village, through breaks in the woodlands, I caught glimpses of the long front of an old ruined house, placed among the trees, about half-way up the picturesque mountainside.

The solitude and melancholy of this ruin piqued my curiosity, and when I had reached the rude thatched public-house, with the sign of St. Columbkill, with robes, mitre, and crozier displayed over its lintel, having seen to my horse and made a good meal myself on a rasher and eggs, I began to think again of the wooded park and the ruinous house, and resolved on a ramble of half an hour among its sylvan solitudes.

The name of the place, I found, was Dunoran; and beside the gate a stile admitted to the grounds, through which, with a pensive enjoyment, I began to saunter towards the dilapidated mansion.

A long grass-grown road, with many turns and windings, led up to the old house, under the shadow of the wood.

The road, as it approached the house, skirted the edge of a precipitous glen, clothed with hazel, dwarf-oak, and thorn, and the silent house stood with its wide-open hall-door facing this dark ravine, the further edge of which was crowned with towering forest; and great trees stood about the house and its deserted court-yard and stables.

I walked in and looked about me, through passages overgrown with nettles and weeds; from room to room with ceilings rotted, and here and there a great beam dark and worn, with tendrils of ivy trailing over it. The tall walls with rotten plaster were stained and mouldy, and in some rooms the remains of decayed wainscoting crazily swung to and fro. The almost sashless windows were darkened also with ivy, and about the tall chimneys the jackdaws were wheeling, while from the huge trees that overhung the glen in sombre masses at the other side, the rooks kept up a ceaseless cawing.

As I walked through these melancholy passages—peeping only into some of the rooms, for the flooring was quite gone in the middle, and bowed down toward the center, and the house was very nearly un-roofed, a state of things which made the exploration a little critical—I began to wonder why so grand a house, in the midst of scenery so picturesque, had been permitted to go to decay; I dreamed of the hospitalities of which it had long ago been the rallying place, and I thought what a scene of Redgauntlet revelries it might disclose at midnight.

The great staircase was of oak, which had stood the weather wonderfully, and I sat down upon its steps, musing vaguely on the transitoriness of all things under the sun.

Except for the hoarse and distant clamor of the rooks, hardly audible where I sat, no sound broke the profound stillness of the spot. Such a sense of solitude I have seldom experienced before. The air was stirless, there was not even the rustle of a withered leaf along the passage. It was oppressive. The tall trees that stood close about the building darkened it, and added something of awe to the melancholy of the scene.

In this mood I heard, with an unpleasant surprise, close to me, a voice that was drawling, and, I fancied, sneering, repeat the words: "Food for worms, dead and rotten; God over all."

There was a small window in the wall, here very thick, which had been built up, and in the dark recess of this, deep in the shadow, I now saw a sharp-featured man, sitting with his feet dangling. His keen eyes were fixed on me, and he was smiling cynically, and before I had well recovered my surprise, he repeated the distich:

" 'If death was a thing that money could buy,
The rich they would live, and the poor they would die.'

"It was a grand house in its day, sir," he continued, "Dunoran House, and the Sarsfields. Sir Dominick Sarsfield was the last of the old stock. He lost his life not six foot away from where you are sitting."

As he thus spoke he let himself down, with a little jump, on to the ground.

He was a dark-faced, sharp-featured, little hunchback, and had a walking-stick in his hand, with the end of which he pointed to a rusty stain in the plaster of the wall.

"Do you mind that mark sir?" he asked.

"Yes," I said, standing up, and looking at it, with a curious anticipation of something worth hearing.

"That's about seven or eight feet from the ground, sir, and you'll not guess what it is."

"I dare say not," said I, "unless it is a stain from the weather."

" 'Tis nothing so lucky, sir," he answered, with the same cynical smile and a wag of his head, still pointing at the mark with his stick.

"That's a splash of brains and blood. It's there this hundred years; and it will never leave it while the wall stands."

"He was murdered, then?"

"Worse than that, sir," he answered.

"He killed himself, perhaps?"

"Worse than that, itself, this cross between us and harm! I'm oulder than I look, sir; you wouldn't guess my years."

He became silent, and looked at me, evidently inviting a guess.

"Well, I should guess you to be about five-and-fifty."

He laughed and took a pinch of snuff, and said:

"I'm that, your honor, and something to the back of it. I was seventy last Candlemas. You would not 'a' thought that, to look at me."

"Upon my word I should not; I can hardly believe it even now. Still, you don't remember Sir Dominick Sarsfield's death?" I said, glancing up at the ominous stain on the wall.

"No, sir, that was a long while before I was born. But my grandfather was butler here long ago, and many a time I heard tell how Sir Dominick came by his death. There was no masther in the great house ever sinst that happened. But there was two sarvants in care of it, and my aunt was one o' them; and she kep' me here wid her till I was nine year old, and she was lavin' the place to go to Dublin; and from that time it was let to go down. The wind sthript the roof, and the rain rotted the timber, and little by little, in sixty years' time, it kem to what you see. But I have a likin' for it still, for the sake of ould times; and I never come this way but I take a look in. I don't think it's many more times I'll be turnin' to see the ould place, for I'll be undher the sod myself before long."

"You'll outlive younger people," I said.

And, quitting that trite subject, I ran on:

"I don't wonder that you like this old place; it is a beautiful spot, such noble trees."

"I wish ye seen the glin when the nuts is ripe; they're the

sweetest nuts in all Ireland, I think," he rejoined, with a practical sense of the picturesque. "You'd fill your pockets while you'd be lookin' about you."

"These are very fine old woods," I remarked. "I have not seen any in Ireland I thought so beautiful."

"Eiah! your honor, the woods about here is nothing to what they wor. All the mountains along here was wood when my father was a gossoon, and Murroa Wood was the grandest of them all. All oak mostly, and all cut down as bare as the road. Not one left here that's fit to compare with them. Which way did your honor come hither— from Limerick?"

"No. Killaloe."

"Well, then, you passed the ground where Murroa Wood was in former times. You kem undher Lisnavourra, the steep knob of a hill about a mile above the village here. 'Twas near that Murroa Wood was, and 'twas there Sir Dominick Sarsfield first met the Devil, the Lord between us and harm, and a bad meeting it was for him and his."

I had become interested in the adventure which had occurred in the very scenery which had so greatly attracted me, and my new acquaintance, the little hunchback, was easily entreated to tell me the story, and spoke thus, so soon as we had each returned his seat . . .

It was a fine estate when Sir Dominick came into it; and grand doings there was entirely, feasting and fiddling, free quarters for all the pipers in the counthry round, and a welcome for every one that liked to come. There was wine, by the hogshead, for the quality; and potteen enough to set a town a-fire, and beer and cidher enough to float a navy, for the boys and girls, and the likes of me. It was kep' up the best part of a month, till the weather broke, and the rain spoilt the sod for the moneen jigs, and the fair of Allybally Killudeen comin' on they wor obliged to give over their divarsion, and attind to the pigs.

But Sir Dominick was only beginnin' when they wor lavin' off. There was no way of gettin' rid of his money and estates he did not try—what with drinkin', dicin', racin', cards, and all soarts, it was not many years before the estates wor in debt, and Sir Dominick a distressed man. He showed a bold front to the world as long as he could; and then he sould off his dogs, and most of his horses, and gev out he was going to thravel in France, and the like; and so off with him for awhile; and no one in these parts heard tale or tidings of him for two or three years. Till at last quite unexpected, one night there comes a rapping at the big kitchen window. It was past ten o'clock, and old Connor Hanlon, the butler, my grandfather, was sittin' by the fire alone, warming his shins over it. There was keen east wind blowing along the mountains that night, and whistling cowld enough through the tops of the trees, and soundin' lonesome through the long chimneys.

(And the story-teller glanced up at the nearest stack visible from his seat.)

So he wasn't quite sure of the knockin' at the window, and up he gets, and sees his master's face.

My grandfather was glad to see him safe, for it was a long time since there was any news of him; but he was sorry, too, for it was a changed place and only himself and old Juggy Broadrick in charge of the house, and a man in the stables, and it was a poor thing to see him comin' back to his own like that.

He shook Con by the hand, and says he:

"I came here to say a word to you. I left my horse with Dick in the stable; I may want him again before morning, or I may never want him."

And with that he turns into the big kitchen, and draws a stool, and sits down to take an air of the fire.

"Sit down, Connor, opposite me, and listen to what I tell you, and don't be afeard to say what you think."

He spoke all the time lookin' into the fire, with his hands stretched over it, and a tired man he looked.

"An' why should I be afeard, Masther Dominick?" says my grandfather. "Yourself was a good masther to me, and so was your father, rest his sould, before you, and I'll say the truth, and dar' the Devil, and more than that, for any Sarsfield of Dunoran, much less yourself, and a good right I'd have."

"It's all over with me, Con," says Sir Dominick.

"Heaven forbid!" says my grandfather.

" 'Tis past praying for," says Sir Dominick. "The last guinea's gone; the ould place will follow it. It must be sold, and I'm come here, I don't know why, like a ghost to have a last look round me, and go off in the dark again."

And with that he tould him to be sure, in case he should hear of his death, to give the oak box, in the closet off his room, to his cousin, Pat Sarsfield, in Dublin, and the sword and pistols his grandfather carried in Aughrim, and two or three thrifling things of the kind.

And says he, "Con, they say if the Divil gives you money overnight, you'll find nothing but a bagful of pebbles, and chips, and nutshells, in the morning. If I thought he played fair, I'm in the humour to make a bargain with him tonight."

"Lord forbid!" says my grandfather, standing up with a start, and crossing himself.

"They say the country's full of men, listin' sogers for the King o' France. If I light on one o' them, I'll not refuse his offer. How contrary things goes! How long is it since me and Captain Waller fought the jewel at New Castle?"

"Six years, Masther Dominick, and ye broke his thigh with the bullet the first shot."

"I did, Con," says he, "and I wish, instead, he had shot me through the heart. Have you any whisky?"

My grandfather took it out of the buffet, and the masther pours out some into a bowl, and drank it off.

"I'll go out and have a look at my horse," says he, standing up. There was a sort of a stare in his eyes, as he pulled his riding-cloak about him, as if there was something bad in his thoughts.

"Sure, I won't be a minute running out myself to the stable, and looking after the horse for you myself," says my grandfather.

"I'm not goin' to the stable," says Sir Dominick; "I may as well tell you, for I see you found it out already—I'm goin' across the deer-park; if I come back you'll see me in an hour's time. But, anyhow, you'd better not follow me, for if you do I'll shoot you, and that'd be a bad ending to our friendship."

And with that he walks down this passage here, and turns the key in the side door at that end of it, and out wid him on the sod into the moonlight and the cowld wind; and my grandfather seen him walkin' hard towards the park-wall, and then he comes in and closes the door with a heavy heart.

Sir Dominick stopped to think when he got to the middle of the deer-park, for he had not made up his mind, when he left the house and the whisky did not clear his head, only it gev him courage.

He did not feel the cowld wind now, nor fear death, nor think much of anything, but the shame and fall of the old family.

And he made up his mind, if no better thought came to him between that and there, so soon as he came to Murroa Wood, he'd hang himself from one of the oak branches with his cravat.

It was a bright moonlight night, there was just a bit of a cloud driving across the moon now and then, but, only for that, as light a'most as day.

Down he goes, right for the wood of Murroa. It seemed to him every step he took was as long as three, and it was no time till he was among the big oak-trees with their roots spreading from one to another, and their branches stretching overhead like the timbers of a naked roof, and the moon shining down through them, and casting their shadows thick and twist abroad on the ground as black as my shoe.

He was sobering a bit by this time, and he slacked his pace, and he thought 'twould be better to list in the French king's army, and thry what that might do for him, for he knew a man might take his own life any time, but it would puzzle him to take it back again when he liked.

Just as he made up his mind not to make away with himself, what should he hear but a step clinkin' along the dry ground under the trees, and soon he sees a grand gentleman right before him comin' up to meet him.

He was a handsome young man like himself, and he wore a cocked-hat with gold-lace round it, such as officers wear on their coats, and he had on a dress the same as French officers wore in them times.

He stopped opposite Sir Dominick, and he cum to a standstill also.

The two gentlemen took off their hats to one another, and says the stranger:

"I am recruiting, sir," says he, "for my sovereign, and you'll find my money won't turn into pebbles, chips, and nutshells, by tomor-row."

At the same time he pulls out a big purse full of gold.

The minute he sets eyes on that gentleman, Sir Dominick had his own opinion of him; and at those words he felt the very hair standing up on his head.

"Don't be afraid," says he, "the money won't burn you. If it proves honest gold, and if it prospers with you, I'm willing to make a bargain. This is the last day of February," says he; "I'll serve you seven years, and at the end of that time you shall serve me, and I'll come for you when the seven years is over, when the clock turns the minute between February and March; and the first of March ye'll come away with me, or never. You'll not find me a bad master, any more than a bad servant. I love my own; and I command all the pleasures and the glory of the world. The bargain dates from this day, and the lease is out at midnight on the last day I told you; and in the year"—he told him the year, it was easy reckoned, but I forget it—"and if you'd rather wait," he says, "for eight months and twenty-eight days, before you sign the writin', you may, if you meet me here. But I can't do a great deal for you in the meantime; and if you don't sign then, all you get from me, up to that time, will vanish away, and you'll be just as you are tonight, and ready to hang yourself on the first tree you meet."

Well, the end of it was, Sir Dominick chose to wait, and he came back to the house with a big bag full of money, as round as your hat a'most.

My grandfather was glad enough, you may be sure, to see the master safe and sound again so soon. Into the kitchen he bangs again, and swings the bag o' money on the table; and he stands up straight, and heaves up his shoulders like a man that has just got shut of a load; and he looks at the bag, and my grandfather looks at him, and from him to it, and back again. Sir Dominick looked as white as a sheet, and says he:

"I don't know, Con, what's in it; it's the heaviest load I ever carried."

He seemed shy of openin' the bag; and he made my grandfather heap up a roaring fire of turf and wood, and then, at last, he opens it, and, sure enough, 'twas stuffed full o' golden guineas, bright and new, as if they were only that minute out o' the Mint.

Sir Dominick made my grandfather sit at his elbow while he counted every guinea in the bag.

When he was done countin', and it wasn't far from daylight when that time came, Sir Dominick made my grandfather swear not to tell a word about it. And a close secret it was for many a day after.

When the eight months and twenty-eight days were pretty near spent and ended, Sir Dominick returned to the house here with a troubled mind, in doubt what was best to be done, and no one alive but my grandfather knew anything about the matter, and he not half what had happened.

As the day drew near, towards the end of October, Sir Dominick grew only more and more troubled in mind.

One time he made up his mind to have no more to say to such things, nor to speak again with the like of them he met with in the wood of Murroa. Then, again, his heart failed him when he thought of his debts, and he not knowing where to turn. Then, only a week before the day, everything began to go wrong with him. One man wrote from London to say that Sir Dominick paid three thousand pounds to the wrong man, and must pay it over again; another demanded a debt he never heard of before; and another, in Dublin, denied the payment of a thundherin' big bill, and Sir Dominick could nowhere find the receipt, and so on, wid fifty other things as bad.

Well, by the time the night of the 28th of October came round, he was a'most ready to lose his senses with all the demands that was risin' up again him on all sides, and nothing to meet them but the help of the one dhreadful friend he had to depind on at night in the oak-wood down there below.

So there was nothing for it but to go through with the business that was begun already, and about the same hour as he went last, he takes off the little crucifix he wore round his neck, for he was a Catholic, and his gospel, and his bit o' the thrue cross that he had in a locket, for since he took the money from the Evil One he was growin' frightful in himself, and got all he could to guard him from the power of the Devil. But tonight, for his life, he daren't take them with him. So he gives them into my grandfather's hands without a word, only he looked as white as a sheet o' paper; and he takes his hat and sword, and telling my grandfather to watch for him, away he goes, to try what would come of it.

It was a fine still night, and the moon—not so bright, though, now as the first time—was shinin' over heath and rock, and down on the lonesome oak-wood below him.

His heart beat thick as he drew near it. There was not a sound, not even the distant bark of a dog from the village behind him. There was not a lonesomer spot in the country round, and if it wasn't for his debts and losses that was drivin' him on half mad, in spite of his fears for his soul and his hopes of paradise, and all his good angel was whisperin' in his ear, he would 'a' turned back, and sent for his clargy, and made his confession and his penance, and changed his ways, and led a good life, for he was frightened enough to have done a great dale.

Softer and slower he stept as he got, once more, in undher the big branches of the oak-threes; and when he got in a bit, near where he met with the bad spirit before, he stopped and looked round him, and felt himself, every bit, turning cowld as a dead man, and you may be sure he did not feel much betther when he seen the same man steppin' from behind the big tree that was touchin' his elbow a'most.

"You found the money good," says he, "but it was not enough. No matter, you shall have enough and to spare. I'll see after your luck, and I'll give you a hint whenever it can serve you; and any time you want to see me you have only to come down here, and call my face to mind, and wish me present. You shan't owe a shilling by the end of the year, and you shall never miss the right card, the best throw, and the winning horse. Are you willing?"

The young gentleman's voice almost stuck in his throat, and his hair was rising on his head, but he did get out a word or two to signify that he consented; and with that the Evil One handed him a needle, and bid him give him three drops of blood from his arm; and he took them in the cup of an acorn, and gave him a pen, and bid him write some words that he repeated, and that Sir Dominick did not understand, on two thin slips of parchment. He took one himself and the other he sunk in Sir Dominick's arm at the place where he drew the blood, and he closed the flesh over it. And that's as true as you're sittin' there!

Well, Sir Dominick went home. He was a frightened man, and well he might be. But in a little time he began to grow aisier in his mind. Anyhow, he got out of debt very quick, and money came tumbling in to make him richer, and everything he took in hand prospered, and he never made a wager, or played a game, but he won; and for all that, there was not a poor man on the estate that was not happier than Sir Dominick.

So he took again to his old ways; for, when the money came back, all came back, and there were hounds and horses, and wine galore, and no end of company, and grand doin's, and divarsion, up here at the great house. And some said Sir Dominick was thinkin' of gettin' married; and more said he wasn't. But, anyhow, there was somethin' troublin' him more than common, and so one night, unknownst to all, away he goes to the lonesome oak-wood. It was something, maybe, my grandfather thought was troublin' him about a beautiful young lady he was jealous of, and mad in love with her. But that was only guess.

Well, when Sir Dominick got into the wood this time, he grew more in dread than ever; and he was on the point of turnin' and lavin' the place, when who should he see, close beside him, but my gentleman, seated on a big stone undher one of the trees. In place of looking the fine young gentleman in goold lace and grand clothes he appeared before, he was now in rags, he looked twice the size he had been, and his face smutted with soot, and he had a murtherin' big steel hammer, as heavy as a half-hundhred, with a handle a yard long, across his knees. It was so dark under the tree, he did not see him quite clear for some time.

He stood up, and he looked awful tall entirely. And what passed between them in that discourse my grandfather never heered. But Sir Dominick was as black as night afterwards, and hadn't a laugh for anything nor a word a'most for any one, and he only grew worse and worse, and darker and darker. And now this thing, whatever it was, used to come to him of its own accord, whether he wanted it or no; sometimes in one shape, and sometimes in another, in lonesome places, and sometimes at his side by night when he'd be ridin' home alone, until at last he lost heart altogether and sent for the priest.

The priest was with him a long time, and when he heered the whole story, he rode off all the way for the bishop, and the bishop came here to the great house next day, and he gev Sir Dominick a good advice. He toult him he must give over dicin', and swearin', and drinkin', and all bad company, and live a vartuous steady life until the seven years' bargain was out, and if the Divil didn't come for him the minute afther the stroke of twelve the first morning of the month of March, he was safe out of the bargain. There was not more than eight or ten months to run now before the seven years wor out, and he lived all the time according to the bishop's advice, as strict as if he was "in retreat."

Well, you may guess he felt quare enough when the mornin' of the 28th of February came.

The priest came up by appointment, and Sir Dominick and his raverence wor together in the room you see there, and kep' up their prayers together till the clock struck twelve, and a good hour after, and not a sign of a disturbance, nor nothing came near them, and the priest slep' that night in the house in the room next Sir Dominick's, and all went over as comfortable as could be, and they shook hands and kissed like two comrades after winning a battle.

So, now, Sir Dominick thought he might as well have a pleasant evening, after all his fastin' and praying; and he sent round to half a dozen of the neighbouring gentlemen to come and dine with him, and his raverence stayed and dined also, and a roarin' bowl o' punch they had, and no end o' wine, and the swearin' and dice, and cards and guineas changing hands, and songs and stories, that wouldn't do any one good to hear, and the priest slipped away, when he seen the turn things was takin', and it was not far from the stroke of twelve when Sir Dominick, sitting at the head of his table, swears, "this is the best first of March I ever sat down with my friends."

"It ain't the first o' March," says Mr. Hiffernan of Ballyvoreen. He was a scholard, and always kep' an almanack.

"What is it, then?" says Sir Dominick, startin' up, and dhroppin' the ladle into the bowl, and starin' at him as if he had two heads.

" 'Tis the twenty-ninth of February, leap year," says he. And just as they were talkin', the clock strikes twelve; and my grandfather, who was half asleep in a chair by the fire in the hall, openin' his eyes, sees a short square fellow with a cloak on, and long black hair bushin' out from under his hat, standin' just there where you see the bit o' light shinin' again' the wall.

(My hunchback friend pointed with his stick to a little patch of red sunset light that relieved the deepening shadow of the passage.)

"Tell your master," says he, in an awful voice, like the growl of a baist, "that I'm here by appointment, and expect him downstairs this minute."

Up goes my grandfather, by these very steps you are sittin' on.

"Tell him I can't come down yet," says Sir Dominick, and he turns to the company in the room, and says he with a cold sweat shinin' on his face, "for God's sake, gentlemen, will any of you jump from the window and bring the priest here?" One looked at another and no one knew what to make of it, and in the meantime, up comes my grandfather again, and says he, tremblin', "He says, sir, unless you go down to him, he'll come up to you."

"I don't understand this, gentlemen, I'll see what it means," says Sir Dominick, trying to put a face on it, and walkin' out o' the room like a man through the press-room, with the hangman waitin' for him outside. Down the stairs he comes, and two or three of the gentlemen peeping over the banisters, to see. My grandfather was walking six or eight steps behind him, and he seen the stranger take a stride out to meet Sir Dominick, and catch him up in his arms, and whirl his head against the wall, and wi' that the hall-doore flies open, and out goes the candles, and the turf and wood-ashes flyin' with the wind out o' the hall-fire, ran in a drift o' sparks along the floore by his feet.

Down runs the gintlemen. Bang goes the hall-doore. Some comes runnin' up, and more runnin' down, with lights. It was all over with Sir Dominick. They lifted up the corpse, and put its shoulders again' the wall; but there was not a gasp left in him. He was cowld and stiffenin' already.

Pat Donovan was comin' up to the great house late that night and after he passed the little brook, that the carriage track up to the house crosses, and about fifty steps to this side of it, his dog, that was by his side, makes a sudden wheel, and springs over the wall, and sets up a yowlin' inside you'd hear a mile away; and that minute two men passed him by in silence, goin' down from the house, one of them short and square, and the other like Sir Dominick in shape, but there was little light under the trees where he was, and they looked only like shadows; and as they passed him by he could not hear the sound of their feet and he drew back to the wall frightened; and when he got up to the great house, he found all in confusion, and the master's body, with the head smashed to pieces, lying just on *that spot.*

The narrator stood up and indicated with the point of his stick the exact site of the body, and, as I looked, the shadow deepened, the red stain of sunlight vanished from the wall, and the sun had gone down behind the distant hill of New Castle, leaving the haunted scene in the deep gray of darkening twilight.

So I and the story-teller parted, not without good wishes on both sides, and a little "tip" which seemed not unwelcome, from me.

It was dusk and the moon up by the time I reached the village, remounted my nag, and looked my last on the scene of the terrible legend of Dunoran.

The Legend of Mont St.-Michel

GUY DE MAUPASSANT

I had first seen it from Cancale, this fairy castle in the sea. I got an indistinct impression of it as of a gray shadow outlined against the misty sky. I saw it again from Avranches at sunset. The immense stretch of sand was red; the horizon was red; the whole boundless bay was red. The rocky castle rising out there in the distance like a weird, seignorial residence, like a dream palace, strange and beautiful—this alone remained black in the crimson light of the dying day.

The following morning at dawn I went toward it across the sands, my eyes fastened on this gigantic jewel, as big as a mountain, cut like a cameo, and as dainty as lace. The nearer I approached, the greater my admiration grew, for nothing in the world could be more wonderful or more perfect.

As surprised as if I had discovered the habitation of a god, I wandered through those halls supported by frail or massive columns, raising my eyes in wonder to those spires which looked like rockets starting for the sky, and to that marvelous assemblage of towers, of gargoyles, of slender and charming ornaments, a regular fireworks of stone, granite lace, a masterpiece of colossal and delicate architecture.

As I was looking up in ecstasy a Lower Normandy peasant came up to me and told me the story of the great quarrel between St. Michael and the Devil.

A skeptical genius has said: "God made man in his image and man has returned the compliment."

This saying is an eternal truth, and it would be very curious to write the history of the local divinity of every continent, as well as the history of the patron saints in each one of our provinces. The Negro has his ferocious man-eating idols; the polygamous Mohammedan fills his paradise with women; the Greeks, like a practical people, deified all the passions.

Every village in France is under the influence of some protecting saint, modeled according to the characteristics of the inhabitants.

St. Michael watches over Lower Normandy, St. Michael, the radiant and victorious angel, the sword carrier, the hero of Heaven, the victorious, the conqueror of Satan.

But this is how the Lower Normandy peasant, cunning, deceitful, and tricky, understands and tells of the struggle between the great saint and the Devil.

To escape from the malice of his neighbor, the Devil, St. Michael built himself, in the open ocean, this habitation worthy of an archangel, and only such a saint could build a residence of such magnificence.

But, as he still feared the approaches of the wicked one, he surrounded his domains by quicksands, more treacherous even than the sea.

The Devil lived in a humble cottage on the hill, but he owned all the salt marshes, the rich lands where grow the finest crops, the wooded valleys, and all the fertile hills of the country, while the saint ruled only over the sands. Therefore, Satan was rich, whereas St. Michael was as poor as a church mouse.

After a few years of fasting the saint grew tired of this state of affairs and began to think of some compromise with the Devil, but the matter was by no means easy, as Satan kept a good hold on his crops.

He thought the thing over for about six months; then one morning he walked across to the shore. The demon was eating his soup in front of his door when he saw the saint. He immediately rushed toward him, kissed the hem of his sleeve, invited him in, and offered him refreshments.

St. Michael drank a bowl of milk and then began: "I have come here to propose to you a good bargain."

The Devil, candid and trustful, answered: "That will suit me."

"Here it is. Give me all your lands."

Satan, growing alarmed, wished to speak. "But—"

The saint continued: "Listen first. Give me all your lands. I will take care of all the work, the plowing, the sowing, the fertilizing, everything, and we will share the crops equally. How does that suit you?"

The Devil, who was naturally lazy, accepted. He only demanded in addition a few of those delicious gray mullet which are caught around the solitary mount. St. Michael promised the fish.

They grasped hands and spat on the ground to show that it was a bargain, and the saint continued: "See here, so that you will have nothing to complain of, choose that part of the crops which you prefer: the part that grows aboveground or the part that stays in the ground."

Satan cried out: "I will take all that will be aboveground."

"It's a bargain!" said the saint. And he went away.

Six months later, all over the immense domain of the Devil, one could see nothing but carrots, turnips, onions, salsify, all the plants whose juicy roots are good and savory and whose useless leaves are good for nothing but for feeding animals.

Satan wished to break the contract, calling St. Michael a swindler. But the saint, who had developed quite a taste for agriculture, went back to see the Devil and said: "Really, I hadn't thought of that at all; it was just an accident, no fault of mine. And to make things fair with you, this year I'll let you take everything that is under the ground."

"Very well," answered Satan.

The following spring all the evil spirit's lands were covered with golden wheat, oats as big as beans, flax, magnificent colza, red clover, peas, cabbage, artichokes, everything that develops into grains or fruit in the sunlight.

Once more Satan received nothing, and this time he completely lost his temper. He took back his fields and remained deaf to all the fresh propositions of his neighbor.

A whole year rolled by. From the top of his lonely manor St. Michael looked at the distant and fertile lands and watched the Devil direct the work, take in his crops, and thresh the wheat. And he grew angry, exasperated at his powerlessness. As he was no longer able to deceive Satan, he decided to wreak vengeance on him, and he went out to invite him to dinner for the following Monday.

"You have been very unfortunate in your dealings with me," he said; "I know it, but I don't want any ill feeling between us, and I expect you to dine with me. I'll give you some good things to eat."

Satan, who was as greedy as he was lazy, accepted eagerly. On the day appointed he donned his finest clothes and set out for the castle.

St. Michael sat him down to a magnificent meal. First there was a *vol-au-vent,* full of cocks' crests and kidneys, with meat balls, then two big gray mullet with cream sauce, a turkey stuffed with chest-nuts soaked in wine, some salt-marsh lamb as tender as cake, vegeta-bles which melted in the mouth, and a nice hot pancake which was brought on smoking and spreading a delicious odor of butter.

They drank new, sweet, sparkling cider and heady red wine, and after each course they whetted their appetites with some old apple brandy.

The Devil drank and ate to his heart's content; in fact, he took so much that he was very uncomfortable and began to retch.

Then St. Michael arose in anger and cried in a voice like thun-der: "What! Before me, rascal! You dare—before me—"

Satan, terrified, ran away, and the saint, seizing a stick, pursued him. They ran through the halls, turning round the pillars, running up the staircases, galloping along the cornices, jumping from gar-goyle to gargoyle. The poor Devil, who was woefully ill, was running about madly and trying hard to escape. At last he found himself at the top of the last terrace, right at the top, from which could be seen the immense bay, with its distant towns, sands, and pastures. He could no longer escape, and the saint came up behind him and gave him a furious kick, which shot him through space like a cannon ball.

He shot through the air like a javelin and fell heavily before the town of Mortain. His horns and claws stuck deep into the rock, which keeps through eternity the traces of this fall of Satan.

He stood up again, limping, crippled until the end of time, and as he looked at this fatal castle in the distance, standing out against the setting sun, he understood well that he would always be van-quished in this unequal struggle, and he went away limping, heading for distant countries, leaving to his enemy his fields, his hills, his valleys, and his marshes.

And this is how St. Michael, the patron saint of Normandy, vanquished the Devil.

Another people would have dreamed of this battle in an entirely different manner.

Madam Lucifer

RICHARD GARNETT

L ucifer sat playing chess with Man for his soul.

The game was evidently going ill for Man. He had but pawns left, few and struggling. Lucifer had rooks, knights, and, of course, bishops.

It was but natural under such circumstances that Man should be in no great hurry to move. Lucifer grew impatient.

"It is a pity," said he at last, "that we did not fix some period within which the player must move, or resign."

"Oh, Lucifer," returned the young man, in heartrending accents, "it is not the impending loss of my soul that thus unmans me, but the loss of my betrothed. When I think of the grief of the Lady Adeliza, the paragon of terrestrial loveliness!" Tears choked his utterance; Lucifer was touched.

"Is the Lady Adeliza's loveliness in sooth so transcendent?" he inquired.

"She is a rose, a lily, a diamond, a morning star!"

"If that is the case," rejoined Lucifer, "thou mayest reassure thyself. The Lady Adeliza shall not want for consolation. I will assume thy shape and woo her in thy stead."

The young man hardly seemed to receive all the comfort from this promise which Lucifer no doubt designed. He made a desperate move. In an instant the Devil checkmated him, and he disappeared.

"Upon my word, if I had known what a business this was going to be, I don't think I should have gone in for it," soliloquized the Devil as, wearing his captive's semblance and installed in his apartments, he surveyed the effects to which he now had to administer. They included coats, shirts, collars, neckties, foils, cigars, and the like *ad libitum;* and very little else except three challenges, ten writs, and seventy-four unpaid bills, elegantly disposed around the looking-glass. To the poor youth's praise be it said, there were no *billets-doux,* except from the Lady Adeliza herself.

Noting the address of these carefully, the Devil sallied forth, and nothing but his ignorance of the topography of the hotel, which made him take the back stairs, saved him from the clutches of two bailiffs lurking on the principal staircase. Leaping into a cab, he thus escaped a perfumer and a bootmaker, and shortly found himself at the Lady Adeliza's feet.

The truth had not been half told him. Such beauty, such wit, such correctness of principle! Lucifer went forth from her presence a love-sick fiend. Not Merlin's mother had produced half the impression upon him; and Adeliza on her part had never found her lover one-hundredth part so interesting as he seemed that morning.

Lucifer proceeded at once to the City, where, assuming his proper shape for the occasion, he negotiated a loan without the smallest difficulty. All debts were promptly discharged, and Adeliza was astonished at the splendor and variety of the presents she was constantly receiving.

Lucifer had all but brought her to name the day, when he was informed that a gentleman of clerical appearance desired to wait upon him.

"Wants money for a new church or mission, I suppose," said he. "Show him up."

But when the visitor was ushered in, Lucifer found with discomposure that he was no earthly clergyman, but a celestial saint; a saint, too, with whom Lucifer had never been able to get on. He had served in the army while on earth, and his address was curt, precise, and peremptory.

"I have called," he said, "to notify to you my appointment as Inspector of Devils."

"What!" exclaimed Lucifer, in consternation. "To the post of my old friend Michael!"

"Too old," said the Saint laconically. "Millions of years older than the world. About your age, I think."

Lucifer winced, remembering the particular business he was then about. The Saint continued:

"I am a new broom, and am expected to sweep clean. I warn you that I mean to be strict, and there is one little matter which I must set right immediately. You are going to marry that poor young fellow's betrothed, are you? Now you know you can not take his wife, unless you give him yours."

"Oh, my dear friend," exclaimed Lucifer, "what an inexpressibly blissful prospect you do open unto me!"

"I don't know that," said the Saint. "I must remind you that the dominion of the infernal regions is unalterably attached to the person of the present Queen thereof. If you part with her you immediately lose all your authority and possessions. I don't care a brass button which you do, but you must understand that you cannot eat your cake and have it too. Good morning!"

Who shall describe the conflict in Lucifer's bosom? If any stronger passion existed therein at that moment than attachment to Adeliza, it was aversion to his consort, and the two combined were wellnigh irresistible. But to disenthrone himself, to descend to the condition of a poor devil!

Feeling himself incapable of coming to a decision, he sent for Belial, unfolded the matter, and requested his advice.

"What a shame that our new inspector will not let you marry Adeliza!" lamented his counsellor. "If you did, my private opinion is that forty-eight hours afterwards you would care just as much for her as you do now for Madam Lucifer, neither more nor less. Are your intentions really honourable?"

"Yes," replied Lucifer, "it is to be a Lucifer match."

"The more fool you," rejoined Belial. "If you tempted her to commit a sin, she would be yours without any conditions at all."

"Oh, Belial," said Lucifer, "I cannot bring myself to be a tempter of so much innocence and loveliness."

And he meant what he said.

"Well then, let me try," proposed Belial.

"You?" replied Lucifer contemptuously; "do you imagine that Adeliza would look at you?

"Why not?" asked Belial, surveying himself complacently in the glass.

He was humpbacked, squinting, and lame, and his horns stood up under his wig.

The discussion ended in a wager: after which there was no retreat for Lucifer.

The infernal Iachimo was introduced to Adeliza as a distinguished foreigner, and was soon prosecuting his suit with all the success which Lucifer had predicted. One thing protected while it baffled him—the entire inability of Adeliza to understand what he meant. At length he was constrained to make the matter clear by producing an enormous treasure, which he offered Adeliza in exchange for the abandonment of her lover.

The tempest of indignation which ensued would have swept away any ordinary demon, but Belial listened unmoved. When Adeliza had exhausted herself he smilingly rallied her upon her affection for an unworthy lover, of whose infidelity he undertook to give her proof. Frantic with jealousy, Adeliza consented, and in a trice found herself in the infernal regions.

Adeliza's arrival in Pandemonium, as Belial had planned, occurred immediately after the receipt of a message from Lucifer, in whose bosom love had finally gained the victory, and who had telegraphed his abdication and resignation of Madam Lucifer to Adeliza's betrothed. The poor young man had just been hauled up from the lower depths, and was beset by legions of demons obsequiously pressing all manner of treasures upon his acceptance. He stared, helpless and bewildered, unable to realize his position in the smallest degree. In the background grave and serious demons, the princes of the infernal realm, discussed the new departure, and consulted especially how to break it to Madam Lucifer—a commission of which no one seemed ambitious.

"Stay where you are," whispered Belial to Adeliza; "stir not: you shall put his constancy to the proof within five minutes."

Not all the hustling, mowing, and gibbering of the fiends would under ordinary circumstances have kept Adeliza from her lover's side: but what is all hell to jealousy?

In even less time than he had promised, Belial returned, accompanied by Madam Lucifer. This lady's black robe, dripping with blood, contrasted agreeably with her complexion of sulphurous yellow; the absence of hair was compensated by the exceptional length of her nails; she was a thousand million years old, and, but for her remarkable muscular vigour, looked every one of them. The rage into which Belial's communication had thrown her was something indescribable; but, as her eye fell on the handsome youth, a different order of thoughts seemed to take possession of her mind.

"Let the monster go!" she exclaimed; "who cares? Come, my love, ascend the throne with me, and share the empire and the treasures of thy fond Luciferetta."

"If you don't, back you go," interjected Belial.

What might have been the young man's decision if Madam Lucifer had borne more resemblance to Madam Vulcan, it would be wholly impertinent to inquire, for the question never arose.

"Take me away!" he screamed, "take me away, anywhere! anywhere out of her reach! Oh, Adeliza!"

With a bound Adeliza stood by his side. She was darting a triumphant glance at the discomfited Queen of Hell, when suddenly her expression changed, and she screamed loudly. Two adorers stood before her, alike in every lineament and every detail of costume, utterly indistinguishable, even by the eye of Love.

Lucifer, in fact, hastening to throw himself at Adeliza's feet and pray her to defer his bliss no longer, had been thunderstruck by the tidings of her elopement with Belial. Fearing to lose his wife and his dominions along with his sweetheart, he had sped to the nether regions with such expedition that he had had no time to change his costume. Hence the equivocation which confounded Adeliza, but at the same time preserved her from being torn to pieces by the no less mystified Madam Lucifer.

Perceiving the state of the case, Lucifer with true gentlemanly feeling resumed his proper semblance, and Madam Lucifer's talons were immediately inserted into his whiskers.

"My dear! my love!" he gasped, as audibly as she would let him, "is this the way it welcomes its own Lucy-pucy?"

"Who is that person?" demanded Madam Lucifer.

"I don't know her," screamed the wretched Lucifer. "I never saw her before. Take her away; shut her up in the deepest dungeon!"

"Not if I know it," sharply replied Madam Lucifer. "You can't bear to part with her, can't you? You would intrigue with her under my nose, would you? Take that! and that! Turn them both out, I say! turn them both out!"

"Certainly, my dearest love, most certainly," responded Lucifer.

"Oh, Sire," cried Moloch and Beelzebub together, "for Heaven's sake let your Majesty consider what he is doing. The Inspector—"

"Bother the Inspector!" screeched Lucifer. "D'ye think I'm not a thousand times more afraid of your mistress than of all the saints in the calendar? There," addressing Adeliza and her betrothed, "be off! You'll find all debts paid, and a nice balance at the bank. Out! Run!"

They did not wait to be told twice. Earth yawned. The gates of Tartarus stood wide. They found themselves on the side of a steep mountain, down which they scoured madly, hand linked in hand. But fast as they ran, it was long ere they ceased to hear the tongue of Madam Lucifer.

Lucifer

ANATOLE FRANCE

And so successful was Spinello with his horrible and portentous Production that it was commonly reported—so great is always the force of fancy—that the said figure (of Lucifer trodden underfoot by St. Michael in the Altar-Piece of the Church of St. Agnolo at Arezzo) painted by him had appeared to the artist in a dream, and asked him in what place he had beheld him under so brutish a form.

—"Life of Spinello," *Lives of the Most Excellent Painters,* by Giorgio Vasari

Andrea Tafi, painter and worker-in-mosaic of Florence, had a wholesome terror of the Devils of Hell, particularly in the watches of the night, when it is given to the powers of Darkness to prevail. And the worthy man's fears were not unreasonable, for in those days the Demons had good cause to hate the Painters, who robbed them of more souls with a single picture than a good little Preaching Friar could do in thirty sermons. No doubt the Monk, to instil a soul-saving horror in the hearts of the faithful, would describe to the utmost of his powers "that day of wrath, that day of mourning," which is to reduce the universe to ashes, *teste David et Sibylla,* borrowing his deepest voice and bellowing through his hands to imitate the Archangel's last trump. But there! it was "all sound and fury, signifying nothing," whereas a painting displayed on a Chapel wall or in the Cloister, showing Jesus Christ sitting on the Great White Throne to judge the living and the dead, spoke unceasingly to the eyes of sinners, and through the eyes chastened such as had sinned by the eyes or otherwise.

It was in the days when cunning masters were depicting at Santa-Croce in Florence and the Campo Santo of Pisa the mysteries of Divine Justice. These works were drawn according to the account in verse which Dante Alighieri, a man very learned in Theology and in Canon Law, wrote in days gone by of his journey to Hell, and Purgatory and Paradise, whither by the singular great merits of his lady, he was able to make his way alive. So everything in these paintings was instructive and true, and we may say surely less profit is to be had of reading the most full and ample Chronicle than from contemplating such representative works of art. Moreover, the Florentine masters took heed to paint, under the shade of orange groves, on the flower-starred turf, fair ladies and gallant knights, with Death lying in wait for them with his scythe, while they were discoursing of love to the sound of lutes and

viols. Nothing was better fitted to convert carnal-minded sinners who quaff forgetfulness of God on the lips of women. To
rebuke the covetous, the painter would show to the life the Devils
pouring molten gold down the throat of Bishop or Abbess, who
had commissioned some work from him and then scamped
his pay.

This is why the Demons in those days were bitter enemies of
the painters, and above all of the Florentine painters, who sur-
passed all the rest in subtlety of wit. Chiefly they reproached them
with representing them under a hideous guise, with the heads of
bird and fish, serpents' bodies and bats' wings. This sore resent-
ment which they felt will come out plainly in the history of
Spinello of Arezzo.

Spinello Spinelli was sprung of a noble family of Florentine
exiles, and his graciousness of mind matched his gentle birth; for he
was the most skilful painter of his time. He wrought many and great
works at Florence; and the Pisans begged him to complete Giotto's
wall-paintings in their Campo Santo, where the dead rest beneath
roses in holy earth shipped from Jerusalem. At last, after working
long years in divers cities and getting much gold, he longed to see
once more the good city of Arezzo, his mother. The men of Arezzo
had not forgotten how Spinello, in his younger days, being enrolled
in the Confraternity of Santa Maria della Misericordia, had visited
the sick and buried the dead in the plague of 1383. They were
grateful to him besides for having by his works spread the fame of
their city over all Tuscany. For all these reasons they welcomed him
with high honours on his return.

Still full of vigour in his old age, he undertook important tasks
in his native town. His wife would tell him:

"You are rich, Spinello. Do you rest, and leave younger men to
paint instead of you. It is meet a man should end his days in a gentle,
religious quiet. It is tempting God to be for ever raising new and

worldly monuments, mere heathen towers of Babel. Quit your colors and your varnishes, Spinello, or they will destroy your peace of mind."

So the good dame would preach, but he refused to listen, for his one thought was to increase his fortune and renown. Far from resting on his laurels, he arranged a price with the Wardens of Sant' Agnolo for a history of St. Michael, that was to cover all the Choir of the Church and contain an infinity of figures. Into this enterprise he threw himself with extraordinary ardor. Re-reading the parts of Scripture that were to be his inspiration, he set himself to study deeply every line and every word of these passages. Not content with drawing all day long in his workshop, he persisted in working both at bed and board; while at dusk, walking below the hill on whose brow Arezzo proudly lifts her walls and towers, he was still lost in thought. And we may say the story of the Archangel was already limned in his brain when he started to sketch out the incidents in red chalk on the plaster of the wall. He was soon done tracing these outlines; then he fell to painting above the high altar the scene that was to outshine all the others in brilliancy. For it was his intent therein to glorify the leader of the hosts of Heaven for the victory he won before the beginning of time. Accordingly Spinello represented St. Michael fighting in the air against the serpent with seven heads and ten horns, and he figured with delight, in the bottom part of the picture, the Prince of the Devils, Lucifer, under the semblance of an appalling monster. The figures seemed to grow to life of themselves under his hand. His success was beyond his fondest hopes; so hideous was the countenance of Lucifer, none could escape the nightmare of its foulness. The face haunted the painter in the streets and even went home with him to his lodging.

Presently when night was come, Spinello lay down in his bed beside his wife and fell asleep. In his slumbers he saw an Angel as comely as St. Michael, but black; and the Angel said to him:

"Spinello, I am Lucifer. Tell me, where had you seen me, that you should paint me as you have, under so ignominious a likeness?"

The old painter answered, trembling, that he had never seen him with his eyes, never having gone down alive into Hell, like Messer Dante Alighieri; but that, in depicting him as he had done, he was for expressing in visible lines and colors the hideousness of sin.

Lucifer shrugged his shoulders, and the hill of San Gemignano seemed of a sudden to heave and stagger.

"Spinello," he went on, "will you do me the pleasure to reason awhile with me? I am no mean Logician; He you pray to knows that."

Receiving no reply, Lucifer proceeded in these terms:

"Spinello, you have read the books that tell of me. You know of my enterprise, and how I forsook Heaven to become the Prince of this World. A tremendous adventure—and a unique one, had not the Giants in like fashion assailed the god Jupiter, as yourself have seen, Spinello, recorded on an ancient tomb where this Titanic war is carved in marble."

"It is true," said Spinello, "I have seen the tomb, shaped like a great tun, in the Church of Santa Reparata at Florence. 'Tis a fine work of the Romans."

"Still," returned Lucifer, smiling, "the Giants are not pictured on it in the shape of frogs or chameleons or the like hideous and horrid creatures."

"True," replied the painter, "but then they had not attacked the true God, but only a false idol of the Pagans. 'Tis a mighty differ-ence. The fact is clear, Lucifer, you raised the standard of revolt against the true and veritable King of Earth and Heaven."

"I will not deny it," said Lucifer. "And how many sorts of sins do you charge me with for that?"

"Seven, it is like enough," the painter answered, "and deadly sins one and all."

"Seven!" exclaimed the Angel of Darkness; "well! the number is canonical. Everything goes by sevens in my history, which is close bound up with God's. Spinello, you deem me proud, angry and envious. I enter no protest, provided you allow that glory was my only aim. Do you deem me covetous? Granted again; Covetousness is a virtue for Princes. For Gluttony and Lust, if you hold me guilty, I will not complain. Remains *Indolence.*"

As he pronounced the word, Lucifer crossed his arms across his breast, and shaking his gloomy head, tossed his flaming locks:

"Tell me, Spinello, do you really think I am indolent? Do you take me for a coward? Do you hold that in my revolt I showed a lack of courage? Nay! you cannot. Then it was but just to paint me in the guise of a hero, with a proud countenance. You should wrong no one, not even the Devil. Cannot you see that you insult Him you make prayer to, when you give Him for adversary a vile, monstrous toad? Spinello, you are very ignorant for a man of your age. I have a great mind to pull your ears, as they do to an ill-conditioned school-boy."

At this threat, and seeing the arm of Lucifer already stretched out towards him, Spinello clapped his hand to his head and began to howl with terror.

His good wife, waking up with a start, asked him what ailed him. He told her with chattering teeth, how he had just seen Lucifer and had been in terror for his ears.

"I told you so," retorted the worthy dame; "I knew all those figures you will go on painting on the walls would end by driving you mad."

"I am not mad," protested the painter. "I saw him with my own eyes; and he is beautiful to look on, albeit proud and sad. First thing tomorrow I will blot out the horrid figure I have drawn and set in its place the shape I beheld in my dream. For we must not wrong even the Devil himself."

"You had best go to sleep again," scolded his wife. "You are talking stark nonsense, and unchristian to boot."

Spinello tried to rise, but his strength failed him and he fell back unconscious on his pillow. He lingered on a few days in a high fever, and then died.

The Devil

MAXIM GORKY

L ife is a burden in the fall—the sad season of decay and death!
The gray days, the weeping, sunless sky, the dark nights, the
growling, whining wind, the heavy, black autumn shadows—all
that drives clouds of gloomy thoughts over the human soul, and fills
it with a mysterious fear of life where nothing is permanent, all is in
an eternal flux; things are born, decay, die . . . why? . . . for
what purpose? . . .

Sometimes the strength fails us to battle against the tenebrous
thoughts that enfold the soul late in the autumn, therefore those
who want to assuage their bitterness ought to meet them half way.

This is the only way by which they will escape from the chaos of despair and doubt, and will enter on the terra firma of self-confidence.

But it is a laborious path, it leads through thorny brambles that lacerate the living heart, and on that path the Devil always lies in ambush. It is that best of all the Devils, with whom the great Goethe has made us acquainted. . . .

My story is about that Devil.

The Devil suffered from ennui.

He is too wise to ridicule everything.

He knows that there are phenomena of life which the Devil himself is not able to rail at; for example, he has never applied the sharp scalpel of his irony to the majestic fact of his existence. To tell the truth, our favorite Devil is more bold than clever, and if we were to look more closely at him, we might discover that, like ourselves, he wastes most of his time on trifles. But we had better leave that alone; we are not children that break their best toys in order to discover what is in them.

The Devil once wandered over the cemetery in the darkness of an autumn night: he felt lonely and whistled softly as he looked around himself in search of a distraction. He whistled an old song—my father's favorite song—

> "When, in autumnal days,
> A leaf from its branch is torn
> And on high by the wind is borne."

And the wind sang with him, soughing over the graves and among the black crosses, and heavy autumnal clouds slowly crawled over the heaven and with their cold tears watered the narrow dwellings of the dead. The mournful trees in the cemetery timidly creaked under the strokes of the wind and stretched their bare branches to the speechless clouds. The branches were now and then caught by the crosses, and then a dull, shuffling, awful sound passed over the churchyard. . . .

The Devil was whistling, and he thought:

"I wonder how the dead feel in such weather! No doubt, the dampness goes down to them, and although they are secure against rheumatism ever since the day of their death, yet, I suppose, they do not feel comfortable. How, if I called one of them up and had a talk with him? It would be a little distraction for me, and, very likely, for him also. I will call him! Somewhere around here they have buried an old friend of mine, an author. . . . I used to visit him when he was alive . . . why not renew our acquaintance? People of his kind are dreadfully exacting. I shall find out whether the grave satisfies him completely. But where is his grave?"

And the Devil who, as is well known, knows everything, wandered for a long time about the cemetery, before he found the author's grave. . . .

"Oh there!" he called out as he knocked with his claws at the heavy stone under which his acquaintance was put away.

"Get up!"

"What for?" came the dull answer from below.

"I need you."

"I won't get up."

"Why?"

"Who are you, anyway?"

"You know me."

"The censor?"

"Ha, ha, ha! No!"

"Maybe a secret policeman?"

"No, no!"

"Not a critic, either?"

"I am the Devil."

"Well, I'll be out in a minute."

The stone lifted itself from the grave, the earth burst open, and a skeleton came out of it. It was a very common skeleton, just the kind that students study anatomy by: only it was dirty, had no wire connections, and in the empty sockets there shone a blue phosphoric light instead of eyes. It crawled out of the ground, shook its bones in order to throw off the earth that stuck to them, making a dry, rattling noise with them, and raising up its skull, looked with its cold, blue eyes at the murky, cloud-covered sky. "I hope you are well!" said the Devil.

"How can I be?" curtly answered the author. He spoke in a strange, low voice, as if two bones were grating against each other.

"Oh, excuse my greeting!" the Devil said pleasantly.

"Never mind! . . . But why have you raised me?"

"I just wanted to take a walk with you, though the weather is very bad.

"I suppose you are not afraid of catching a cold?" asked the Devil.

"Not at all, I got used to catching colds during my lifetime."

"Yes, I remember, you died pretty cold."

"I should say I did! They had poured enough cold water over me all my life."

They walked beside each other over the narrow path, between graves and crosses. Two blue beams fell from the author's eyes upon the ground and lit the way for the Devil. A drizzling rain sprinkled over them, and the wind freely passed between the author's bare ribs and through his breast where there was no longer a heart.

"We are going to town?" he asked the Devil.

"What interests you there?"

"Life, my dear sir," the author said impassionately.

"What! It still has a meaning for you?"

"Indeed it has!"

"But why?"

"How am I to say it? A man measures all by the quantity of his effort, and if he carries a common stone down from the summit of Ararat, that stone becomes a gem to him."

"Poor fellow!" smiled the Devil.

"But also happy man!" the author retorted coldly.

The Devil shrugged his shoulders.

They left the churchyard, and before them lay a street—two rows of houses, and between them was darkness in which the miserable lamps clearly proved the want of light upon earth.

"Tell me," the Devil spoke after a pause, "how do you like your grave?"

"Now I am used to it, and it is all right: it is very quiet there."

"Is it not damp down there in the fall?" asked the Devil.

"A little. But you get used to that. The greatest annoyance comes from those various idiots who ramble over the cemetery and accidentally stumble on my grave. I don't know how long I have been lying in my grave, for I and everything around me is unchangeable, and the concept of time does not exist for me."

"You have been in the ground four years—it will soon be five," said the Devil.

"Indeed? Well then, there have been three people at my grave during that time. Those accursed people make me nervous. One, you see, straight away denied the fact of my existence: he read my name on the tombstone and said confidently: 'There never was such a man! I have never read him, though I remember such a name: when I was a boy, there lived a man of that name who had a broker's shop in our street.' How do you like that? And my articles appeared for sixteen years in the most popular periodicals, and three times during my lifetime my books came out in separate editions."

"There were two more editions since your death," the Devil informed him.

"Well, you see? Then came two, and one of them said: 'Oh, that's that fellow!' 'Yes, that is he!' answered the other. 'Yes, they used to read him in the auld lang syne.' 'They read a lot of them.' 'What was it he preached?' 'Oh, generally, ideas of beauty, goodness, and so forth.' 'Oh, yes, I remember.' 'He had a heavy tongue.' 'There is a lot of them in the ground—yes, Russia is rich in talents' . . . And those asses went away. It is true, warm words do not raise the temperature of the grave, and I do not care for that, yet it hurts me. And oh, how I wanted to give them a piece of my mind!"

"You ought to have given them a fine tongue-lashing!" smiled the Devil.

"No, that would not have done. On the verge of the twentieth century it would be absurd for dead people to scold, and, besides, it would be hard on the materialists."

The Devil again felt the ennui coming over him.

This author had always wished in his lifetime to be a bridegroom at all weddings and a corpse at all burials, and now that all is dead in him, his egotism is still alive. Is man of any importance to life? Of importance is only the human spirit, and only the spirit deserves applause and recognition. . . . How annoying people are! The Devil was on the point of proposing to the author to return to his grave, when an idea flashed through his evil head. They had just reached a square, and heavy masses of buildings surrounded them on all sides. The dark, wet sky hung low over the square; it seemed as though it rested on the roofs and murkily looked at the dirty earth.

"Say," said the Devil as he inclined pleasantly towards the author, "don't you want to know how your wife is getting on?"

"I don't know whether I want to," the author spoke slowly.

"I see, you are a thorough corpse!" called out the Devil to annoy him.

"Oh, I don't know?" said the author and jauntily shook his bones. "I don't mind seeing her; besides, she will not see me, or if she will, she cannot recognize me!"

"Of course!" the Devil assured him.

"You know, I only said so because she did not like for me to go away long from home," explained the author.

And suddenly the wall of a house disappeared or became as transparent as glass. The author saw the inside of large apartments, and it was so light and cosy in them.

"Elegant appointments!" he grated his bones approvingly: "Very fine appointments! If I had lived in such rooms, I would be alive now."

"I like it, too," said the Devil and smiled. "And it is not expensive—it only costs some three thousands."

"Hem, that not expensive? I remember my largest work brought me 815 roubles, and I worked over it a whole year. But who lives here?"

"Your wife," said the Devil.

"I declare! That is good . . . for her."

"Yes, and here comes her husband."

"She is so pretty now, and how well she is dressed! Her husband, you say? What a fine looking fellow! Rather a bourgeois phiz—kind, but somewhat stupid! He looks as if he might be cunning—well, just the face to please a woman."

"Do you want me to heave a sigh for you?" the Devil proposed and looked maliciously at the author. But he was taken up with the scene before him.

"What happy, jolly faces both have! They are evidently satisfied with life. Tell me, does she love him?"

"Oh, yes, very much!"

"And who is he?"

"A clerk in a millinery shop."

"A clerk in a millinery shop," the author repeated slowly and did not utter a word for some time. The Devil looked at him and smiled a merry smile.

"Do you like that?" he asked.

The author spoke with an effort:

"I had some children. . . . I know they are alive. . . . I had some children . . . a son and a daughter. . . . I used to think then that my son would turn out in time a good man. . . ."

"There are plenty of good men, but what the world needs is perfect men," said the Devil coolly and whistled a jolly march.

"I think the clerk is probably a poor pedagogue . . . and my son . . ."

The author's empty skull shook sadly.

"Just look how he is embracing her! They are living an easy life!" exclaimed the Devil.

"Yes. Is that clerk a rich man?"

"No, he was poorer than I, but your wife is rich."

"My wife? Where did she get the money from?"

"From the sale of your books!"

"Oh!" said the author and shook his bare and empty skull. "Oh! Then it simply means that I have worked for a certain clerk?"

"I confess it looks that way," the Devil chimed in merrily.

The author looked at the ground and said to the Devil: "Take me back to my grave!"

. . . It was late. A rain fell, heavy clouds hung in the sky, and the author rattled his bones as he marched rapidly to his grave. . . . The Devil walked behind him and whistled merrily.

My reader is, of course, dissatisfied. My reader is surfeited with literature, and even the people that write only to please him, are rarely to his taste. In the present case my reader is also dissatisfied because I have said nothing about hell. As my reader is justly convinced that after death he will find his way there, he would like to know something about hell during his lifetime. Really, I can't tell anything pleasant to my reader on that score, because there is no hell, no fiery hell which it is so easy to imagine. Yet, there is something else and infinitely more terrible.

The moment the doctor will have said about you to your friends: "He is dead!" you will enter an immeasurable, illuminated space, and that is the space of the consciousness of your mistakes.

You lie in the grave, in a narrow coffin, and your miserable life rotates about you like a wheel.

It moves painfully slow, and passes before you from your first conscious step to the last moment of your life.

You will see all that you have hidden from yourself during your lifetime, all the lies and meanness of your existence: you will think over anew all your past thoughts, and you will see every wrong step of yours—all your life will be gone over, to its minutest details!

And to increase your torments, you will know that on that narrow and stupid road which you have traversed, others are marching, and pushing each other, and hurrying, and lying. . . . And you understand that they are doing it all only to find out in time how shameful it is to live such a wretched, soulless life.

And though you see them hastening on towards their destruction, you are in no way able to warn them: you will not move nor cry, and your helpless desire to aid them will tear your soul to pieces.

Your life passes before you, and you see it from the start, and there is no end to the work of your conscience, and there will be no end . . . and to the horror of your torments there will never be an end . . . never!

The Devil and the Old Man

JOHN MASEFIELD

Up away north, in the old days, in Chester, there was a man who never throve. Nothing he put his hand to ever prospered, and as his state worsened, his friends fell away and he grew desperate. So one night when he was alone in his room, thinking of the rent due in two or three days and the money he couldn't scrape together, he cried out, "I wish I could sell my soul to the Devil like that man the old books tell about."

Now just as he spoke the clock struck twelve, and, while it chimed, a sparkle began to burn about the room, and the air, all at once, began to smell of brimstone, and a voice said:

"Will these terms suit you?"

He then saw that someone had just placed a parchment there. He picked it up and read it through; and being in despair, and not knowing what he was doing, he answered, "Yes," and looked round for a pen.

"Take and sign," said the voice again, "but first consider what it is you do; do nothing rashly. Consider."

So he thought awhile; then, "Yes," he said, "I'll sign," and with that he groped for the pen.

"Blood from your left thumb and sign," said the voice.

So he pricked his left thumb and signed.

"Here is your earnest money," said the voice, "nine and twenty silver pennies. This day twenty years hence I shall see you again."

Now early next morning our friend came to himself and felt like one of the drowned. "What a dream I've had," he said. Then he woke up and saw the nine and twenty silver pennies and smelled a faint smell of brimstone.

So he sat in his chair there and remembered that he had sold his soul to the Devil for twenty years of heart's desire; and whatever fears he may have had as to what might come at the end of those twenty years, he found comfort in the thought that, after all, twenty years is a good stretch of time, and that throughout them he could eat, drink, merrymake, roll in gold, dress in silk, and be carefree, heart at ease, and jib sheet to windward.

So for nineteen years and nine months he lived in great state, having his heart's desire in all things; but, when his twenty years were nearly run through, there was no wretcheder man in all the world than that poor fellow. So he threw up his house, his position, riches, everything, and away he went to the port of Liverpool, where he signed on as A.B., aboard a Black Ball packet, a tea clipper, bound to the China Seas.

They made a fine passage out, and when our friend had only

three days more, they were in the Indian Ocean, lying lazy, be-calmed.

Now it was his wheel that forenoon, and it being dead calm, all he had to do was just to think of things, the ship of course having no way on her.

So he stood there, hanging onto the spokes, groaning and weeping till, just twenty minutes or so before eight bells were made, up came the captain for a turn on deck.

He went aft of course, took a squint aloft, and saw our friend crying at the wheel. "Hello, my man," he says, "why, what's all this? Ain't you well? You'd best lay aft for a dose o' salts at four bells tonight."

"No, Cap'n," said the man, "there's no salts'll ever cure my sickness."

"Why, what's all this?" says the old man. "You must be sick if it's as bad as all that. But come now; your cheek is all sunk, and you look as if you ain't slept well. What is it ails you, anyway? Have you anything on your mind?"

"Captain," he answers very solemn, "I have sold my soul to the Devil."

"Oh," said the old man, "why, that's bad. That's powerful bad. I never thought them sort of things ever happened outside a book."

"But," said our friend, "that's not the worst of it, Captain. At this time three days hence the Devil will fetch me home."

"Good Lord!" groaned the old man. "Here's a nice hurrah's nest to happen aboard my ship. But come now," he went on, "did the Devil give you no chance—no saving clause like? Just think quietly for a moment."

"Yes, Captain," said our friend, "just when I made the deal, there came a whisper in my ear. And," he said, speaking very quietly, so as not to let the mate hear, "if I can give the Devil three jobs to do which he cannot do, why, then, Captain," he says, "I'm saved, and that deed of mine is canceled."

Well, at this the old man grinned and said, "You just leave things to me, my son. *I'll* fix the Devil for you. Aft there, one o' you, and relieve the wheel. Now you run forrard, and have a good watch below, and be quite easy in your mind, for I'll deal with the Devil for you. You rest and be easy."

And so that day goes by, and the next, and the one after that, and the one after that was the day the Devil was due.

Soon as eight bells was made in the morning watch, the old man called all hands aft.

"Men," he said, "I've got an all-hands job for you this forenoon.

"Mr. Mate," he cried, "get all hands onto the main-tops'l halyards and bouse the sail stiff up and down."

So they passed along the halyards and took the turns off, and old John Chantyman piped up:

> "There's a Black Ball clipper
> Comin' down the river."

And away the yard went to the masthead till the bunt robands jammed in the sheave.

"Very well that," said the old man. "Now get my dinghy off o' the half deck and let her drag alongside."

So they did that too.

"Very well that," said the old man. "Now forrard with you, to the chain locker, and rouse out every inch of chain you find there."

So forrard they went, and the chain was lighted up and flaked along the deck all clear for running.

"Now, Chips," says the old man to the carpenter, "just bend the spare anchor to the end of that chain and clear away the fo'c'sle rails ready for when we let go."

So they did this too.

"Now," said the old man, "get them tubs of slush from the galley. Pass that slush along there, doctor. Very well that. Now turn to, all hands, and slush away every link in that chain a good inch thick in grease.

So they did that, too, and wondered what the old man meant.

"Very well that," cries the old man. "Now get below, all hands! Chips, onto the fo'c'sle head with you and stand by! I'll keep the deck, Mr. Mate! Very well that."

So all hands tumbled down below; Chips took a fill o' 'baccy to the leeward of the capstan, and the old man walked the weather poop, looking for a sign of hell-fire.

It was still dead calm—but presently, toward six bells, he raised a black cloud away to leeward and saw the glimmer of the lightning in it; only the flashes were too red and came too quick.

"Now," says he to himself, "stand by."

Very soon that black cloud worked up to windward, right alongside, and there came a red flash, and a strong sulphurous smell, and then a loud peal of thunder as the Devil steps aboard.

"Mornin', Cap'n," says he.

"Mornin', Mr. Devil," says the old man, "and what in blazes do you want aboard *my* ship?"

"Why, Captain," said the Devil, "I've come for the soul of one of your hands as per signed agreement; and, as my time's pretty full up in these wicked days, I hope you won't keep me waiting for him longer than need be."

"Well, Mr. Devil," says the old man, "the man you come for is down below, sleeping, just at this moment. It's a fair pity to call him till it's right time. So supposin' I set you them three tasks. How would that be? Have you any objections?"

"Why, no," said the Devil, "fire away as soon as you like."

"Mr. Devil," said the old man, "you see that main-tops'l yard? Suppose you lay out on that main-tops'l yard and take in three reefs singlehanded."

"Ay, ay, sir," the Devil said, and he ran up the ratlines, into the top, up the topmast rigging, and along the yard.

Well, when he found the sail stiff up and down, he hailed the deck:

"Below there! On deck there! Lower away ya halyards!"

"I will not," said the old man, "nary a lower."

"Come up your sheets, then," said the Devil. "This main-topsail's stiff up and down. How'm I to take in three reefs when the sail's stiff up and down?"

"Why," said the old man, *you can't do it.* Come out o' that! Down from aloft, you hoof-footed son. That's one to me."

"Yes," says the Devil, when he got on deck again, "I don't deny it, Cap'n. That's one to you."

"Now, Mr. Devil," said the old man, going toward the rail, "suppose you was to step into that little boat alongside there. Will you please?"

"Ay, ay, sir," he said, and he slid down the forrard fall, got into the stern sheets, and sat down.

"Now, Mr. Devil," said the skipper, taking a little salt spoon from his vest pocket, "supposin' you bail all the water on that side the boat onto this side the boat, using this spoon as your dipper."

Well!—the Devil just looked at him.

"Say!" he said at length. "Which of the New England States d'ye hail from anyway?"

"Not Jersey, anyway," said the old man. "That's two up, all right; ain't it, sonny?"

"Yes," growls the Devil as he climbs aboard. "That's two up. Two to you and one to play. Now, what's your next contraption?"

"Mr. Devil," said the old man, looking very innocent, "you see, I've ranged my chain ready for letting go anchor. Now Chips is forrard there, and when I sing out, he'll let the anchor go. Supposin' you stopper the chain with them big hands o' yourn and keep it from running out clear. Will you, please?"

So the Devil takes off his coat and rubs his hands together and gets away forrard by the bitts and stands by.

"All ready, Cap'n," he says.

"All ready, Chips?" asked the old man.

"All ready, sir," replies Chips.

"Then, stand by. Let *go* the anchor," and clink, clink, old Chips knocks out the pin, and away goes the spare anchor and greased chain into a five-mile deep of God's sea. As I said, they were in the Indian Ocean.

Well—there was the Devil, making a grab here and a grab there, and the slushy chain just slipping through his claws, and at whiles a bight of chain would spring clear and rap him in the eye.

So at last the cable was nearly clean gone, and the Devil ran to the last big link (which was seized to the heel of the foremast), and he put both his arms through it and hung onto it like grim death.

But the chain gave such a *yank* when it came to that the big link carried away, and oh, roll and go, out it went through the hawsehole, in a shower of bright sparks, carrying the Devil with it. There is no Devil now. The Devil's dead.

As for the old man, he looked over the bows, watching the bubbles burst, but the Devil never rose. Then he went to the fo'c'sle scuttle and banged thereon with a hand spike.

"Rouse out, there, the port watch," he called, "an' get my dinghy inboard."

Enoch Soames

MAX BEERBOHM

When a book about the literature of the eighteen-nineties was given by Mr. Holbrook Jackson to the world, I looked eagerly in the index for SOAMES, ENOCH. I had feared he would not be there. He was not there. But everybody else was. Many writers whom I had quite forgotten, or remembered but faintly, lived again for me, they and their work, in Mr. Holbrook Jackson's pages. The book was as thorough as it was brilliantly written. And thus the omission found by me was an all the deadlier record of poor Soames' failure to impress himself on his decade.

I daresay I am the only person who noticed the omission.

Soames had failed so piteously as all that! Nor is there a counterpoise in the thought that if he had had some measure of success he might have passed, like those others, out of my mind, to return only at the historian's beck. It is true that had his gifts, such as they were, been acknowledged in his lifetime, he would never have made the bargain I saw him make—that strange bargain whose results have kept him always in the foreground of my memory. But it is from those very results that the full piteousness of him glares out.

Not my compassion, however, impels me to write of him. For his sake, poor fellow, I should be inclined to keep my pen out of the ink. It is ill to deride the dead. And how can I write about Enoch Soames without making him ridiculous? Or rather, how am I to hush up the horrid fact that he *was* ridiculous? I shall not be able to do that. Yet, sooner or later, write about him I must. You will see, in due course, that I have no option. And I may as well get the thing done now.

In the Summer Term of '93 a bolt from the blue flashed down on Oxford. It drove deep, it hurtlingly embedded itself in the soil. Dons and undergraduates stood around, rather pale, discussing nothing but it. Whence came it, this meteorite? From Paris. Its name? Will Rothenstein. Its aim? To do a series of twenty-four portraits in lithograph. These were to be published from the Bodley Head, London. The matter was urgent. Already the Warden of A, and the Master of B, and the Regius Professor of C, had meekly "sat." Dignified and doddering old men, who had never consented to sit to anyone, could not withstand this dynamic little stranger. He did not sue: he invited; he did not invite: he commanded. He was twenty-one years old. He wore spectacles that flashed more than any other pair ever seen. He was a wit. He was brimful of ideas. He knew Whistler. He knew Edmond de Goncourt. He knew every one in

Paris. He knew them all by heart. He was Paris in Oxford. It was whispered that, so soon as he had polished off his selection of dons, he was going to include a few undergraduates. It was a proud day for me when I—I—was included. I liked Rothenstein not less than I feared him; and there arose between us a friendship that has grown ever warmer, and been more and more valued by me, with every passing year.

At the end of Term he settled in—or rather, meteoritically into—London. It was to him I owed my first knowledge of that forever enchanting little world-in-itself, Chelsea, and my first acquaintance with Walter Sickert and other august elders who dwelt there. It was Rothenstein that took me to see, in Cambridge Street, Pimlico, a young man whose drawings were already famous among the few—Aubrey Beardsley, by name. With Rothenstein I paid my first visit to the Bodley Head. By him I was inducted into another haunt of intellect and daring, the domino room of the Café Royal.

There, on that October evening—there, in that exuberant vista of gilding and crimson velvet set amidst all those opposing mirrors and upholding caryatids, with fumes of tobacco ever rising to the painted and pagan ceiling, and with the hum of presumably cynical conversation broken into so sharply now and again by the clatter of dominoes shuffled on marble tables, I drew a deep breath, and "This indeed," said I to myself, "is life!"

It was the hour before dinner. We drank vermouth. Those who knew Rothenstein were pointing him out to those who knew him only by name. Men were constantly coming in through the swing-doors and wandering slowly up and down in search of vacant tables, or of tables occupied by friends. One of these rovers interested me because I was sure he wanted to catch Rothenstein's eye. He had twice passed our table, with a hesitating look; but Rothenstein, in the thick of a disquisition on Puvis de Chavannes, had not seen him. He was a stooping, shambling person, rather tall, very pale, with longish and brownish hair. He had a thin vague beard—or rather, he had a chin on which a large number of hairs weakly curled and clustered to cover its retreat. He was an odd-looking person; but in the 'nineties odd apparitions were more frequent, I think, than they are now. The young writers of that era—and I was sure this man was a writer—strove earnestly to be distinct in aspect. This man had striven unsuccessfully. He wore a soft black hat of clerical kind but of Bohemian intention, and a gray waterproof cape which, perhaps because it was waterproof, failed to be romantic. I decided that "dim" was the *mot juste* for him. I had already essayed to write, and was immensely keen on the *mot juste,* that Holy Grail of the period.

The dim man was now again approaching our table, and this time he made up his mind to pause in front of it. "You don't remember me," he said in a toneless voice.

Rothenstein brightly focussed him. "Yes, I do," he replied after a moment, with pride rather than effusion—pride in a retentive memory. "Edwin Soames."

"Enoch Soames," said Enoch.

"Enoch Soames," repeated Rothenstein in a tone implying that it was enough to have hit on the surname. "We met in Paris two or three times when you were living there. We met at the Café Groche."

"And I came to your studio once."

"Oh yes; I was sorry I was out."

"But you were in. You showed me some of your paintings, you know. . . . I hear you're in Chelsea now."

"Yes."

I almost wondered that Mr. Soames did not, after this monosyllable, pass along. He stood patiently there, rather like a dumb animal, rather like a donkey looking over a gate. A sad figure, his. It occurred to me that "hungry" was perhaps the *mot juste* for him; but—hungry for what? He looked as if he had little appetite for anything. I was sorry for him; and Rothenstein, though he had not invited him to Chelsea, did ask him to sit down and have something to drink.

Seated, he was more self-assertive. He flung back the wings of his cape with a gesture which—had not those wings been waterproof—might have seemed to hurl defiance at things in general. And he ordered an absinthe. *"Je me tiens toujours fidèle,"* he told Rothenstein, *"à la sorcière glauque."*

"It is bad for you," said Rothenstein drily.

"Nothing is bad for one," answered Soames. *"Dans ce monde il n'y a ni de bien ni de mal."*

"Nothing good and nothing bad? How do you mean?"

"I explained it all in the preface to *Negations.*"

"Negations?"

"Yes; I gave you a copy of it."

"Oh yes, of course. But did you explain—for instance—that there was no such thing as bad or good grammar?"

"N-no," said Soames. "Of course in Art there is the good and the evil. But in Life—no." He was rolling a cigarette. He had weak white hands, not well washed, and with fingertips much stained by nicotine. "In Life there are illusions of good and evil, but"—his voice trailed away to a murmur in which the words "vieux jeu" and "rococo" were faintly audible. I think he felt he was not doing himself justice, and feared that Rothenstein was going to point out fallacies. Anyway, he cleared his throat and said *"Parlons d'autre chose."*

It occurs to you that he was a fool? It didn't to me. I was young, and had not the clarity of judgment that Rothenstein already had. Soames was quite five or six years older than either of us. Also, he had written a book.

It was wonderful to have written a book.

If Rothenstein had not been there, I should have revered

Soames. Even as it was, I respected him. And I was very near indeed to reverence when he said he had another book coming out soon. I asked if I might ask what kind of book it was to be.

"My poems," he answered. Rothenstein asked if this was to be the title of the book. The poet meditated on this suggestion, but said he rather thought of giving the book no title at all. "If a book is good in itself—" he murmured, waving his cigarette.

Rothenstein objected that absence of title might be bad for the sale of a book. "If," he urged, "I went into a bookseller's and said simply 'Have you got?' or 'Have you a copy of?' how would they know what I wanted?"

"Oh, of course I should have my name on the cover," Soames answered earnestly. "And I rather want," he added, looking hard at Rothenstein, "to have a drawing of myself as frontispiece." Rothenstein admitted that this was a capital idea, and mentioned that he was going into the country and would be there for some time. He then looked at his watch, exclaimed at the hour, paid the waiter, and went away with me to dinner. Soames remained at his post of fidelity to the glaucous witch.

"Why were you so determined not to draw him?" I asked.

"Draw him? Him? How can one draw a man who doesn't exist?"

"He is dim," I admitted. But my *mot juste* fell flat. Rothenstein repeated that Soames was nonexistent.

Still, Soames had written a book. I asked if Rothenstein had read *Negations*. He said he had looked into it, "but," he added crisply, "I don't profess to know anything about writing." A reservation very characteristic of the period! Painters would not then allow that any one outside their own order had a right to any opinion about painting. This law (graven on the tablets brought down by Whistler from the summit of Fujiyama) imposed certain limitations. If other arts than painting were not utterly unintelligible to all but the men who practiced them, the law tottered—the Monroe Doctrine, as it were, did not hold good. Therefore no painter would offer an opinion of a book without warning you at any rate that his opinion was worthless. No one is a better judge of literature than Rothenstein; but it wouldn't have done to tell him so in those days; and I knew that I must form an unaided judgment on *Negations*.

Not to buy a book of which I had met the author face to face would have been for me in those days an impossible act of self-denial. When I returned to Oxford for the Christmas Term I had duly secured *Negations*. I used to keep it lying carelessly on the table in my room, and whenever a friend took it up and asked what it was about I would say "Oh, it's rather a remarkable book. It's by a man whom I know." Just "what it was about" I never was able to say. Head or tail was just what I hadn't made of that slim green volume. I found in the preface no clue to the exiguous labyrinth of contents, and in that labyrinth nothing to explain the preface.

> Lean near to life. Lean very near—nearer.
> Life is web, and therein nor warp nor woof is, but web only.
> It is for this I am Catholick in church and in thought, yet do let swift Mood weave there what the shuttle of Mood wills.

These were the opening phrases of the preface, but those which followed were less easy to understand. Then came "Stark: A Conte," about a midinette who, so far as I could gather, murdered, or was about to murder, a mannequin. It seemed to me like a story by Catulle Mendès in which the translator had either skipped or cut out every alternate sentence. Next, a dialogue between Pan and St. Ursula—lacking, I rather felt, in "snap." Next, some aphorisms (entitled). Throughout, in fact, there was a great variety of form; and the forms had evidently been wrought with much care. It was rather the substance that eluded me. Was there, I wondered, any substance at all? It did now occur to me: suppose Enoch Soames was a fool! Up cropped a rival hypothesis: suppose *I* was! I inclined to give Soames the benefit of the doubt. I had read "L'Après-midi d'un Faune" without extracting a glimmer of meaning. Yet Mallarmé—of course—was a master. How was I to know that Soames wasn't another? There was a sort of music in his prose, not indeed arresting, but perhaps, I thought, haunting, and laden perhaps with meanings as deep as Mallarmé's own. I awaited his poems with an open mind.

And I looked forward to them with positive impatience after I had had a second meeting with him. This was on an evening in January. Going into the aforesaid domino room, I passed a table at which sat a pale man with an open book before him. He looked from his book to me, and I looked back over my shoulder with a vague sense that I ought to have recognized him. I returned to pay my respects. After exchanging a few words, I said with a glance to the open book, "I see I am interrupting you," and was about to pass on, but "I prefer," Soames replied in his toneless voice, "to be interrupted," and I obeyed his gesture that I should sit down.

I asked him if he often read here. "Yes; things of this kind I read here," he answered, indicating the title of his book—*The Poems of Shelley*.

"Anything that you really"—and I was going to say "admire?" But I cautiously left my sentence unfinished, and was glad that I had done so, for he said, with unwonted emphasis, "Anything second-rate."

I had read little of Shelley, but "Of course," I murmured, "he's very uneven."

"I should have thought evenness was just what was wrong with him. A deadly evenness. That's why I read him here. The noise of this place breaks the rhythm. He's tolerable here." Soames took up the book and glanced through the pages. He laughed. Soames' laugh was a short, single and mirthless sound from the throat, unaccompanied by any movement of the face or brightening of the eyes. "What a period!" he uttered, laying the book down. And "What a country!" he added.

I asked rather nervously if he didn't think Keats had more or less held his own against the drawbacks of time and place. He admitted that there were "passages in Keats," but did not specify them. Of "the older men," as he called them, he seemed to like only Milton. "Milton," he said, "wasn't sentimental." Also, "Milton had a dark insight." And again, "I can always read Milton in the reading room."

"The reading room?"

"Of the British Museum. I go there every day."

"You do? I've only been there once. I'm afraid I found it rather a depressing place. It—it seemed to sap one's vitality."

"It does. That's why I go there. The lower one's vitality, the more sensitive one is to great art. I live near the Museum. I have rooms in Dyott Street."

"And you go round to the reading room to read Milton?"

"Usually Milton." He looked at me. "It was Milton," he certificatively added, "who converted me to Diabolism."

"Diabolism? Oh yes? Really?" said I, with that vague discomfort and that intense desire to be polite which one feels when a man speaks of his own religion. "You—worship the Devil?"

Soames shook his head. "It's not exactly worship," he qualified, sipping his absinthe. "It's more a matter of trusting and encouraging."

"Ah, yes. . . . But I had rather gathered from the preface to *Negations* that you were a—a Catholic."

"*Je l'étais à cette époque.*Perhaps I still am. Yes, I'm a Catholic Diabolist."

This profession he made in an almost cursory tone. I could see that what was upmost in his mind was the fact that I had read *Negations.* His pale eyes had for the first time gleamed. I felt as one who is about to be examined, *viva voce,* on the very subject in which he is shakiest. I hastily asked him how soon his poems were to be published. "Next week," he told me.

"And are they to be published without a title?"

"No. I found a title, at last. But I shan't tell you what it is," as though I had been so impertinent as to inquire. "I am not sure that it wholly satisfies me. But it is the best I can find. It does suggest something of the quality of the poems. . . . Strange growths, natural and wild; yet exquisite," he added, "and many-hued, and full of poisons."

I asked him what he thought of Baudelaire. He uttered the snort that was his laugh, and "Baudelaire," he said, "was a *bourgeois malgré lui.*" France had had only one poet: Villon; "and two-thirds of Villon were sheer journalism." Verlaine was "an *épicier malgré lui.*" Altogether, rather to my surprise, he rated French literature lower than English. There were "passages" in Villiers de l'Isle-Adam. But "I," he summed up, "owe nothing to France." He nodded at me. "You'll see," he predicted.

I did not, when the time came, quite see that. I thought the author of *Fungoids* did—unconsciously, no doubt—owe something to the young Parisian décadents, or to the young English ones who owed something to *them.* I still think so. The little book—bought by me in Oxford—lies before me as I write. Its pale gray buckram cover and silver lettering have not worn well. Nor have its contents. Through these, with a melancholy interest, I have again been looking. They are not much. But at the time of their publication I had a vague suspicion that they *might* be. I suppose it is my capacity for faith, not poor Soames' work, that is weaker than it once was. . . .

To a Young Woman

Thou art, who hast not been!
Pale tunes irresolute
And traceries of old sounds

> Blown from a rotted flute
> Mingle with noise of cymbals rouged with rust,
> Nor not strange forms and epicene
> Lie bleeding in the dust,
> Being wounded with wounds.
> For this it is
> That is thy counterpart
> Of age-long mockeries
> *Thou hast not been nor art!*

There seemed to me a certain inconsistency as between the first and last lines of this. I tried, with bent brows, to resolve the discord. But I did not take my failure as wholly incompatible with a meaning in Soames' mind. Might it not rather indicate the depth of his meaning? As for the craftsmanship, "rouged with rust" seemed to me a fine stroke, and "nor not" instead of "and" had a curious felicity. I wondered who the Young Woman was, and what she had made of it all. I sadly suspect that Soames could not have made more of it than she. Yet, even now, if one doesn't try to make any sense at all of the poem, and reads it just for the sound, there is a certain grace of cadence. Soames was an artist—in so far as he was anything, poor fellow!

It seemed to me, when first I read *Fungoids,* that, oddly enough, the Diabolistic side of him was the best. Diabolism seemed to be a cheerful, even a wholesome, influence in his life.

Nocturne

> Round and round the shutter'd Square
> I stroll'd with the Devil's arm in mine.
> No sound but the scrape of his hoofs was there

And the ring of his laughter and mine.
　　We had drunk black wine.

I scream'd "I will race you, Master!"
"What matter," he shriek'd, "tonight
Which of us runs the faster?
There is nothing to fear tonight
　　In the foul moon's light!"

Then I look'd him in the eyes,
And I laugh'd full shrill at the lie he told
And the gnawing fear he would fain disguise.
It was true, what I'd time and again been told:
　　He was old—old.

There was, I felt, quite a swing about that first stanza—a joyous and rollicking note of comradeship. The second was slightly hysterical perhaps. But I liked the third: it was so bracingly unorthodox, even according to the tenets of Soames' peculiar sect in the faith. Not much "trusting and encouraging" here! Soames triumphantly exposing the Devil as a liar, and laughing "full shrill," cut a quite heartening figure, I thought—then! Now, in the light of what befell, none of his poems depresses me so much as "Nocturne."

I looked out for what the metropolitan reviewers would have to say. They seemed to fall into two classes: those who had little to say and those who had nothing. The second class was the larger, and the words of the first were cold; insomuch that

　　Strikes a note of modernity throughout. . . . These tripping numbers.—*Preston Telegraph.*

was the sole lure offered in advertisements by Soames' publisher. I
had hoped that when next I met the poet I could congratulate him
on having made a stir; for I fancied he was not so sure of his intrinsic
greatness as he seemed. I was but able to say, rather coarsely, when
next I did see him, that I hoped *Fungoids* was "selling splendidly."
He looked at me across his glass of absinthe and asked if I had
bought a copy. His publisher had told him that three had been sold.
I laughed, as at a jest.

"You don't suppose I *care,* do you?" he said, with something like
a snarl. I disclaimed the notion. He added that he was not a tradesman. I said mildly that I wasn't, either, and murmured that an artist
who gave truly new and great things to the world had always to wait
long for recognition. He said he cared not a sou for recognition. I
agreed that the act of creation was its own reward.

His moroseness might have alienated me if I had regarded myself
as a nobody. But ah! hadn't both John Lane and Aubrey Beardsley
suggested that I should write an essay for the great new venture that
was afoot—the *Yellow Book?* And hadn't Henry Harland, as editor,
accepted my essay? And wasn't it to be in the very first number? At
Oxford I was still *in statu pupillari.* In London I regarded myself as
very much indeed a graduate now—one whom no Soames could
ruffle. Partly to show off, partly in sheer goodwill, I told Soames he
ought to contribute to the *Yellow Book.* He uttered from the throat a
sound of scorn for that publication.

Nevertheless, I did, a day or two later, tentatively ask Harland if
he knew anything of the work of a man called Enoch Soames.
Harland paused in the midst of his characteristic stride around the
room, threw up his hands towards the ceiling, and groaned aloud: he
had often met "that absurd creature" in Paris, and this very morning
had received some poems in manuscript from him.

"Has he *no* talent?" he asked.

"He has an income. He's all right." Harland was the most joyous of men and most generous of critics, and he hated to talk of anything about which he couldn't be enthusiastic. So I dropped the subject of Soames. The news that Soames had an income did take the edge off solicitude. I learned afterwards that he was the son of an unsuccessful and deceased bookseller in Preston, but had inherited an annuity of £300 from a married aunt, and had no surviving relatives of any kind. Materially, then, he was "all right." But there was still a spiritual pathos about him, sharpened for me now by the possibility that even the praises of the *Preston Telegraph* might not have been forthcoming had he not been the son of a Preston man. He had a sort of weak doggedness which I could not but admire. Neither he nor his work received the slightest encouragement; but he persisted in behaving as a personage: always he kept his dingy little flag flying. Wherever congregated the *jeunes féroces* of the arts, in whatever Soho restaurant they had just discovered, in whatever music hall they were most frequenting, there was Soames in the midst of them, or rather on the fringe of them, a dim but inevitable figure. He never sought to propitiate his fellow writers, never bated a jot of his arrogance about his own work or of his contempt for theirs. To the painters he was respectful, even humble; but for the poets and prosaists of the *Yellow Book*, and later of *The Savoy*, he had never a word but of scorn. He wasn't resented. It didn't occur to anybody that he or his Catholic Diabolism mattered. When, in the autumn of '96, he brought out (at his own expense, this time) a third book, his last book, nobody said a word for or against it. I meant, but forgot, to buy it. I never saw it, and am ashamed to say I don't even remember what it was called. But I did, at the time of its publication, say to Rothenstein that I thought poor old Soames was really a rather tragic figure, and that I believed he would literally die for want of recognition. Rothenstein scoffed. He said I was trying to get credit for a kind heart which I didn't possess; and perhaps this was so. But at the private view of the New English Art Club, a few weeks later, I beheld a pastel portrait of "Enoch Soames, Esq." It was very like him, and very like Rothenstein to have done it. Soames was standing near it, in his soft hat and his waterproof cape, all through the afternoon. Anybody who knew him would have recognized the portrait at a glance, but nobody who didn't know him would have recognized the portrait from its bystander: it "existed" so much more than he; it was bound to. Also, it had not that expression of faint happiness which on this day was discernible, yes, in Soames' countenance. Fame had breathed on him. Twice again in the course of the month I went to the New English, and on both occasions Soames himself was on view there. Looking back, I regard the close of that exhibition as having been virtually the close of his career. He had felt the breath of Fame against his cheek—so late, for such a little while; and at its withdrawal he gave in, gave up, gave out. He, who had never looked strong or well, looked ghastly now—a shadow of the shade he had once been. He still frequented the domino room, but, having lost all wish to excite curiosity, he no longer read books there. "You read only at the Museum now?" asked I, with attempted cheerfulness. He said he never went there now. "No absinthe there," he muttered. It was the sort of thing that in the old days he would have said for effect; but it carried conviction now. Absinthe, erst but a point in the "personality" he had striven so hard to build up, was solace and necessity now. He no longer called it "la sorcière glauque." He had shed away all his French phrases. He had become a plain, unvarnished, Preston man.

Failure, if it be a plain, unvarnished, complete failure, and even though it be a squalid failure, has always a certain dignity. I avoided Soames because he made me feel rather vulgar. John Lane had published, by this time, two little books of mine, and they had had a pleasant little success of esteem. I was a—slight but definite—"personality." Frank Harris had engaged me to kick up my heels in the *Saturday Review,* Alfred Harmsworth was letting me do likewise in

The Daily Mail. I was just what Soames wasn't. And he shamed my gloss. Had I known that he really and firmly believed in the greatness of what he as an artist had achieved, I might not have shunned him. No man who hasn't lost his vanity can be held to have altogether failed. Soames' dignity was an illusion of mine. One day in the first week of June, 1897, that illusion went. But on the evening of that day Soames went too.

I had been out most of the morning, and, as it was too late to reach home in time for luncheon, I sought "the Vingtième." This little place—Restaurant du Vingtième Siècle, to give it its full title—had been discovered in '96 by the poets and prosaists, but had now been more or less abandoned in favor of some later find. I don't think it lived long enough to justify its name; but at that time there it still was, in Greek Street, a few doors from Soho Square, and almost opposite to that house where, in the first years of the century, a little girl, and with her a boy named De Quincey, made nightly encampment in darkness and hunger among dust and rats and old legal parchments. The Vingtième was but a small whitewashed room, leading out into the street at one end and into a kitchen at the other. The proprietor and cook was a Frenchman, known to us as Monsieur Vingtième; the waiters were his two daughters, Rose and Berthe; and the food, according to faith, was good. The tables were so narrow, and were set so close together, that there was space for twelve of them, six jutting from either wall.

Only the two nearest to the door, as I went in, were occupied. On one side sat a tall, flashy, rather Mephistophelian man whom I had seen from time to time in the domino room and elsewhere. On the other side sat Soames. They made a queer contrast in that sunlit room—Soames sitting haggard in that hat and cape which nowhere at any season had I seen him doff, and this other, this keenly vital man, at sight of whom I more than ever wondered whether he were a diamond merchant, a conjurer, or the head of a private detective

agency. I was sure Soames didn't want my company; but I asked, as
it would have seemed brutal not to, whether I might join him, and
took the chair opposite to his. He was smoking a cigarette, with an
untasted salmi of something on his plate and a half-empty bottle of
Sauterne before him; and he was quite silent. I said that the preparations for the Jubilee made London impossible. (I rather liked them,
really.) I professed a wish to go right away till the whole thing was
over. In vain did I attune myself to his gloom. He seemed not to hear
me nor even to see me. I felt that his behavior made me ridiculous in
the eyes of the other man. The gangway between the two rows of
tables at the Vingtième was hardly more than two feet wide (Rose
and Berthe, in their ministrations, had always to edge past each
other, quarreling in whispers as they did so), and anyone at the table
abreast of yours was practically at yours. I thought our neighbor was
amused at my failure to interest Soames, and so, as I could not
explain to him that my insistence was merely charitable, I became
silent. Without turning my head, I had him well within my range of
vision. I hoped I looked less vulgar than he in contrast with Soames.
I was sure he was not an Englishman, but what *was* his nationality?
Though his jet-black hair was *en brosse,* I did not think he was
French. To Berthe, who waited on him, he spoke French fluently,
but with a hardly native idiom and accent. I gathered that this was
his first visit to the Vingtième; but Berthe was offhand in her manner to him: he had not made a good impression. His eyes were
handsome, but—like the Vingtième's tables—too narrow and set
too close together. His nose was predatory, and the points of his
moustache, waxed up beyond his nostrils, gave a fixity to his smile.
Decidedly, he was sinister. And my sense of discomfort in his presence was intensified by the scarlet waistcoat which tightly, and so
unseasonably in June, sheathed his ample chest. This waistcoat
wasn't wrong merely because of the heat, either. It was somehow all
wrong in itself. It wouldn't have done on Christmas morning. It

would have struck a jarring note at the first night of *Hernani*. I was trying to account for its wrongness when Soames suddenly and strangely broke silence. "A hundred years hence!" he murmured, as in a trance.

"We shall not be here!" I briskly but fatuously added.

"We shall not be here. No," he droned, "but the Museum will still be just where it is. And the reading room, just where it is. And people will be able to go and read there." He inhaled sharply, and a spasm as of actual pain contorted his features.

I wondered what train of thought poor Soames had been following. He did not enlighten me when he said, after a long pause, "You think I haven't minded."

"Minded what, Soames?"

"Neglect. Failure."

"*Failure?*" I said heartily. "Failure?" I repeated vaguely. "Neglect—yes, perhaps; but that's quite another matter. Of course you haven't been—appreciated. But what then? Any artist who—who gives—" What I wanted to say was, "Any artist who gives truly new and great things to the world has always to wait long for recognition"; but the flattery would not out: in the face of his misery, a misery so genuine and so unmasked, my lips would not say the words.

And then—he said them for me. I flushed. "That's what you were going to say, isn't it?" he asked.

"How did you know?"

"It's what you said to me three years ago, when *Fungoids* was published." I flushed the more. I need not have done so at all, for "It's the only important thing I ever heard you say," he continued. "And I've never forgotten it. It's a true thing. It's a horrible truth. But—d'you remember what I answered? I said 'I don't care a sou for recognition.' And you believed me. You've gone on believing I'm above that sort of thing. You're shallow. What should *you* know of the feelings of a man like me? You imagine that a great artist's faith in himself and in the verdict of posterity is enough to keep him happy. . . . You've never guessed at the bitterness and loneliness, the"—his voice broke; but presently he resumed, speaking with a force that I had never known in him. "Posterity! What use is it to *me?* A dead man doesn't know that people are visiting his grave— visiting his birthplace—putting up tablets to him—unveiling statues of him. A dead man can't read the books that are written about him. A hundred years hence! Think of it! If I could come back to life *then*—just for a few hours—and go to the reading room, and *read!* Or better still: if I could be projected, now, at this moment, into that future, into that reading room, just for this one afternoon! I'd sell myself body and soul to the devil, for that! Think of the pages and pages in the catalogue: 'SOAMES, ENOCH' endlessly—endless editions, commentaries, prolegomena, biographies"—but here he was inter-rupted by a sudden loud creak of the chair at the next table. Our neighbor had half risen from his place. He was leaning towards us, apologetically intrusive.

"Excuse—permit me," he said softly. "I have been unable not to hear. Might I take a liberty? In this little restaurant-sans-façon"—he spread wide his hands—"might I, as the phrase is, 'cut in'?"

I could but signify our acquiescence. Berthe had appeared at the kitchen door, thinking the stranger wanted his bill. He waved her away with his cigar, and in another moment had seated himself beside me, commanding a full view of Soames.

"Though not an Englishman," he explained, "I know my Lon-don well, Mr. Soames. Your name and fame—Mr. Beerbohm's too—very known to me. Your point is: who am *I?*" He glanced quickly over his shoulder, and in a lowered voice said "I am the Devil."

I couldn't help it: I laughed. I tried not to, I knew there was nothing to laugh at, my rudeness shamed me, but—I laughed with increasing volume. The Devil's quiet dignity, the surprise and disgust of his raised eyebrows, did but the more dissolve me. I rocked to and fro, I lay back aching. I behaved deplorably.

"I am a gentleman, and," he said with intense emphasis, "I thought I was in the company of *gentlemen.*"

"Don't!" I gasped faintly. "Oh, don't!"

"Curious, *nicht wahr?*" I heard him say to Soames. "There is a type of person to whom the very mention of my name is—oh-so-awfully-funny! In your theatres the dullest comédien needs only to say 'The Devil!' and right away they give him 'the loud laugh that speaks the vacant mind.' Is it not so?"

I had now just breath enough to offer my apologies. He accepted them, but coldly, and readdressed himself to Soames.

"I am a man of business," he said, "and always I would put things through 'right now,' as they say in the States. You are a poet. *Les affaires*—you detest them. So be it. But with me you will deal, eh? What you have said just now gives me furiously to hope."

Soames had not moved, except to light a fresh cigarette. He sat crouched forward, with his elbows squared on the table, and his head just above the level of his hands, staring up at the Devil. "Go on," he nodded. I had no remnant of laughter in me now.

"It will be the more pleasant, our little deal," the Devil went on, "because you are—I mistake not?—a Diabolist."

"A Catholic Diabolist," said Soames.

The Devil accepted the reservation genially. "You wish," he resumed, "to visit now—this afternoon as-ever-is—the reading room of the British Museum, yes? but of a hundred years hence, yes? *Parfaitement.* Time—an illusion. Past and future—they are as ever-present as the present, or at any rate only what you call 'just-round-the-corner.' I switch you on to any date. I project you—pouf! You wish to be in the reading room just as it will be on the afternoon of June 3rd, 1997? You wish to find yourself standing in that room, just past the swing-doors, this very minute, yes? and to stay there till closing time? Am I right?"

Soames nodded.

The Devil looked at his watch. "Ten past two," he said. "Closing time in summer same then as now: seven o'clock. That will give you almost five hours. At seven o'clock—pouf!—you find yourself again here, sitting at this table. I am dining tonight *dans le monde—dans le higlif.* That concludes my present visit to your great city. I come and fetch you here, Mr. Soames, on my way home."

"Home?" I echoed.

"Be it never so humble!" said the Devil lightly.

"All right," said Soames.

"Soames!" I entreated. But my friend moved not a muscle.

The Devil had made as though to stretch forth his hand across the table and touch Soames' forearm; but he paused in his gesture.

"A hundred years hence, as now," he smiled, "no smoking allowed in the reading room. You would better therefore——"

Soames removed the cigarette from his mouth and dropped it into his glass of Sauterne.

"Soames!" again I cried. "Can't you"—but the Devil had now stretched forth his hand across the table. He brought it slowly down on—the tablecloth. Soames' chair was empty. His cigarette floated sodden in his wine-glass. There was no other trace of him.

For a few moments the Devil let his hand rest where it lay, gazing at me out of the corners of his eyes, vulgarly triumphant.

A shudder shook me. With an effort I controlled myself and rose from my chair. "Very clever," I said condescendingly. "But—'The Time Machine' is a delightful book, don't you think? So entirely original!"

"You are pleased to sneer," said the Devil, who had also risen, "but it is one thing to write about a not possible machine; it is a quite other thing to be a Supernatural Power." All the same, I had scored.

Berthe had come forth at the sound of our rising. I explained to her that Mr. Soames had been called away, and that both he and I would be dining here. It was not until I was out in the open air that I began to feel giddy. I have but the haziest recollection of what I did, where I wandered, in the glaring sunshine of that endless afternoon. I remember the sound of carpenters' hammers all along Piccadilly, and the bare chaotic look of the half-erected "stands." Was it in the Green Park, or in Kensington Gardens, or *where* was it that I sat on a chair beneath a tree, trying to read an evening paper? There was a phrase in the leading article that went on repeating itself in my fagged mind—"Little is hidden from this august Lady full of the garnered wisdom of sixty years of Sovereignty." I remember wildly conceiving a letter (to reach Windsor by express messenger told to await answer):

> "MADAM—Well knowing that your Majesty is full of the garnered wisdom of sixty years of Sovereignty, I venture to ask your advice in the following delicate matter. Mr. Enoch Soames, whose poems you may or may not know," . . .

Was there *no* way of helping him—saving him? A bargain was a bargain, and I was the last man to aid or abet any one in wriggling out of a reasonable obligation. I wouldn't have lifted a little finger to save Faust. But poor Soames!—doomed to pay without respite an eternal price for nothing but a fruitless search and a bitter disillusioning. . . .

Odd and uncanny it seemed to me that he, Soames, in the flesh, in the waterproof cape, was at this moment living in the last decade of the next century, poring over books not yet written, and seeing and seen by men not yet born. Uncannier and odder still, that tonight and evermore he would be in Hell. Assuredly, truth was stranger than fiction.

Endless that afternoon was. Almost I wished I had gone with

Soames—not indeed to stay in the reading room, but to sally forth for a brisk sightseeing walk around a new London. I wandered restlessly out of the Park I had sat in. Vainly I tried to imagine myself an ardent tourist from the eighteenth century. Intolerable was the strain of the slow-passing and empty minutes. Long before seven o'clock I was back at the Vingtième.

I sat there just where I had sat for luncheon. Air came in listlessly through the open door behind me. Now and again Rose or Berthe appeared for a moment. I had told them I would not order any dinner till Mr. Soames came. A hurdy-gurdy began to play, abruptly drowning the noise of a quarrel between some Frenchmen further up the street. Whenever the tune was changed I heard the quarrel still raging. I had bought another evening paper on my way. I unfolded it. My eyes gazed ever away from it to the clock over the kitchen door. . . .

Five minutes, now, to the hour! I remembered that clocks in restaurants are kept five minutes fast. I concentrated my eyes on the paper. I vowed I would not look away from it again. I held it upright, at its full width, close to my face, so that I had no view of anything but it. . . . Rather a tremulous sheet? Only because of the draught, I told myself.

My arms gradually became stiff; they ached; but I could not drop them—now. I had a suspicion, I had a certainty. Well, what then? . . . What else had I come for? Yet I held tight that barrier of newspaper. Only the sound of Berthe's brisk footstep from the kitchen enabled me, forced me, to drop it, and to utter:

"What shall we have to eat, Soames?"

"*Il est souffrant, ce pauvre Monsieur Soames?*" asked Berthe.

"He's only—tired." I asked her to get some wine—Burgundy— and whatever food might be ready. Soames sat crouched forward against the table, exactly as when last I had seen him. It was as though he had never moved—he who had moved so unimaginably far. Once or twice in the afternoon it had for an instant occurred to

me that perhaps his journey was not to be fruitless—that perhaps we
had all been wrong in our estimate of the works of Enoch Soames.
That we had been horribly right was horribly clear from the look of
him. But "Don't be discouraged," I falteringly said. "Perhaps it's
only that you—didn't leave enough time. Two, three centuries
hence, perhaps——"

"Yes," his voice came. "I've thought of that."

"And now—now for the more immediate future! Where are you
going to hide? How would it be if you caught the Paris express from
Charing Cross? Almost an hour to spare. Don't go on to Paris. Stop
at Calais. Live in Calais. He'd never think of looking for you in
Calais."

"It's like my luck," he said, "to spend my last hours on earth
with an ass." But I was not offended. "And a treacherous ass," he
strangely added, tossing across to me a crumpled bit of paper which
he had been holding in his hand. I glanced at the writing on it—
some sort of gibberish, apparently. I laid it impatiently aside.

"Come, Soames! pull yourself together! This isn't a mere matter
of life and death. It's a question of eternal torment, mind you! You
don't mean to say you're going to wait limply here till the Devil
comes to fetch you?"

"I can't do anything else. I've no choice."

"Come! This is 'trusting and encouraging' with a vengeance!
This is Diabolism run mad!" I filled his glass with wine. "Surely,
now that you've *seen* the brute——"

"It's no good abusing him."

"You must admit there's nothing Miltonic about him, Soames."

"I don't say he's not rather different from what I expected."

"He's a vulgarian, he's a swell-mobsman, he's the sort of man
who hangs about the corridors of trains going to the Riviera and
steals ladies' jewel-cases. Imagine eternal torment presided over by
him!"

"You don't suppose I look forward to it, do you?"

"Then why not slip quietly out of the way?"

Again and again I filled his glass, and always, mechanically, he emptied it; but the wine kindled no spark of enterprise in him. He did not eat, and I myself ate hardly at all. I did not in my heart believe that any dash for freedom could save him. The chase would be swift, the capture certain. But better anything than this passive, meek, miserable waiting. I told Soames that for the honor of the human race he ought to make some show of resistance. He asked what the human race had ever done for him. "Besides," he said, "can't you understand that I'm in his power? You saw him touch me, didn't you? There's an end of it. I've no will. I'm sealed."

I made a gesture of despair. He went on repeating the word "sealed." I began to realize that the wine had clouded his brain. No wonder! Foodless he had gone into futurity, foodless he still was. I urged him to eat at any rate some bread. It was maddening to think that he, who had so much to tell, might tell nothing. "How was it all," I asked, "yonder? Come! Tell me your adventures."

"They'd make first-rate 'copy,' wouldn't they?"

"I'm awfully sorry for you, Soames, and I make all possible allowances; but what earthly right have you to insinuate that I should make 'copy,' as you call it, out of you?"

The poor fellow pressed his hands to his forehead. "I don't know," he said. "I had some reason, I'm sure. . . . I'll try to remember."

"That's right. Try to remember everything. Eat a little more bread. What did the reading room look like?"

"Much as usual," he at length muttered.

"Many people there?"

"Usual sort of number."

"What did they look like?"

Soames tried to visualize them. "They all," he presently remembered, "looked very like one another."

My mind took a fearsome leap. "All dressed in Jaeger?"

"Yes. I think so. Grayish-yellowish stuff."

"A sort of uniform?" He nodded. 'With a number on it, per-haps?—a number on a large disc of metal sewn on to the left sleeve? DKF 78,910—that sort of thing?" It was even so. "And all of them—men and women alike—looking very well-cared-for? very Utopian? and smelling rather strongly of carbolic? and all of them quite hairless?' I was right every time. Soames was only not sure whether the men and women were hairless or shorn. "I hadn't time to look at them very closely," he explained.

"No, of course not. But—"

"They stared at *me,* I can tell you. I attracted a great deal of attention." At last he had done that! "I think I rather scared them. They moved away whenever I came near. They followed me about at a distance, wherever I went. The men at the round desk in the middle seemed to have a sort of panic whenever I went to make inquiries."

"What did you do when you arrived?"

Well, he had gone straight to the catalogue, of course—to the S volumes, and had stood long before SN-SOF, unable to take this volume out of the shelf, because his heart was beating so. . . . At first, he said, he wasn't disappointed—he only thought there was some new arrangement. He went to the middle desk and asked where the catalogue of *twentieth*-century books was kept. He gath-ered that there was still only one catalogue. Again he looked up his name, stared at the three little pasted slips he had known so well. Then he went and sat down for a long time. . . .

"And then," he droned, "I looked up the 'Dictionary of Na-tional Biography' and some encyclopædias. . . . I went back to the middle desk and asked what was the best modern book on late nineteenth-century literature. They told me Mr. T. K. Nupton's book was considered the best. I looked it up in the catalogue and filled in a form for it. It was brought to me. My name wasn't in the index, but— Yes!" he said with a sudden change of tone. "That's what I'd forgotten. Where's that bit of paper? Give it back to me."

I, too, had forgotten that cryptic screed. I found it fallen on the floor, and handed it to him.

He smoothed it out, nodding and smiling at me disagreeably. "I found myself glancing through Nupton's book," he resumed. "Not very easy reading. Some sort of phonetic spelling. . . . All the modern books I saw were phonetic."

"Then I don't want to hear anymore, Soames, please."

"The proper names seemed all to be spelt in the old way. But for that, I mightn't have noticed my own name."

"Your own name? Really? Soames, I'm *very* glad."

"And yours."

"No!"

"I thought I should find you waiting here tonight. So I took the trouble to copy out the passage. Read it."

I snatched the paper. Soames' handwriting was characteristically dim. It, and the noisome spelling, and my excitement, made me all the slower to grasp what T. K. Nupton was driving at.

The document lies before me at this moment. Strange that the words I here copy out for you were copied out for me by poor Soames just seventy-eight years hence. . . .

From p. 234 of "Inglish Littracher 1890–1900," bi T. K. Nupton, published bi th Stait, 1992:

"Fr. egzarmpl, a riter ov th time, naimd Max Beerbohm, hoo woz stil alive in th twentieth senchri, rote a stauri in wich e pautraid an immajnari karrakter kauld "Enoch Soames"—a thurd-rait poit hoo beleevz imself a grate jeneus an maix a bargin with th Devvl in auder ter no wot posterriti thinx ov im! It iz a sumwot labud sattire but not without vallu az showing hou seriusli the yung men ov th aiteenninetiz took themselvz. Nou that the littreri profeshn haz bin auganized az a department of publik servis, our riters hav found their levvl an hav lernt ter doo their duti without thort ov th morro. 'Th laibrer iz werthi ov hiz hire,' an that iz aul. Thank hevvn we hav no Enoch Soameses amung us to-dai!"

I found that by murmuring the words aloud (a device which I commend to my reader) I was able to master them, little by little. The clearer they became, the greater was my bewilderment, my distress and horror. The whole thing was a nightmare. Afar, the great grisly background of what was in store for the poor dear art of letters; here, at the table, fixing on me a gaze that made me hot all over, the poor fellow whom—whom evidently . . . but no: whatever down-grade my character might take in coming years, I should never be such a brute as to——

Again I examined the screed. "Immajnari"—but here Soames was, no more imaginary, alas! than I. And "labud"—what on earth was that? (To this day, I have never made out that word.) "It's all very—baffling," I at length stammered.

Soames said nothing, but cruelly did not cease to look at me.

"Are you sure," I temporized, "quite sure you copied the thing out correctly?"

"Quite."

"Well, then it's this wretched Nupton who must have made— must be going to make—some idiotic mistake. . . . Look here, Soames! you know me better than to suppose that I . . . After all, the name 'Max Beerbohm' is not at all an uncommon one, and there must be several Enoch Soameses running around—or rather, 'Enoch Soames' is a name that might occur to any one writing a story. And I don't write stories: I'm an essayist, an observer, a recorder. . . . I admit that it's an extraordinary coincidence. But you must see——"

"I see the whole thing," said Soames quietly. And he added, with a touch of his old manner, but with more dignity than I had ever known in him, *"Parlons d'autre chose."*

I accepted that suggestion very promptly. I returned straight to the more immediate future. I spent most of the long evening in renewed appeals to Soames to slip away and seek refuge somewhere. I remember saying at last that if indeed I was destined to write about him, the supposed "stauri" had better have at least a happy ending. Soames repeated those last three words in a tone of intense scorn. "In Life and in Art," he said, "all that matters is an *inevitable* ending."

"But," I urged, more hopefully than I felt, "an ending that can be avoided *isn't* inevitable."

"You aren't an artist," he rasped. "And you're so hopelessly not an artist that, so far from being able to imagine a thing and make it seem true, you're going to make even a true thing seem as if you'd made it up. You're a miserable bungler. And it's like my luck."

I protested that the miserable bungler was not I—was not going to be I—but T. K. Nupton; and we had a rather heated argument, in the thick of which it suddenly seemed to me that Soames saw he was in the wrong: he had quite physically cowered. But I wondered why—and now I guessed with a cold throb just why—he stared so, past me. The bringer of that "inevitable ending" filled the doorway.

I managed to turn in my chair and to say, not without a semblance of lightness, "Aha, come in!" Dread was indeed rather blunted in me by his looking so absurdly like a villain in a melodrama. The sheen of his tilted hat and of his shirtfront, the repeated twists he was giving to his moustache, and most of all the magnificence of his sneer, gave token that he was there only to be foiled.

He was at our table in a stride. "I am sorry," he sneered witheringly, "to break up your pleasant party, but—"

"You don't: you complete it," I assured him. "Mr. Soames and I want to have a little talk with you. Won't you sit? Mr. Soames got

d and round the shutter'd Square"—that line came back t
my lonely beat, and with it the whole stanza, ringing in my
and bearing in on me how tragically different from the happy
imagined by him was the poet's actual experience of that
e in whom of all princes we should put not our trust.

But—strange how the mind of an essayist, be it never so
ken, roves and ranges!—I remember pausing before a wide door-
and wondering if perchance it was on this very one that the
ng De Quincey lay ill and faint while poor Ann flew as fast as her
t would carry her to Oxford Street, the "stony-hearted step-
other" of them both, and came back bearing that "glass of port
ine and spices" but for which he might, so he thought, actually
ave died. Was this the very doorstep that the old De Quincey used
o revisit in homage? I pondered Ann's fate, the cause of her sudden
vanishing from the ken of her boyfriend; and presently I blamed
myself for letting the past override the present. Poor vanished
Soames!

And for myself, too, I began to be troubled. What had I better
do? Would there be a hue and cry—Mysterious Disappearance of an
Author, and all that? He had last been seen lunching and dining in
my company. Hadn't I better get a hansom and drive straight to
Scotland Yard? . . . They would think I was a lunatic. After all, I
reassured myself, London was a very large place, and one very dim
figure might easily drop out of it unobserved—now especially, in the
blinding glare of the near Jubilee. Better say nothing at all, I
thought.

And I was right. Soames' disappearance made no stir at all. He
was utterly forgotten before anyone, so far as I am aware, noticed
that he was no longer hanging around. Now and again some poet or
prosaist may have said to another, "What has become of that man
Soames?" but I never heard any such question asked. The solicitor
through whom he was paid his annuity may be presumed to have

nothing—frankly nothing—by his journey
wish to say that the whole thing was a swindl
On the contrary, we believe you meant we
bargain, such as it was, is off."

The Devil gave no verbal answer. He mere
and pointed with rigid forefinger to the door.
edly rising from his chair when, with a despera
swept together two dinner-knives that were on t
their blades across each other. The Devil stepped sh
the table behind him, averting his face and shudde

"You are not superstitious!" he hissed.

"Not at all," I smiled.

"Soames!" he said as to an underling, but withou
face, "put those knives straight!"

With an inhibitive gesture to my friend, "Mr. Soar
emphatically to the Devil, "is a *Catholic* Diabolist"; bu
friend did the Devil's bidding, not mine; and now, with h
eyes again fixed on him, he arose, he shuffled past me.
speak. It was he that spoke. "Try," was the prayer he threw
me as the Devil pushed him roughly out through the door,
make them know that I did exist!"

In another instant I too was through that door. I stood stari
ways—up the street, across it, down it. There was moonlight
lamplight, but there was not Soames nor that other.

Dazed, I stood there. Dazed, I turned back, at length, into
little room; and I suppose I paid Berthe or Rose for my dinner an
luncheon, and for Soames': I hope so, for I never went to the
Vingtième again. Ever since that night I have avoided Greek Street
altogether. And for years I did not set foot even in Soho Square,
because on that same night it was there that I paced and loitered,
long and long, with some such dull sense of hope as a man has in not
straying far from the place where he has lost something. . . .

made inquiries, but no echo of these resounded. There was something rather ghastly to me in the general unconsciousness that Soames had existed, and more than once I caught myself wondering whether Nupton, that babe unborn, were going to be right in thinking him a figment of my brain.

In that extract from Nupton's repulsive book there is one point which perhaps puzzles you. How is it that the author, though I have here mentioned him by name and have quoted the exact words he is going to write, is not going to grasp the obvious corollary that I have invented nothing? The answer can but be this: Nupton will not have read the later passages of this memoir. Such lack of thoroughness is a serious fault in anyone who undertakes to do scholar's work. And I hope these words will meet the eye of some contemporary rival to Nupton and be the undoing of Nupton.

I like to think that some time between 1992 and 1997 somebody will have looked up this memoir, and will have forced on the world his inevitable and startling conclusions. And I have reasons for believing that this will be so. You realize that the reading room into which Soames was projected by the Devil was in all respects precisely as it will be on the afternoon of June 3rd, 1997. You realize, therefore, that on that afternoon, when it comes round, there the selfsame crowd will be, and there Soames too will be, punctually, he and they doing precisely what they did before. Recall now Soames' account of the sensation he made. You may say that the mere difference of his costume was enough to make him sensational in that uniformed crowd. You wouldn't say so if you had ever seen him. I assure you that in no period could Soames be anything but dim. The fact that people are going to stare at him, and follow him around, and seem afraid of him, can be explained only on the hypothesis that they will somehow have been prepared for his ghostly visitation. They will have been awfully waiting to see whether he really would come. And when he does come the effect will of course be—awful.

An authentic, guaranteed, proven ghost, but—only a ghost, alas!
Only that. In his first visit, Soames was a creature of flesh and blood,
whereas the creatures into whose midst he was projected were but
ghosts, I take it—solid, palpable, vocal, but unconscious and auto-
matic ghosts, in a building that was itself an illusion. Next time, that
building and those creatures will be real. It is of Soames that there
will be but the semblance. I wish I could think him destined to
revisit the world actually, physically, consciously. I wish he had this
one brief escape, this one small treat, to look forward to. I never
forget him for long. He is where he is, and forever. The more rigid
moralists among you may say he has only himself to blame. For my
part, I think he has been very hardly used. It is well that vanity
should be chastened; and Enoch Soames' vanity was, I admit, above
the average, and called for special treatment. But there was no need
for vindictiveness. You say he contracted to pay the price he is
paying; yes; but I maintain that he was induced to do so by fraud.
Well-informed in all things, the Devil must have known that my
friend would gain nothing by his visit to futurity. The whole thing
was a very shabby trick. The more I think of it, the more detestable
the Devil seems to me.

Of him I have caught sight several times, here and there, since
that day at the Vingtième. Only once, however, have I seen him at
close quarters. This was in Paris. I was walking, one afternoon, along
the Rue d'Antin, when I saw him advancing from the opposite
direction—over-dressed as ever, and swinging an ebony cane, and
altogether behaving as though the whole pavement belonged to him.
At thought of Enoch Soames and the myriads of other sufferers
eternally in this brute's dominion, a great cold wrath filled me, and I
drew myself up to my full height. But—well, one is so used to
nodding and smiling in the street to anybody whom one knows, that
the action becomes almost independent of oneself: to prevent it
requires a very sharp effort and great presence of mind. I was miser-

ably aware, as I passed the Devil, that I nodded and smiled to him. And my shame was the deeper and hotter because he, if you please, stared straight at me with the utmost haughtiness.

To be cut—deliberately cut—by *him!* I was, I still am, furious at having had that happen to me.

The Devil in a Nunnery

FRANCIS OSCAR MANN

Buckingham is as pleasant a shire as a man shall see on a seven days' journey. Neither was it any less pleasant in the days of our Lord King Edward, the third of that name, he who fought and put the French to shameful discomfiture at Crecy and Poitiers and at many another hard-fought field. May God rest his soul, for he now sleeps in the great Church at Westminster.

Buckinghamshire is full of smooth round hills and woodlands of hawthorn and beech, and it is a famous country for its brooks and shaded waterways running through the low hay meadows. Upon its hills feed a thousand sheep, scattered like the remnants of the spring snow, and it was from these that the merchants made themselves fat purses, sending the wool into Flanders in exchange for silver crowns. There were many strong castles there too, and rich abbeys, and the King's Highway ran through it from North to South, upon which the pilgrims went in crowds to worship at the Shrine of the Blessed Saint Alban. Thereon also rode noble knights and stout men-at-arms, and these you could follow with the eye by their glistening armor, as they wound over hill and dale, mile after mile, with shining spears and shields and fluttering pennons, and anon a trumpet or two sounding the same keen note as that which rang out dreadfully on those bloody fields of France. The girls used to come to the cottage doors or run to hide themselves in the wayside woods to see them go trampling by; for Buckinghamshire girls love a soldier above all men. Nor, I warrant you, were jolly friars lacking in the highways and the byways and under the hedges, good men of religion, comfortable of penance and easy of life, who could tip a wink to a housewife, and drink and crack a joke with the good man, going on their several ways with tight paunches, skins full of ale and a merry salutation for every one. A fat pleasant land was this Buckinghamshire; always plenty to eat and drink therein, and pretty girls and lusty fellows; and God knows what more a man can expect in a world where all is vanity, as the Preacher truly says.

There was a nunnery at Maids Moreton, two miles out from Buckingham Borough, on the road to Stony Stratford, and the place was called Maids Moreton because of the nunnery. Very devout creatures were the nuns, being holy ladies out of families of gentle blood. They punctually fulfilled to the letter all the commands of the pious founder, just as they were blazoned on the great parchment Regula, which the Lady Mother kept on her reading-desk in her little cell. If ever any of the nuns, by any chance or subtle machination of the Evil One, was guilty of the smallest backsliding from the conduct that beseemed them, they made full and devout confession thereof to the Holy Father who visited them for this purpose. This good man loved swan's meat and galingale, and the charitable nuns never failed to provide of their best for him on his visiting days; and whatsoever penance he laid upon them they performed to the utmost, and with due contrition of heart.

From Matins to Compline they regularly and decently carried out the services of Holy Mother Church. After dinner, one read aloud to them from the Rule, and again after supper there was reading from the life of some notable Saint or Virgin, that thereby they might find ensample for themselves on their own earthly pilgrimage. For the rest, they tended their herb garden, reared their chickens, which were famous for miles around, and kept strict watch over their haywards and swineherds. If time was when they had nothing more important on hand, they set to and made the prettiest blood bandages imaginable for the Bishop, the Bishop's Chaplain, the Archdeacon, the neighboring Abbot and other godly men of religion round about, who were forced often to bleed themselves for their health's sake and their eternal salvation, so that these venerable men in process of time came to have by them great chests full of these useful articles. If little tongues wagged now and then as the sisters sat at their sewing in the great hall, who shall blame them, *Eva peccatrice?* Not I; besides, some of them were something stricken in years, and old women are garrulous and hard to be constrained from chattering and gossiping. But being devout women they could have spoken no evil.

One evening after Vespers all these good nuns sat at supper, the Abbess on her high dais and the nuns ranged up and down the hall at the long trestled tables. The Abbess had just said *"Gratias"* and the sisters had sung *"Qui vivit et regnat per omnia saecula saeculorum, Amen,"* when in came the Manciple mysteriously, and, with many deprecating bows and outstretchings of the hands, sidled himself up upon the dais, and, permission having been given him, spoke to the Lady Mother thus:

"Madam, there is a certain pilgrim at the gate who asks refreshment and a night's lodging." It is true he spoke softly, but little pink ears are sharp of hearing, and nuns, from their secluded way of life, love to hear news of the great world.

"Send him away," said the Abbess. "It is not fit that a man should lie within this house."

"Madam, he asks food and a bed of straw lest he should starve of hunger and exhaustion on his way to do penance and worship at the Holy Shrine of the Blessed Saint Alban."

"What kind of pilgrim is he?"

"Madam, to speak truly, I know not; but he appears of a reverend and gracious aspect, a young man well spoken and well disposed. Madam knows it waxeth late, and the ways are dark and foul."

"I would not have a young man, who is given to pilgrimages and good works, to faint and starve by the wayside. Let him sleep with the haywards."

"But, Madam, he is a young man of goodly appearance and conversation; saving your reverence, I would not wish to ask him to eat and sleep with churls."

"He must sleep without. Let him, however, enter and eat of our poor table."

"Madam, I will strictly enjoin him what you command. He hath with him, however, an instrument of music and would fain cheer you with spiritual songs."

A little shiver of anticipation ran down the benches of the great hall, and the nuns fell to whispering.

"Take care, Sir Manciple, that he be not some light juggler, a singer of vain songs, a mocker. I would not have these quiet halls disturbed by wanton music and unholy words. God forbid." And she crossed herself.

"Madam, I will answer for it."

The Manciple bowed himself from the dais and went down the

middle of the hall, his keys rattling at his belt. A little buzz of conversation rose from the sisters and went up to the oak roof-trees, like the singing of bees. The Abbess told her beads.

The hall door opened and in came the pilgrim. God knows what manner of man he was; I cannot tell you. He certainly was lean and lithe like a cat, his eyes danced in his head like the very devil, but his cheeks and jaws were as bare of flesh as any hermit's that lives on roots and ditchwater. His yellow-hosed legs went like the tune of a May game, and he screwed and twisted his scarlet-jerkined body in time with them. In his left hand he held a cithern, on which he twanged with his right, making a cunning noise that titillated the backbones of those who heard it, and teased every delicate nerve in the body. Such a tune would have tickled the ribs of Death himself. A queer fellow to go pilgrimaging certainly, but why, when they saw him, all the young nuns tittered and the old nuns grinned, until they showed their red gums, it is hard to tell. Even the Lady Mother on the dais smiled, though she tried to frown a moment later.

The pilgrim stepped lightly up to the dais, the infernal devil in his legs making the nuns think of the games the village folk play all night in the churchyard on Saint John's Eve.

"Gracious Mother," he cried, bowing deeply and in comely wise, "allow a poor pilgrim on his way to confess and do penance at the shrine of Saint Alban to take food in your hall, and to rest with the haywards this night, and let me thereof make some small recompense with a few sacred numbers, such as your pious founder would not have disdained to hear."

"Young man," returned the Abbess, "right glad am I to hear that God has moved thy heart to godly works and to go on pilgrimages, and verily I wish it may be to thy soul's health and to the respite of thy pains hereafter. I am right willing that thou shouldst refresh thyself with meat and rest at this holy place."

"Madam, I thank thee from my heart, but as some slight token of gratitude for so large a favor, let me, I pray thee, sing one or two of my divine songs, to the uplifting of these holy Sisters' hearts."

Another burst of chatter, louder than before, from the benches in the hall. One or two of the younger Sisters clapped their plump white hands and cried, "Oh!" The Lady Abbess held up her hand for silence.

"Verily, I should be glad to hear some sweet songs of religion, and I think it would be to the uplifting of these Sisters' hearts. But, young man, take warning against singing any wanton lines of vain imagination, such as the ribalds use on the highways, and the idlers and haunters of taverns. I have heard them in my youth, although my ears tingle to think of them now, and I should think it shame that any such light words should echo among these sacred rafters or disturb the slumber of our pious founder, who now sleeps in Christ. Let me remind you of what saith Saint Jeremie, *Onager solitarius, in desiderio animae suae, attraxit ventum amoris;* the wild ass of the wilderness, in the desire of his heart, snuffeth up the wind of love; whereby that holy man signifies that vain earthly love, which is but wind and air, and shall avail nothing at all, when this weak, impure flesh is sloughed away."

"Madam, such songs as I shall sing, I learnt at the mouth of our holy parish priest, Sir Thomas, a man of all good learning and purity of heart."

"In that case," said the Abbess, "sing in God's name, but stand at the end of the hall, for it suits not the dignity of my office a man should stand so near this dais."

Whereon the pilgrim, making obeisance, went to the end of the hall, and the eyes of all the nuns danced after his dancing legs, and their ears hung on the clear, sweet notes he struck out of his cithern as he walked. He took his place with his back against the great hall door, in such attitude as men use when they play the cithern. A little trembling ran through the nuns, and some rose from their seats and knelt on the benches, leaning over the table, the better to see and hear him. Their eyes sparkled like dew on meadowsweet on a fair morning.

Certainly his fingers were bewitched or else the devil was in his cithern, for such sweet sounds had never been heard in the hall since the day when it was built and consecrated to the service of the servants of God. The shrill notes fell like a tinkling rain from the high roof in mad, fantastic trills and dying falls that brought all one's soul to one's lips to suck them in. What he sang about, God only knows; not one of the nuns or even the holy Abbess herself could have told you, although you had offered her a piece of the True Cross or a hair of the Blessed Virgin for a single word. But a divine yearning filled all their hearts; they seemed to hear ten thousand thousand angels singing in choruses, Alleluia, Alleluia, Alleluia; they floated up on impalpable clouds of azure and silver, up through the blissful paradises of the uppermost heaven; their nostrils were filled with the odors of exquisite spices and herbs and smoke of incense; their eyes dazzled at splendors and lights and glories; their ears were full of gorgeous harmonies and all created concords of sweet sounds; the very fibers of being were loosened within them, as though their souls would leap forth from their bodies in exquisite dissolution. The eyes of the younger nuns grew round and large and tender, and their breath almost died upon their velvet lips. As for the old nuns, the great, salt tears coursed down their withered cheeks and fell like rain on their gnarled hands. The Abbess sat on her dais with her lips apart, looking into space, ten thousand thousand miles away. But no one saw her and she saw no one; everyone had forgotten every one else in that delicious intoxication.

Then with a shrill cry, full of human yearnings and desire, the minstrel came to a sudden stop—

"Western wind, when wilt thou blow,
And the small rain will down rain?
Christ, if my love were in my arms,
And I in my bed again."

Silence!—not one of the holy Sisters spoke, but some sighed; some put their hands over their hearts, and one put her hand in her hood, but when she felt her hair shorn close to her scalp, drew it out again sharply, as though she had touched red-hot iron, and cried, "O Jesu."

Sister Peronelle, a toothless old woman, began to speak in a cracked, high voice, quickly and monotonously, as though she spoke in a dream. Her eyes were wet and red, and her thin lips trembled. "God knows," she said, "I loved him; God knows it. But I bid all those who be maids here, to be mindful of the woods. For they are green, but they are deep and dark, and it is merry in the springtime with the thick turf below and the good boughs above, all alone with your heart's darling—all alone in the green wood. But God help me, he would not stay anymore than snow at Easter. I thought just now that I was back with him in the woods. God keep all those that be maids from the green woods."

The pretty Sister Ursula, who had only just finished her novitiate, was as white as a sheet. Her breath came thickly and quick as though she bore a great burden up hill. A great sigh made her comely shoulders rise and fall. "Blessed Virgin," she cried. "Ah, ye ask too much; I did not know; God help me, I did not know," and her gray eyes filled with sudden tears, and she dropped her head on her arms on the table, and sobbed aloud.

Then cried out Sister Katherine, who looked as old and dead as a twig dropped from a tree of last autumn, and at whom the younger Sisters privily mocked, "It is the wars, the wars, the cursed wars. I have held his head in this lap, I tell you; I have kissed his soul into mine. But now he lies dead, and his pretty limbs all dropped away into earth. Holy Mother, have pity on me. I shall never kiss his sweet lips again or look into his jolly eyes. My heart is broken long since. Holy Mother! Holy Mother!"

"He must come oftener," said a plump Sister of thirty, with a little nose turned up at the end, eyes black as sloes and lips round as a plum. "I go to the orchard day after day, and gather my lap full of apples. He is my darling. Why does he not come? I look for him every time that I gather the ripe apples. He used to come; but that was in the spring, and Our Lady knows that is long ago. Will it not be spring again soon? I have gathered many ripe apples."

Sister Margarita rocked herself to and fro in her seat and crossed her arms on her breast. She was singing quietly to herself.

"Lulla, lullay, thou tiny little child,
    Lulla, lullay, lullay;
Suck at my breast that am thereat beguiled,
    Lulla, lullay, lullay."

She moaned to herself, "I have seen the village women go to the well, carrying their babies with them, and they laugh as they go by on the way. Their babies hold them tight round the neck, and their mothers comfort them, saying, 'Hey, hey, my little son; hey, hey, my sweeting.' Christ and the blessed Saints know that I have never felt a baby's little hand in my bosom—and now I shall die without it, for I am old and past the age of bearing children.

"Lulla, lullay, thou tiny little boy,
    Lulla, lullay, lullay;
To feel thee suck doth soothe my great annoy,
    Lulla, lullay, lullay."

"I have heard them on a May morning, with their pipes and tabors and jolly, jolly music," cried Sister Helen; "I have seen them too, and my heart has gone with them to bring back the white hawthorn from the woods. 'A man and a maid to a hawthorn bough,' as it says in the song. They sing outside my window all Saint John's Eve so that I cannot say my prayers for the wild thoughts they put into my brain, as they go dancing up and down in the church-yard; I cannot forget the pretty words they say to each other, 'Sweet love, a kiss'; 'kiss me, my love, nor let me go'; 'As I went through the garden gate'; 'A bonny black knight, a bonny black knight, and what will you give to me? A kiss, and a kiss, and no more than a kiss, under the wild rose tree.' Oh, Mary Mother, have pity on a poor girl's heart, I shall die, if no one love me, I shall die."

"In faith, I am truly sorry, William," said Sister Agnes, who was gaunt and hollow-eyed with long vigils and overfasting, for which the good father had rebuked her time after time, saying that she overtasked the poor weak flesh. "I am truly sorry that I could not wait. But the neighbors made such a clamor, and my father and mother buffeted me too sorely. It is under the oak tree, no more than a foot deep, and covered with the red and brown leaves. It was a pretty sight to see the red blood on its neck, as white as whalebone, and it neither cried nor wept, so I put it down among the leaves, the pretty poppet; and it was like thee, William, it was like thee. I am sorry I did not wait, and now I'm worn and wan for thy sake, this many a long year, and all in vain, for thou never comst. I am an old woman now, and I shall soon be quiet and not complain any more."

Some of the Sisters were sobbing as if their hearts would break; some sat quiet and still, and let the tears fall from their eyes un-checked; some smiled and cried together; some sighed a little and trembled like aspen leaves in a southern wind. The great candles in the hall were burning down to their sockets. One by one they spluttered out. A ghostly, flickering light fell upon the legend over the broad dais, *"Connubium mundum sed virginitas paradisum complet"*—"Marriage replenisheth the World, but virginity Paradise."

"Dong, dong, dong." Suddenly the great bell of the Nunnery began to toll. With a cry the Abbess sprang to her feet; there were tear stains on her white cheeks, and her hand shook as she pointed fiercely to the door.

"Away, false pilgrim," she cried. "Silence, foul blasphemer! *Retro me, Satanas."* She crossed herself again and again, saying *Pater Noster.*

The nuns screamed and trembled with terror. A little cloud of blue smoke arose from where the minstrel had stood. There was a little tongue of flame, and he had disappeared. It was almost dark in the hall. A few sobs broke the silence. The dying light of a single candle fell on the form of the Lady Mother.

"Tomorrow," she said, "we shall fast and sing *Placebo* and *Dirige* and the *Seven Penitential Psalms*. May the Holy God have mercy upon us for all we have done and said and thought amiss this night. Amen."

The Devil and Daniel Webster

STEPHEN VINCENT BENÉT

I

It's a story they tell in the border country, where Massachusetts joins Vermont and New Hampshire.

Yes, Dan'l Webster's dead—or, at least, they buried him. But every time there's a thunderstorm around Marshfield, they say you can hear his rolling voice in the hollows of the sky. And they say that if you go to his grave and speak loud and clear, "Dan'l Webster—Dan'l Webster!" the ground'll begin to shiver and the trees begin to shake. And after a while you'll hear a deep voice saying, "Neighbor, how stands the Union?" Then you better answer the Union stands as she stood, rock-bottomed and copper-sheathed, one and indivisible, or he's liable to rear right out of the ground. At least, that's what I was told when I was a youngster.

You see, for a while, he was the biggest man in the country. He never got to be President, but he was the biggest man. There were thousands that trusted in him right next to God Almighty, and they told stories about him and all the things that belonged to him that were like the stories of patriarchs and such. They said, when he stood up to speak, stars and stripes came right out in the sky, and once he spoke against a river and made it sink into the ground. They said, when he walked the woods with his fishing rod, Killall, the trout would jump out of the streams right into his pockets, for they knew it was no use putting up a fight against him; and, when he argued a case, he could turn on the harps of the blessed and the shaking of the earth underground. That was the kind of man he was, and his big farm up at Marshfield was suitable to him. The chickens he raised were all white meat down through the drumsticks, the cows were tended like children, and the big ram he called Goliath had horns with a curl like a morning-glory vine and could butt through an iron door. But Dan'l wasn't one of your gentlemen farmers; he knew all the ways of the land, and he'd be up by candlelight to see that the chores got done. A man with a mouth like a mastiff, a brow like a mountain and eyes like burning anthracite—that was Dan'l Webster in his prime. And the biggest case he argued never got written down in the books, for he argued it against the devil, nip and tuck and no holds barred. And this is the way I used to hear it told.

There was a man named Jabez Stone, lived at Cross Corners, New Hampshire. He wasn't a bad man to start with, but he was an unlucky man. If he planted corn, he got borers; if he planted potatoes, he got blight. He had good-enough land, but it didn't prosper him; he had a decent wife and children, but the more children he had, the less there was to feed them. If stones cropped up in his neighbor's field, boulders boiled up in his; if he had a horse with the spavins, he'd trade it for one with the staggers and give something extra. There's some folks bound to be like that, apparently. But one day Jabez Stone got sick of the whole business.

He'd been plowing that morning and he'd just broke the plowshare on a rock that he could have sworn hadn't been there yesterday. And, as he stood looking at the plowshare, the off horse began to cough—that ropy kind of cough that means sickness and horse doctors. There were two children down with the measles, his wife was ailing, and he had a whitlow on his thumb. It was about the last straw for Jabez Stone. "I vow," he said, and he looked around him kind of desperate—"I vow it's enough to make a man want to sell his soul to the devil! And I would, too, for two cents!"

Then he felt a kind of queerness come over him at having said what he'd said; though, naturally, being a New Hampshireman, he wouldn't take it back. But, all the same, when it got to be evening and, as far as he could see, no notice had been taken, he felt relieved in his mind, for he was a religious man. But notice is always taken, sooner or later, just like the Good Book says. And, sure enough, next day, about suppertime, a soft-spoken, dark-dressed stranger drove up in a handsome buggy and asked for Jabez Stone.

Well, Jabez told his family it was a lawyer, come to see him about a legacy. But he knew who it was. He didn't like the looks of the stranger, nor the way he smiled with his teeth. They were white teeth, and plentiful—some say they were filed to a point, but I wouldn't vouch for that. And he didn't like it when the dog took one look at the stranger and ran away howling, with his tail between his legs. But having passed his word, more or less, he stuck to it, and they went out behind the barn and made their bargain. Jabez Stone had to prick his finger to sign, and the stranger lent him a silver pin. The wound healed clean, but it left a little white scar.

II

After that, all of a sudden, things began to pick up and prosper for
Jabez Stone. His cows got fat and his horses sleek, his crops were the
envy of the neighborhood, and lightning might strike all over the
valley, but it wouldn't strike his barn. Pretty soon, he was one of
the prosperous people of the country; they asked him to stand for
selectman, and he stood for it; there began to be talk of running him
for state senate. All in all, you might say the Stone family was as
happy and contented as cats in a dairy. And so they were, except for
Jabez Stone.

He'd been contented enough, the first few years. It's a great
thing when bad luck turns; it drives most other things out of your
head. True, every now and then, especially in rainy weather, the little
white scar on his finger would give him a twinge. And once a year,
punctual as clockwork, the stranger with the handsome buggy would
come driving by. But the sixth year, the stranger lighted, and, after
that, his peace was over for Jabez Stone.

The stranger came up through the lower field, switching his
boots with a cane—they were handsome black boots, but Jabez
Stone never liked the look of them, particularly the toes. And, after
he'd passed the time of day, he said, "Well, Mr. Stone, you're a
hummer! It's a very pretty property you've got here, Mr. Stone."

"Well, some might favor it and others might not," said Jabez
Stone, for he was a New Hampshireman.

"Oh, no need to decry your industry!" said the stranger, very
easy, showing his teeth in a smile. "After all, we know what's been
done, and it's been according to contract and specifications. So
when—ahem—the mortgage falls due next year, you shouldn't have
any regrets."

"Speaking of that mortgage, mister," said Jabez Stone, and he looked around for help to the earth and the sky, "I'm beginning to have one or two doubts about it."

"Doubts?" said the stranger, not quite so pleasantly.

"Why, yes," said Jabez Stone. "This being the U.S.A. and me always having been a religious man." He cleared his throat and got bolder. "Yes, sir," he said, "I'm beginning to have considerable doubts as to that mortgage holding in court."

"There's courts and courts," said the stranger, clicking his teeth. "Still, we might as well have a look at the original document." And he hauled out a big black pocketbook, full of papers. "Sherwin, Slater, Stevens, Stone," he muttered. "I, Jabez Stone, for a term of seven years—Oh, it's quite in order, I think."

But Jabez Stone wasn't listening, for he saw something else flutter out of the black pocketbook. It was something that looked like a moth, but it wasn't a moth. And as Jabez Stone stared at it, it seemed to speak to him in a small sort of piping voice, terrible small and thin, but terrible human.

"Neighbor Stone!" it squeaked. "Neighbor Stone! Help me! For God's sake, help me!"

But before Jabez Stone could stir hand or foot, the stranger whipped out a big bandanna handkerchief, caught the creature in it, just like a butterfly, and started tying up the ends of the bandanna.

"Sorry for the interruption," he said. "As I was saying—"

But Jabez Stone was shaking all over like a scared horse.

"That's Miser Stevens' voice!" he said, in a croak. "And you've got him in your handkerchief!"

The stranger looked a little embarrassed.

"Yes, I really should have transferred him to the collecting box," he said with a simper, "but there were some rather unusual specimens there and I didn't want them crowded. Well, well, these little contretemps will occur."

"I don't know what you mean by contertan," said Jabez Stone, "but that was Miser Stevens' voice! And he ain't dead! You can't tell me he is! He was just as spry and mean as a woodchuck, Tuesday!"

"In the midst of life—" said the stranger, kind of pious. "Listen!" Then a bell began to toll in the valley and Jabez Stone listened, with the sweat running down his face. For he knew it was tolled for Miser Stevens and that he was dead.

"These longstanding accounts," said the stranger with a sigh; "one really hates to close them. But business is business."

He still had the bandanna in his hand, and Jabez Stone felt sick as he saw the cloth struggle and flutter.

"Are they all as small as that?" he asked hoarsely.

"Small?" said the stranger. "Oh, I see what you mean. Why, they vary." He measured Jabez Stone with his eyes, and his teeth showed. "Don't worry, Mr. Stone," he said. "You'll go with a very good grade. I wouldn't trust you outside the collecting box. Now, a man like Dan'l Webster, of course—well, we'd have to build a special box for him, and even at that, I imagine the wing spread would astonish you. He'd certainly be a prize. I wish we could see our way clear to him. But, in your case, as I was saying—"

"Put that handkerchief away!" said Jabez Stone, and he began to beg and to pray. But the best he could get at the end was a three years' extension, with conditions.

But till you make a bargain like that, you've got no idea of how fast four years can run. By the last months of those years, Jabez Stone's known all over the state and there's talk of running him for governor—and it's dust and ashes in his mouth. For every day, when he gets up, he thinks, "There's one more night gone," and every night when he lies down, he thinks of the black pocketbook and the soul of Miser Stevens, and it makes him sick at heart. Till, finally, he can't bear it any longer, and, in the last days of the last year, he hitches up his horse and drives off to seek Dan'l Webster. For Dan'l was born in New Hampshire, only a few miles from Cross Corners, and it's well known that he has a particular soft spot for old neighbors.

III

It was early in the morning when he got to Marshfield, but Dan'l was up already, talking Latin to the farm hands and wrestling with the ram, Goliath, and trying out a new trotter and working up speeches to make against John C. Calhoun. But when he heard a New Hampshireman had come to see him, he dropped everything else he was doing, for that was Dan'l's way. He gave Jabez Stone a breakfast that five men couldn't eat, went into the living history of every man and woman in Cross Corners, and finally asked him how he could serve him.

Jabez Stone allowed that it was a kind of mortgage case.

"Well, I haven't pleaded a mortgage case in a long time, and I don't generally plead now, except before the Supreme Court," said Dan'l, "but if I can, I'll help you."

"Then I've got hope for the first time in ten years," said Jabez Stone, and told him the details.

Dan'l walked up and down as he listened, hands behind his back, now and then asking a question, now and then plunging his eyes at the floor, as if they'd bore through it like gimlets. When Jabez Stone had finished, Dan'l puffed out his cheeks and blew. Then he turned to Jabez Stone and a smile broke over his face like the sunrise over Monadnock.

"You've certainly given yourself the devil's own row to hoe, Neighbor Stone," he said, "but I'll take your case."

"You'll take it?" said Jabez Stone, hardly daring to believe.

"Yes," said Dan'l Webster. "I've got about seventy-five other things to do and the Missouri Compromise to straighten out, but I'll take your case. For if two New Hampshiremen aren't a match for the devil, we might as well give the country back to the Indians."

Then he shook Jabez Stone by the hand and said, "Did you come down here in a hurry?"

"Well, I admit I made time," said Jabez Stone.

"You'll go back faster," said Dan'l Webster, and he told 'em to hitch up Constitution and Constellation to the carriage. They were matched grays with one white forefoot, and they stepped like greased lightning.

Well, I won't describe how excited and pleased the whole Stone family was to have the great Dan'l Webster for a guest, when they finally got there. Jabez Stone had lost his hat on the way, blown off when they overtook a wind, but he didn't take much account of that. But after supper he sent the family off to bed, for he had most particular business with Mr. Webster. Mrs. Stone wanted them to sit in the front parlor, but Dan'l Webster knew front parlors and said he preferred the kitchen. So it was there they sat, waiting for the stranger, with a jug on the table between them and a bright fire on the hearth—the stranger being scheduled to show up on the stroke of midnight, according to specification.

Well, most men wouldn't have asked for better company than Dan'l Webster and a jug. But with every tick of the clock Jabez Stone got sadder and sadder. His eyes roved round, and though he sampled the jug you could see he couldn't taste it. Finally, on the stroke of 11:30 he reached over and grabbed Dan'l Webster by the arm.

"Mr. Webster, Mr. Webster!" he said, and his voice was shaking with fear and a desperate courage. "For God's sake, Mr. Webster, harness your horses and get away from this place while you can!"

"You've brought me a long way, neighbor, to tell me you don't like my company," said Dan'l Webster, quite peaceable, pulling at the jug.

"Miserable wretch that I am!" groaned Jabez Stone. "I've brought you a devilish way, and now I see my folly. Let him take me if he wills. I don't hanker after it, I must say, but I can stand it. But you're the Union's stay and New Hampshire's pride! He mustn't get you, Mr. Webster! He mustn't get you!"

Dan'l Webster looked at the distracted man, all gray and shaking in the firelight, and laid a hand on his shoulder.

"I'm obliged to you, Neighbor Stone," he said gently. "It's kindly thought of. But there's a jug on the table and a case in hand. And I never left a jug or a case half finished in my life."

And just at that moment there was a sharp rap on the door.

"Ah," said Dan'l Webster, very coolly, "I thought your clock was a trifle slow, Neighbor Stone." He stepped to the door and opened it. "Come in!" he said.

The stranger came in—very dark and tall he looked in the firelight. He was carrying a box under his arm—a black, japanned box with little air holes in the lid. At the sight of the box, Jabez Stone gave a low cry and shrank into a corner of the room.

"Mr. Webster, I presume," said the stranger, very polite, but with his eyes glowing like a fox's deep in the woods.

"Attorney of record for Jabez Stone," said Dan'l Webster, but his eyes were glowing too. "Might I ask your name?"

"I've gone by a good many," said the stranger carelessly. "Perhaps Scratch will do for the evening. I'm often called that in these regions."

Then he sat down at the table and poured himself a drink from the jug. The liquor was cold in the jug, but it came steaming into the glass.

"And now," said the stranger, smiling and showing his teeth, "I shall call upon you, as a law-abiding citizen, to assist me in taking possession of my property."

Well, with that the argument began—and it went hot and heavy.

At first, Jabez Stone had a flicker of hope, but when he saw Dan'l Webster being forced back at point after point, he just sat scrunched in his corner, with his eyes on that japanned box. For there wasn't any doubt as to the deed or the signature—that was the worst of it. Dan'l Webster twisted and turned and thumped his fist on the table, but he couldn't get away from that. He offered to compromise the case; the stranger wouldn't hear of it. He pointed out the property had increased in value, and state senators ought to be worth more; the stranger stuck to the letter of the law. He was a great lawyer, Dan'l Webster, but we know who's the King of Lawyers, as the Good Book tells us, and it seemed as if, for the first time, Dan'l Webster had met his match.

Finally, the stranger yawned a little. "Your spirited efforts on behalf of your client do you credit, Mr. Webster," he said, "but if you have no more arguments to adduce, I'm rather pressed for time—" and Jabez Stone shuddered.

Dan'l Webster's brow looked dark as a thundercloud. "Pressed or not, you shall not have this man!" he thundered. "Mr. Stone is an American citizen, and no American citizen may be forced into the service of a foreign prince. We fought England for that in '12 and we'll fight all hell for it again!"

"Foreign?" said the stranger. "And who calls me a foreigner?"

"Well, I never yet heard of the dev—of your claiming American citizenship," said Dan'l Webster with surprise.

"And who with better right?" said the stranger, with one of his terrible smiles. "When the first wrong was done to the first Indian, I was there. When the first slaver put out for the Congo, I stood on her deck. Am I not in your books and stories and beliefs, from the first settlements on? Am I not spoken of, still, in every church in New England? 'Tis true the North claims me for a Southerner, and the South for a Northerner, but I am neither. I am merely an honest American like yourself—and of the best descent—for, to tell the truth, Mr. Webster, though I don't like to boast of it, my name is older in this country than yours."

"Aha!" said Dan'l Webster, with the veins standing out in his forehead. "Then I stand on the Constitution! I demand a trial for my client!"

"The case is hardly one for an ordinary court," said the stranger, his eyes flickering. "And, indeed, the lateness of the hour—"

"Let it be any court you choose, so it is an American judge and an American jury!" said Dan'l Webster in his pride. "Let it be the quick or the dead; I'll abide the issue!"

"You have said it," said the stranger, and pointed his finger at the door. And with that, and all of a sudden, there was a rushing of wind outside and a noise of footsteps. They came, clear and distinct, through the night. And yet, they were not like the footsteps of living men.

"In God's name, who comes by so late?" cried Jabez Stone, in an ague of fear.

"The jury Mr. Webster demands," said the stranger, sipping at his boiling glass. "You must pardon the rough appearance of one or two; they will have come a long way."

I V

And with that the fire burned blue and the door blew open and twelve men entered, one by one.

If Jabez Stone had been sick with terror before, he was blind with terror now. For there was Walter Butler, the loyalist, who spread fire and horror through the Mohawk Valley in the times of the Revolution; and there was Simon Girty, the renegade, who saw white men burned at the stake and whooped with the Indians to see them burn. His eyes were green, like a catamount's, and the stains on his hunting shirt did not come from the blood of the deer. King Philip was there, wild and proud as he had been in life, with the great gash in his head that gave him his death wound, and cruel Governor Dale, who broke men on the wheel. There was Morton of Merry Mount, who so vexed the Plymouth Colony, with his flushed, loose, handsome face and his hate of the godly. There was Teach, the bloody pirate, with his black beard curling on his breast. The Reverend John Smeet, with his strangler's hands and his Geneva gown, walked as daintily as he had to the gallows. The red print of the rope was still around his neck, but he carried a perfumed handkerchief in one hand. One and all, they came into the room with the fires of hell still upon them, and the stranger named their names and their deeds as they came, till the tale of twelve was told. Yet the stranger had told the truth—they had all played a part in America.

"Are you satisfied with the jury, Mr. Webster?" said the stranger mockingly, when they had taken their places.

The sweat stood upon Dan'l Webster's brow, but his voice was clear.

"Quite satisfied," he said. "Though I miss General Arnold from the company."

"Benedict Arnold is engaged upon other business," said the stranger, with a glower. "Ah, you asked for a justice, I believe."

He pointed his finger once more, and a tall man, soberly clad in Puritan garb, with the burning gaze of the fanatic, stalked into the room and took his judge's place.

"Justice Hathorne is a jurist of experience," said the stranger. "He presided at certain witch trials once held in Salem. There were others who repented of the business later, but not he."

"Repent of such notable wonders and undertakings?" said the stern old justice. "Nay, hang them—hang them all!" And he muttered to himself in a way that struck ice into the soul of Jabez Stone.

Then the trial began, and, as you might expect, it didn't look anyways good for the defense. And Jabez Stone didn't make much of a witness in his own behalf. He took one look at Simon Girty and screeched, and they had to put him back in his corner in a kind of swoon.

It didn't halt the trial, though; the trial went on, as trials do. Dan'l Webster had faced some hard juries and hanging judges in his time, but this was the hardest he'd ever faced, and he knew it. They sat there with a kind of glitter in their eyes, and the stranger's smooth voice went on and on. Every time he'd raise an objection, it'd be "Objection sustained," but whenever Dan'l objected, it'd be "Objection denied." Well, you couldn't expect fair play from a fellow like this Mr. Scratch.

It got to Dan'l in the end, and he began to heat, like iron in the forge. When he got up to speak he was going to flay that stranger with every trick known to the law, and the judge and jury too. He didn't care if it was contempt of court or what would happen to him for it. He didn't care any more what happened to Jabez Stone. He just got madder and madder, thinking of what he'd say. And yet, curiously enough, the more he thought about it, the less he was able to arrange his speech in his mind.

Till, finally, it was time for him to get up on his feet, and he did so, all ready to bust out with lightnings and denunciations. But before he started he looked over the judge and jury for a moment, such being his custom. And he noticed the glitter in their eyes was twice as strong as before, and they all leaned forward. Like hounds just before they get the fox, they looked, and the blue mist of evil in the room thickened as he watched them. Then he saw what he'd been about to do, and he wiped his forehead, as a man might who's just escaped falling into a pit in the dark.

For it was him they'd come for, not only Jabez Stone. He read it in the glitter of their eyes and in the way the stranger hid his mouth with one hand. And if he fought them with their own weapons, he'd fall into their power; he knew that, though he couldn't have told you how. It was his own anger and horror that burned in their eyes; and he'd have to wipe that out or the case was lost. He stood there for a moment, his black eyes burning like anthracite. And then he began to speak.

He started off in a low voice, though you could hear every word. They say he could call on the harps of the blessed when he chose. And this was just as simple and easy as a man could talk. But he didn't start out by condemning or reviling. He was talking about the things that make a country a country, and a man a man.

And he began with the simple things that everybody's known and felt—the freshness of a fine morning when you're young, and the taste of food when you're hungry, and the new day that's every day when you're a child. He took them up and he turned them in his hands. They were good things for any man. But without freedom, they sickened. And when he talked of those enslaved, and the sorrows of slavery, his voice got like a big bell. He talked of the early days of America and the men who had made those days. It wasn't a spread-eagle speech, but he made you see it. He admitted all the wrong that had ever been done. But he showed how, out of the wrong and the right, the suffering and the starvations, something new had come. And everybody had played a part in it, even the traitors.

Then he turned to Jabez Stone and showed him as he was—an ordinary man who'd had hard luck and wanted to change it. And, because he'd wanted to change it, now he was going to be punished for all eternity. And yet there was good in Jabez Stone, and he showed that good. He was hard and mean, in some ways, but he was a man. There was sadness in being a man, but it was a proud thing too. And he showed what the pride of it was till you couldn't help feeling it. Yes, even in hell, if a man was a man, you'd know it. And he wasn't pleading for any one person anymore, though his voice rang like an organ. He was telling the story and the failures and the endless journey of mankind. They got tricked and trapped and bamboozled, but it was a great journey. And no demon that was ever foaled could know the inwardness of it—it took a man to do that.

V

The fire began to die on the hearth and the wind before morning to blow. The light was getting gray in the room when Dan'l Webster finished. And his words came back at the end to New Hampshire ground, and the one spot of land that each man loves and clings to. He painted a picture of that, and to each one of that jury he spoke of things long forgotten. For his voice could search the heart, and that was his gift and his strength. And to one, his voice was like the forest and its secrecy, and to another like the sea and the storms of the sea; and one heard the cry of his lost nation in it, and another saw a little harmless scene he hadn't remembered for years. But each saw something. And when Dan'l Webster finished he didn't know whether or not he'd saved Jabez Stone. But he knew he'd done a miracle. For the glitter was gone from the eyes of judge and jury, and, for the moment, they were men again, and knew they were men.

"The defense rests," said Dan'l Webster, and stood there like a mountain. His ears were still ringing with his speech, and he didn't hear anything else till he heard Judge Hathorne say, "The jury will retire to consider its verdict."

Walter Butler rose in his place and his face had a dark, gay pride on it.

"The jury has considered its verdict," he said, and looked the stranger full in the eye. "We find for the defendant, Jabez Stone."

With that, the smile left the stranger's face, but Walter Butler did not flinch.

"Perhaps 'tis not strictly in accordance with the evidence," he said, "but even the damned may salute the eloquence of Mr. Webster."

With that, the long crow of a rooster split the gray morning sky, and judge and jury were gone from the room like a puff of smoke and as if they had never been there. The stranger turned to Dan'l Webster, smiling wryly. "Major Butler was always a bold man," he said. "I had not thought him quite so bold. Nevertheless, my congratulations, as between two gentlemen."

"I'll have that paper first, if you please," said Dan'l Webster, and he took it and tore it into four pieces. It was queerly warm to the touch. "And now," he said, "I'll have you!" and his hand came down like a bear trap on the stranger's arm. For he knew that once you bested anybody like Mr. Scratch in fair fight, his power on you was gone. And he could see that Mr. Scratch knew it too.

The stranger twisted and wriggled, but he couldn't get out of that grip. "Come, come, Mr. Webster," he said, smiling palely. "This sort of thing is ridic—ouch!—is ridiculous. If you're worried about the costs of the case, naturally, I'd be glad to pay—"

"And so you shall!" said Dan'l Webster, shaking him till his teeth rattled. "For you'll sit right down at that table and draw up a document, promising never to bother Jabez Stone nor his heirs or assigns nor any other New Hampshireman till doomsday! For any hades we want to raise in this state, we can raise ourselves, without assistance from strangers."

"Ouch!" said the stranger. "Ouch! Well, they never did run very big to the barrel, but—ouch!—I agree!"

So he sat down and drew up the document. But Dan'l Webster kept his hand on his coat collar all the time.

"And, now, may I go?" said the stranger, quite humble, when Dan'l'd seen the document was in proper and legal form.

"Go?" said Dan'l, giving him another shake. "I'm still trying to figure out what I'll do with you. For you've settled the costs of the case, but you haven't settled with me. I think I'll take you back to Marshfield," he said, kind of reflective. "I've got a ram there named Goliath that can butt through an iron door. I'd kind of like to turn you loose in his field and see what he'd do."

Well, with that the stranger began to beg and to plead. And he begged and he pled so humble that finally Dan'l, who was naturally kindhearted, agreed to let him go. The stranger seemed terrible grateful for that and said, just to show they were friends, he'd tell Dan'l's fortune before leaving. So Dan'l agreed to that, though he didn't take much stock in fortunetellers ordinarily.

But, naturally, the stranger was a little different. Well, he pried and he peered at the lines in Dan'l's hands. And he told him one thing and another that was quite remarkable. But they were all in the past.

"Yes, all that's true, and it happened," said Dan'l Webster. "But what's to come in the future?"

The stranger grinned, kind of happily, and shook his head. "The future's not as you think it," he said. "It's dark. You have a great ambition, Mr. Webster."

"I have," said Dan'l firmly, for everybody knew he wanted to be President.

"It seems almost within your grasp," said the stranger, "but you will not attain it. Lesser men will be made President and you will be passed over."

"And, if I am, I'll still be Daniel Webster," said Dan'l. "Say on."

"You have two strong sons," said the stranger, shaking his head. "You look to found a line. But each will die in war and neither reach greatness."

"Live or die, they are still my sons," said Dan'l Webster. "Say on."

"You have made great speeches," said the stranger. "You will make more."

"Ah," said Dan'l Webster.

"But the last great speech you make will turn many of your own against you," said the stranger. "They will call you Ichabod; they will call you by other names. Even in New England some will say you have turned your coat and sold your country, and their voices will be loud against you till you die."

"So it is an honest speech, it does not matter what men say," said Dan'l Webster. Then he looked at the stranger and their glances locked.

"One question," he said. "I have fought for the Union all my life. Will I see that fight won against those who would tear it apart?"

"Not while you live," said the stranger, grimly, "but it will be won. And after you are dead, there are thousands who will fight for your cause, because of words that you spoke."

"Why, then, you long-barreled, slab-sided, lantern-jawed, for-tune-telling note shaver!" said Dan'l Webster, with a great roar of laughter, "be off with you to your own place before I put my mark on you! For, by the thirteen original colonies, I'd go to the Pit itself to save the Union!"

And with that he drew back his foot for a kick that would have stunned a horse. It was only the tip of his shoe that caught the stranger, but he went flying out of the door with his collecting box under his arm.

"And now," said Dan'l Webster, seeing Jabez Stone beginning to rouse from his swoon, "let's see what's left in the jug, for it's dry work talking all night. I hope there's pie for breakfast, Neighbor Stone."

But they say that whenever the devil comes near Marshfield, even now, he gives it a wide berth. And he hasn't been seen in the state of New Hampshire from that day to this. I'm not talking about Massachusetts or Vermont.